"Choosing Hope is a harrowing story of passion and deceit, the things we do for love and the rabbit holes we tumble into chasing elusive fairy-tale endings. Dark around the edges with a shocking twist I didn't see coming, this is the kind of book you'll be passing around to your friends so you can talk about it together. Holly Kammier delivers romance, suspense, and a strong, smart heroine who turns out to be nobody's victim. Don't miss this one!"

– KAT ROSS,
BEST-SELLING AUTHOR *of THE MIDNIGHT SEA*

"Contemporary family drama and dysfunction at its very best. The well-drawn, deeply authentic characters, stayed in my thoughts long after I finished the book. I highly recommend this enthralling, inspirational read, and look forward to more from this author."

– CAROLINE MITCHELL,
USA TODAY BESTSELLING THRILLER AUTHOR

"A beautifully crafted novel that will take you on a heart-breaking journey full of hard choices, the dark feverish passion of an affair, and all the anguish that comes with it. Despite the main character's inner conflict, Kammier does a breathtaking job leaving readers feeling empowered and uplifted."

– JESSICA THERRIEN,
BEST-SELLING AUTHOR *of*
THE CHILDREN OF THE GODS SERIES

"Holly Kammier digs deep into relationships, families, and has an extraordinary message about strength in oneself, even if you need to take it one day at a time."

– CHRISTA YELICH-KOTH,
BEST-SELLING AUTHOR *of ILLUSION*

"An intense and inspiring tale of life in the present. Replete with betrayals and hard choices, this novel showcases one woman's journey to self-respect as she finds the courage to embrace her conviction that she, too, is deserving of love."

– LAURA TAYLOR,
6-TIME ROMANTIC TIMES AWARD WINNING
AUTHOR

"In her riveting follow-up to *Kingston Court*, Holly Kammier's *Choosing Hope* once again takes us behind the façade of a perfect life to a crumbling core where the choices we make turn us into our own worst enemies - - or challenge us to rise above our inner conflicts to become our own saviors in this life affirming, passionate adventure that is anything but predictable."

– MATTHEW J. PALLAMARY,
AWARD WINNING AUTHOR *of* LAND WITHOUT EVIL,
and SPIRIT MATTERS

"When it comes to love, one of the toughest things any of us can do is to follow our heart, even when to follow it means to upset the delicate balance of the life we've known. There's only one thing harder: admitting that your choice was the wrong one. Disastrously wrong.

Choosing Hope is the gripping novel that will resonate with anyone who has chosen passion over safety, or wondered what it would be like to make that choice. Well-paced, deeply relatable, and wise in the ways of the human heart, Holly Kammier's page-turner is one you won't just not want to put down – it's one you'll talk about and share."

-HUGO SHWYZER,
CONTRIBUTOR *to JEZEBEL, THE ATLANTIC, SALON, and* CO-AUTHOR *of BEAUTY, DISRUPTED: A MEMOIR*, A BIGORAPHY OF SUPERMODEL CARRÉ OTTIS

Choosing HOPE

A NOVEL

HOLLY KAMMIER

FROM THE TINY ACORN…
GROWS THE MIGHTY OAK

Choosing Hope

Cover design by Dane Low of eBook Launch
Author photo by Julia Badei of Studio Bijou

ISBN-13: 978-1-947392-00-7

For my Warrior Mama, Joan McAllaster,
and Danielle Forester, the Sister of my Heart.

Your unwavering light encouraged me
to write a new story.

And the day came when the risk to remain tight in a bud was more painful than the risk it took to blossom.

~ Anais Nin

PROLOGUE

I DON'T REMEMBER my breaking point, the exact moment when I decided to abandon my role as faithful wife and surrender to the intoxication of an affair. I play things over in my head. If just one thing had happened differently, maybe I'd still be who I used to be. I'd be content in my marriage. I wouldn't know any better.

If my sister hadn't called that morning to tell me my mother had a stroke. If I'd crashed my car in a mad panic as I swerved in and out of traffic at top speeds to reach her. If my husband had called to comfort me instead of texting me a cold *you should have taken the kids with you* message three hours into my drive.

But none of those things happened. My husband failed to make that call.

Adrian didn't.

Maybe that was the moment.

His voice. My vulnerability.

His question, "What can I do to help you?"

CHAPTER 1

...

TUESDAY, OCTOBER 11, 2016
Morning

I DIALED MY husband, using the Bluetooth device in our black Audi Crossroad. Pushing harder on the gas pedal, I sped into the glare of the morning sun, past our small Northern California town's *City of Good Living* sign, and onto the US-101 heading South.

"Hey," he answered in his stiff work-voice.

"I need you to pick up the boys from school this afternoon." Our seven and eleven-year-old sons attended the highly coveted Lavender Hills Elementary school in our affluent, tree-lined suburb twenty miles south of San Francisco.

"Why?"

I could picture his previously chiseled cheeks, puffy from decades of drink and weed, turning red in frustration.

"Skye called. My mom had a stroke. I'm driving home right now."

"To San Diego?"

"Yes."

"That's ridiculous. Why didn't you call me first to discuss this?"

"I panicked. I knew it would be quicker to throw some clothes in a suitcase and get there."

"I can't pick up the boys today, I've got meetings all afternoon. You should have thought of this."

"I told you, my mother had a stroke. Don't you even care how she's doing?"

"Of course I do. I'm also trying to figure out why you jumped in the car and left town when I'm in the middle of a huge project to try and get promoted. When did you leave?"

"I don't know. Ten minutes ago."

"Good. Turn around."

"I can't."

"I know you're scared, Hon, but it's at least an eight hour drive, and that's if you don't hit LA traffic. What did Skye say?"

My hands trembled as I fought back tears. "Curtis found her soaking wet and naked on the bathroom floor, slumped over with her arm all messed up and her face twitching. She'd just gotten out of the shower. He called 911."

"And?"

"The paramedics came to the house. They took her to the hospital. She's there now. They're getting her set up, or checked in, or whatever it is they do. She needs a brain scan. That's all I know. It just happened."

"So she's being taken care of. You can fly down there for a couple of days at the end of the week. Leave Friday night with the boys and maybe pull them out of school on Monday if you want to stay a little longer."

"It's Tuesday." My heart raced. "You want me to wait three days and then take both the boys?"

"I'm sure she'll want to see her grandsons."

I couldn't speak.

"Hope."

He only called me Hope when he was angry. I hated the sound of my name on his lips.

"What?"

"You're a stay-at-home mom. Your sole job is to take care of the kids."

I stared straight ahead, blind to everything.

I'd left my beloved job as a journalist two years ago to concentrate on our older son. Michael's high functioning autism prompted me to make it my mission to immerse him in intense behavioral therapy while he was still young enough to mold.

Kevin considered the endeavor a huge waste of time. "Why don't you go find some other make-believe problem to waste your time on and leave our son alone?" he'd recently snapped at me across the family dinner table.

Kevin didn't believe Michael's diagnosis or the therapy were real, let alone necessary, and he resented his wealthier co-workers' double incomes. "Can't you go back to work and bring in money like the rest of the wives?" he asked on a regular basis. Our one and a half million dollar home and vacations abroad – admittedly on a budget - weren't enough.

"My mother could die. I need to see her today, and I'm not turning around."

"You're leaving me in a very bad position. This promotion to Marketing Director is for all of us, so you can continue to do what you like around the house while I provide. How am I supposed to do that and take care of children?"

A text came through as Kevin continued to talk. I slid my hand over the screen to unlock it.

I should've felt guilty seeing Adrian's name pop up on my phone. Instead, I felt a rush of sweet relief.

Adrian: *Hey.*

I typed back, trying to focus on the road.

Me: *Hey.*

Adrian: *No call?*

Me: *Very bad morning. Give me twenty.*

"Kevin, I'm sorry. I have to concentrate on my driving. My friend Isabel can walk the boys to and from school. I'll call her now and ask her. All you'd need to do is get them ready in the mornings and work from home in the afternoons. Your boss will understand. It's a family emergency. I'll be back by Sunday. You will all be fine."

I ended the call.

CHAPTER 2

...

TUESDAY, OCTOBER 11, 2016
Morning

AT THIRTY-EIGHT, I hadn't made a single major decision in my life without first getting Mom's opinion. She was my center. I needed her more than ever.

A white pick-up truck veered into my lane. I swerved hard, and he barely missed me. Before my heartbeat had time to recover, I propped my knee against the wheel to keep the car straight and wrapped my frazzled brown hair in a tight bun.

Pushing down further on the gas pedal, I checked myself in the rear-view mirror. Small hazel eyes, puffy from tears, stared back at me. Prominent cheekbones protruded too much. Over the past few months, stress had stolen my appetite. I'd dropped a good five pounds off my already petite frame. If a cop pulled me over, it wouldn't be hard to convince him I was rushing home for an emergency.

Before I called Adrian, I dialed my sister.

"How is she?" I asked.

"I'm not sure, the doctors ordered an MRI. The technician came for her and she's down there now."

"Who all is there?" Mom had remarried a man with four children after her divorce from Dad, making me one of eight siblings. Our family defined complicated.

"Obviously I'm here," Skye responded. "So is Claire. Jonas is around for now. Pete's on his way down from LA, and Tawny had already planned on flying in on Friday for a business trip, so she'll be here then. Kimmie can't make it, she has to work."

"That bad, huh?"

"We could've lost her. The doctors won't know the extent of the damage until they review the MRI and see how she is when she wakes up."

I pictured my little sister pacing the hospital hallway as she spoke. Skye was a hair taller than five-foot-one, with dimpled cheeks and the sweetest smile. Her looks could be deceiving.

When we were kids, she nearly broke my nose. In a fit of anger, she hurled a tap shoe at me during a fight over a box of cereal. Skye was tough. I trusted her to keep the hospital staff hopping until Mom recovered.

"Did you talk to Dad yet?" I asked.

"No, I've been too busy coordinating with everyone. Besides, he'll get all amped and stressed, find some way to make it about him. My other line is beeping. Gotta go."

When the call ended, tears broke, blurring the white lines on the pavement. A horn honked, and a man waved his fist. I swerved and nearly ran off the side of the road for a second time.

The phone rang again. I answered, barely able to breathe.

"What's wrong? Why didn't you call me back?" It was him.

"My mom had a stroke." I choked out the words. "I'm driving down to San Diego."

"You need to pull over."

"No."

"Please. You're not that great a driver to begin with."

"Thanks." I wiped at my tears.

"It's the truth."

I cracked a small smile. "I know."

"Is she okay?" he asked.

"They don't know if she is going to…" I began to sob again, unable to finish my sentence.

"What can I do to help you?"

The most romantic question a man had ever asked me.

"Listening is good."

"I'll meet you down there, for support."

"No."

"You need me."

"Not now, Adrian." I already knew, one way or another, Mom's crisis would force me to confront a reality that couldn't be fixed. "I can't do this right now with my family."

"I'll stay in the hospital lobby. No one will see me if that's what you're worried about."

"My mother is sick. It could be serious. This isn't the time for a big romantic reunion between the two of us. Okay? I'm gonna hang up now."

"Wait, I wasn't looking for anything romantic. I want to support you. I've known your mom since I was fourteen. She's one of the strongest women I know. She's going to pull through this. I promise."

The road narrowed. Curved. Our past unraveled before me. Adrian and I had met twenty-five years ago when I was thirteen and he was fourteen.

It was right around dusk at the open-air University Town Center mall in La Jolla. I was shopping for boys with my BFF at the time, Lauren Lewis.

She was the prettier one, the girl with the sparkly blue eyes and long, tanned legs. We'd worn matching acid-washed Guess jeans that night. I'd begged Mom to buy me the same ones as Lauren, with the cool zippers at the ankles.

Lauren led the way into the mall's air-conditioned Taco Bell for a bean burrito with extra sauce and spotted a group of cute boys from school sitting in a booth toward the back. Bright fluorescent lights reflected against their orangey Sun-In highlights. Two of them caught her eye and waved her over.

The waistline on my copy-cat jeans constricted as we sauntered toward them. They slouched, blew the paper off their straws at one another, and wrapped their hands around sweating paper cups loaded with soda and ice. The leader, the cute one in a white t-shirt with a swoopy surfer-boy haircut, laid a half-eaten taco on its paper wrapper as he made awkward small talk with Lauren.

I recognized another boy in the group, a cocky guy with dark hair and brooding green eyes. He was of mixed race, Caucasian and probably Hispanic. Compared to my pale complexion, his light brown skin seemed exotic.

I'd recently caught sight of him on campus, breakdancing for a handful of the popular kids. When Lauren noticed me watching him that day, she told me he was in love with a pretty redhead. She said I didn't have a chance. But there was no redhead hanging around that evening in Taco Bell, and to my surprise, he couldn't be bothered to even glance at Lauren.

He stared only at me. Even when I looked away, I felt him watching. Sitting with his legs parted and his hands cupped together between his knees, he wasn't the best looking boy in the group. He was average height and build, and his 80's blue jeans were far too baggy. Yet, just like the day I spied him breakdancing, he exuded a rugged teen sex appeal.

His attention made me feel shy and even more self-conscious. To my relief, I noticed him picking at a hangnail and glancing down at his shoes. The cool guy from school, the one whose name I couldn't quite remember, suddenly seemed unsure of himself and, by the way he looked at me, almost star-struck.

He asked for my phone number. His name was Adrian Sicario. He could hold a conversation in Dutch and Spanish, as well as English. We dated for a month. The first boy I ever kissed. When he told me he would marry me someday, I promptly broke up with him.

That was our beginning.

I rubbed at my eyes and tried to keep my focus on the road ahead. Dried chaparral and yellowing grass carpeted the sloping mountainsides as I sped along the endless ribbon of Highway 152 through Pacheco Pass. I was near Gilroy by this point. One hour in.

Adrian cleared his throat, reminding me he was still on the phone. "I remember all the times I dropped by your house when you were in high school and your mom would open the door and ask me if I was hungry. She'd look me up and down and point toward the kitchen. Your mom made me feel welcome. She's a special lady."

I chuckled at the memory. "Typical Jewish mom, needing to make sure nobody is going to starve to death. She really liked you though. You were one of the good ones."

"So, when am I gonna see her again?"

"Never."

"Ouch."

"I'm being honest. I'm married. You live a whole state away in Oregon with your soon-to-be ex and all three of your kids. This thing between us needs to stop."

A life with Adrian would be messy and complicated. Crossing that line, somehow ending up with him instead of my husband seemed ridiculous. When I started flirting with Adrian on Facebook, looking for a little attention, he felt safe. A distant flame from the past. Nothing more. I thought at my age I couldn't possibly fall for someone so different.

A real relationship with Adrian would mean five children under one roof, a miniscule income, and angry exes. I would be throwing away the American dream, a life of privilege and a proper in-tact family, for the one thing I lacked, the attention and support of a romantic partner. Despite it all, I loved my husband. Adrian wasn't enough.

"This isn't the right time to talk about this."

"You're probably right," I agreed.

The thought of my mother unconscious and getting her brain scanned shot a new wave of panic through me. I needed to concentrate on what mattered most. "I gotta go."

"Promise you'll call me as soon as you get there. I need to know you're safe."

"Promise." I slid the phone off as I picked up speed, purposely darting across thick double yellow lines on a winding section of the two-lane highway. My car flew past a truck carrying a load of garlic. The translucent skins floated in the air like angel wings.

CHAPTER 3

...

TUESDAY, OCTOBER 11, 2016
Evening

STEPPING INSIDE THE hospital's hushed corridors, I felt instantly cut off from the hustle of life outside. There was no day or night in these fluorescent hallways. The antiseptic smell, the chill, the unyielding knowledge that behind each door lay a person suffering – reminders of our collective vulnerability. If a cell mutates or our blood fails to clot, if the body inhales an invisible virus or an emergency doctor runs behind schedule, any of us could lose ourselves. Worse, we could lose the life of someone we love.

As I peeked inside Mom's room, I saw the faces of my family gathered in seats around her; my stepdad, stepsister Claire and stepbrother Jonas, and, of course, my sister, Skye. I greeted them quietly.

"Hey," Claire replied, the former homecoming queen half hidden behind her long blonde hair.

"Hi kiddo." My stepdad Curtis stood from his chair as Jonas nodded a silent hello.

Mom had a private room with a large window overlooking the I-5 freeway. A heavy yellow sun hung low in the sky. The multitude of cars and trucks doing their best to traverse the eight lanes were jammed jelly tight in rush hour traffic, trapped in the same holding pattern as my family.

Curtis stepped forward, wrapping me in his big arms for a delicate hug. "Your mama's doing great."

"Yeah?" I asked, tucking a loose curl back into my bun.

"Who's here *now*?" Mom's raspy voice cut through the tender moment. Hearing her speak, I felt I could breathe again.

"It's me, Mom. Hope." I walked toward her.

She scowled in my direction. Mom's short, thinning blonde hair lay matted against her small head. Gray roots and weathered laugh lines emphasized her age and vulnerability. Her lips, however, stood out strongest. They rested in a narrow, defiant sliver.

"Did you bring anyone else?" she asked in irritation.

Never a fan of entertaining, Mom often left her own dinner parties to take an extended bathroom break or a short nap. Having people, even close friends and family, watching her lie weakened in a hospital had to have been painful.

"I'm alone," I assured her, reaching for her hand.

Her scowl relaxed by a quarter inch.

"I left the boys at home with Kevin." I squeezed her finger, setting my purse on the floor beside her bed.

Dressed in a white hospital gown with an I.V. taped to her left hand, Mom raised her bed into a sitting position. "I wake up and everyone is hovering over me."

I leaned in to kiss her forehead. "I'm sorry, Mama, but we're all worried."

Tears of relief welled heavy in my eyes. Mom was speaking, and she was fully coherent. I couldn't help stare at her face.

"Honey, I'm fine." She patted my hand. "Go say 'hi' to everyone else."

"I already did."

Curtis turned toward the bed and massaged her shoulder. Dark circles underscored the red rim of exhaustion in his eyes. "She already told the doctor her age and what year it is," he said in his deep voice. "She even listed the names of all you kiddos, including your mystery brother."

"What did the doctors say happened?"

"Definitely a stroke. They're pretty sure it was due to high blood pressure. They've got her on meds now to control it."

"I'm right here." Mom tilted her head toward Curtis in agitation. "I can speak for myself."

I chuckled. "What happens now, Mama?"

"Ask Curtis."

He grimaced. "They want to keep her here for about a week while they do more blood tests. They need to make sure her meds are working right."

"I'm not staying." Mom crossed her arms over her chest. I worried she'd rip out the I.V. by accident. "I don't want to be here with people coming in and out, poking at me, waking me up asking questions."

Curtis raised his hands in surrender. "The doctor said if your medications aren't dosed correctly, you could have a second stroke. But you do what you think is best."

"I'll take my medication correctly." Mom fought back. "Do you think insurance is going to cover this place for a whole week? I'm getting out of here tomorrow. Maybe sooner."

Panic began to rise, tightening in my chest. "Wait, there's a chance of a second stroke?" I asked.

"It's pretty common," Jonas, dressed in his paramedic uniform, interjected. "She could bust another blood vessel and have a fatal brain hemorrhage."

"Mom! That's terrifying. You should definitely stay here."

"Life is terrifying. I could die crossing the street." Her scowl returned, deeper this time. The menacing little line on her heart monitor escalated.

"Well," Skye said, sliding off her chair. Her thick brown hair was tied back into a messy ponytail, unusual for the perfectionist. "I'm heading to the cafeteria. You want anything?"

"No," Mom answered. "I just want everyone to leave."

Sykes eyes scanned the rest of the room before locking in with mine. "You look good," she mouthed, motioning to my multi-colored maxi skirt and nearly see through white top. True to our hippie roots, I usually dressed slightly off center.

"Thank you," I mouthed back to her. I missed my family, especially Skye.

Claire stood to join her. "I'll tag along. I could stand to stretch my legs."

The two of them shrugged a goodbye, and Jonas trailed behind them. "Glad you made it, Hope," he said on his way out.

"Thanks, Jonas. Good to see you." I went to collect my purse, searching for an easy excuse to give Mom her requested space. I had a text. From Adrian.

Adrian: *How is your mom?*

I tried to text him back discreetly, angling the phone away from Mom's view.

Me: *She's good. I'll probably be going back home soon.*

Adrian: *Before you leave town, let me see you.*

Me: *No.*

I shook my head. Why did he have to do this now?

Adrian: *I've been deprived of you for 20 years. You're in San Diego, away from Kevin and the boys. I know you have feelings for me. Let me see you. Let's find out if it's real. If you feel nothing, I'll let you go, and I'll walk away. At least give me this chance.*

"Who's that?" Mom asked.

"A friend." I tossed the phone back into my purse. "I need to make a call. I'll be back in a little."

"Why don't you meet your sister in the cafeteria? You're too thin, Hope." Mom looked at me as if I were the one she needed to be concerned about.

"Okay." I inched my purse strap up my shoulder, feeling like an insecure child. Gazing down at myself, I reevaluated my body through Mom's eyes.

At my age, thin wasn't necessarily attractive. It made me look haggard. My body was also the exact opposite of celebrities like Beyonce's or J.Lo's strong sexy curves. "I'll get a donut or something to make you happy."

Meandering along the silent hallways, I took out my phone to call home.

"Hey," Kevin answered. "What's up? How's your mom?"

I leaned against the wall and slid down to a squatting position. "Stubborn. She's in her bed now, resting."

"She's awake?"

"Yeah, she kicked us all out of the room so she could have a little privacy. She's acting like nothing serious happened."

"That's great news."

I took a deep breath, wanting to share his enthusiasm. "It is."

"So, when do you think you'll come home?"

"I think I should stay here at least until the end of the week, to make sure she's really okay."

"Hope, I can't keep missing work. If she needed you, of course we'd do whatever's necessary to keep you there. But if your mom's already awake and kicking you out of her room... I didn't get a thing done, taking care of all their needs throughout the day."

"I know it's hard."

"It's hard on all of us. Michael had a really tough time this afternoon. He's been a lot more difficult than usual."

"Michael's always difficult."

"He's much more agitated."

Anger flared. I was exhausted by the stress of the day, and Kevin's prodding tore away at my patience. "You say this whenever you're watching him. Michael doesn't suddenly get worse when I'm not around."

"I'm saying he is going through an especially difficult time, worrying about his mom and his Bubby, and it would be nice if you were around to help out. I have a big meeting Thursday. You don't want me to lose my job."

Kevin's shtick sounded legit. Large chunks of my non-confrontational, keep-the-peace brain wanted to agree with him. The rest of me knew the truth.

There wasn't a day I could remember that our older son didn't have a meltdown. If it wasn't this issue with my mom, it would be someone in his class who was sick and blew their germs on him, or he'd have to get a haircut, which he hated, or he'd lose his favorite jacket that he couldn't possibly live without. Michael would sneak and read articles in my news magazines, then obsess for hours over the terrible death he could suffer from the Zika virus or a bomb being dropped in our backyard in an act of terrorism.

As far as Kevin claiming he needed to focus on work, he skipped out well before the end of business hours all the time. Despite his claims, it seemed to me it was slow at work. In the last few months he'd come home early nearly every Thursday and rarely went into the office on Fridays for more than a few hours. I was positive Kevin was more concerned about being stuck having to take care of the boys than he was about losing his job.

A nurse in bright hospital scrubs swished by. Her shiny black hair swung in a long ponytail, giving her an air of confidence. She had an important job saving people's lives, and she probably had a boyfriend or husband more like Adrian. I was positive she left work each night and went home to someone who appreciated her and treated her as an equal.

Since the boys were born, I'd asked for less and less of my husband's time and attention. It had been my idea to have kids, hence my responsibility to handle all of their wants and needs. Quitting my job had been the tipping point.

I no longer felt worthy of asking for anything more than what Kevin offered. In response, he offered less and less. Dinner dates stopped. He opted out of family barbecues and cousins' birthday parties. Even on holidays he preferred to stay home alone while I took the boys on hiking excursions or get-togethers with friends.

I had set the wrong precedent. I'd given too much. I couldn't even visit my sick mother without upsetting him.

"Of course, I don't want you to lose your job," I said. "But I'm worried about my mom. We could have lost her."

"I love your mom," Kevin said. "We all want what's best for her."

"I know." It was easier not to argue.

"It sounds like she isn't really in the mood for company right now, and it's going to take time for her to get all her strength back. You could go down with the boys over Christmas break if you want."

Once again, a reminder that he didn't want to come with us.

Tears of frustration started to build. Thanks to Adrian, I believed I deserved more. "Can you put the boys on the phone? I want to say 'hi.'"

"Sure. Give me a second."

I heard the phone rustle and the sound of a cartoon on the television. Michael, never much of a conversationalist, moaned he was busy. Zach said 'okay.'

"Hey, Mom." He spoke in his adorable high-pitched, I'll-be-your-baby-forever voice.

"Hi, hon. How are you?"

"Good. Dad fed us pizza and let us watch TV."

Television and junk food were strictly limited when Mommy was in charge. The boys were fine. "Lucky you. Sounds like you're having fun."

"Yeah."

"That's good," I said.

"Yeah." He breathed into the speaker. "Well…" A loud honking noise emanated through the phone, no doubt something to do with the cartoon they were watching. "Mom?"

"Yes?"

"I love you a billion, the sky and the moon."

I imagined his sweet freckled face and it crushed me. He was the reason I should have remained faithful. My children, not my husband, were the ones I was supposed to protect.

"I love you, too, Zacky, all the way around and back again. Infinity."

"Kay. Here's Dad. Bye."

"Hon?" Kevin asked as he took back the phone. "We need you here. We miss you."

Ten years ago I would have found his words sweet. He needed me. But that fresh feeling of loving someone beyond their faults had been stripped away to reveal the bare bones of our truth. He felt no desperate need to hold me or to be near me. I was his workhorse. Nothing more. "I understand."

"I love you." Kevin's words slipped off his tongue with habit.

I hung up, unable to respond in kind. I knew what would happen next. I was going to see Adrian. Just once.

CHAPTER 4

...

TUESDAY, OCTOBER 11, 2016
Night

WE'D BEEN BUILDING toward this romantic relationship since early July, nearly three months. Daily conversations. Texts throughout the day. Even if I'd told him not to come, the thought of not seeing Adrian when I had the chance made me feel like an emerging heroin addict desperate for the intoxicating rush. The newly addicted mind is a selfish mind, no doubt, but also sometimes, a helpless one.

When else would I be able to get away from Kevin, the kids, and all of my gossiping neighbors in Andalucía, long enough to see Adrian without getting caught? I'd talk to him in person, I reasoned, and get him out of my system. Let the fantasy in my head unravel in the unforgiving light of reality.

At the very worst, there'd be intense chemistry. I would be right where I was, tortured, but I'd get over it. At best, I wouldn't feel a thing. Our emotional affair would be over.

I paced the kitchen of Mom's cramped beach house, bargaining with myself that it was okay to see Adrian one single time. I'd almost lost my mom, and my husband barely cared. I deserved to be with someone who wanted to give me comfort.

We'd meet in a public space. Adrian and I were old friends. Even if someone saw us, they wouldn't think a thing of it.

My phone buzzed. I let the call go to voicemail. I needed to collect myself before I told Adrian my plan. Yanking my suitcase from the floor in the living room, I dragged my things to the guest room, tossing the red carry-on bag onto the queen-size bed. I unzipped it and began to search for my toothbrush and skincare products.

I hated that I wanted him so much, regretted my reckless decision to crack open a window and nudge him back into my life. When we first started speaking, I was so eager for attention I hadn't thought about the repercussions. Telling Adrian over a Facebook chat I had feelings for him hadn't seemed dangerous.

I sent him a quick text to let him know I was back at my mom's.

He responded immediately.

Adrian: *Talk?*

Me: *Sure. My mom kicked me out of the hospital. I'll take the dog out on a walk.*

I clicked the leash to the collar on Mom's German Shephard mix, Bishop, heading for the front door without a jacket. Mom had allowed Curtis to stay with her at the hospital. If I didn't have the insatiable need to move, I could plop onto the couch and have the house to myself for this conversation. That wouldn't work, though. I needed to stay ahead of my nerves.

Clouds had rolled in late. Even though it was close to ten, the October air, blocks from the ocean, felt thick and muggy. I took a deep breath, wrapping Bishop's leash twice around my hand to keep him close.

"Hi," I said when I heard Adrian's deep scratchy voice on the line. The first time I'd called him on the phone after so many years of not speaking, his grown-up voice took me by surprise. At first I didn't like the rough-around-the-edges sound, so different from my husband's soft, almost delicate voice. After a few late-night conversations, I began to long for that voice.

Adrian had taken up mixed martial arts after college and fought in a caged ring for sport. He joked that decades of acid reflux, Crown Royal, and getting his windpipe crushed on more than one occasion had given him that sexy reverberation which drove the ladies crazy. I found myself agreeing with his assessment, although I had yet to say so.

"It's good to talk you," I said.

"You, too." I could hear the smile in his voice. "I can't believe your mom tossed you out of the hospital."

I guided Bishop down Bermuda Avenue toward Ocean Beach's Sunset Cliffs. We crossed the boulevard and stepped along the unpaved path edging the Pacific Ocean. Dark crashing waves thundered in greeting, thrashing against sharp sandstone edges.

"My mom's not a fan of crowds. Or sympathy. It's no surprise she tossed us all out."

"I told you she's a tough old broad."

I smiled at his optimism. "You were right."

"Have you heard from him?"

He meant my husband. Adrian refused to call Kevin by his name. "A few texts and a phone call about what was going on and if I could come home sooner. He's not used to having the boys on his own."

"Maybe he'll appreciate what you do a little more."

"Oh, for sure. He'll be super grateful for a few days and then forget about it."

"Piece of work."

"He has a full-time job, Adrian. I normally take care of everything related to the boys."

"I work long hours at least five days a week, and I'm still very involved in my children's lives, make their lunches, take them to school, help with homework."

"Good for you."

"Why do you defend him?"

"Why do you attack him?"

"Because you refuse to see his faults. Anyway, I don't want to talk about him. How are you?"

"I've been thinking." I stepped over a piece of driftwood left behind on the path. "I'd like to see you."

"Give me three hours."

"I'm serious," I said.

"I am, too."

The path veered. A section of the cliff's edge had collapsed under erosion, and was blocked off with chain link fence. The sign ahead read *Sheer Unstable Cliff. Stay Back*.

Only a few feet of space existed between the meandering dirt path and a steep drop into the ocean. In the cloudy darkness, I was tiptoeing along the precipice of infidelity.

"That's a lot of travel for such a short amount of time, and they don't even have a major airport in Grants Pass."

"You're worth it."

Bishop tugged on his leash, sniffing at the scrub brush. "It would only be for a few hours. I wouldn't want anyone to notice I was missing. And we're not going to do anything, just talk. I could meet you for coffee or a drink."

"Okay."

"How about Thursday?" I asked, still feeling unsure.

"I'll be there."

"You sure?"

I kicked at some loose gravel waiting for his response. The rocks clicked and stumbled off the cliff into the ocean below, like pieces of me making the leap.

"Hope?"

He was going to change his mind. A handful of hours with no touching wasn't worth the trouble.

"Yes?" I asked, waiting for the rejection.

"I'd walk a year to spend ten minutes with you."

A genuine smile spread into my cheeks. "You're pretty sweet."

"I'm not trying to be. It's the truth."

"What are you going to tell your wife? Isn't it going to seem weird with your taking off out of nowhere for a day?"

"We're separated. I don't have to tell her anything."

"Yeah, but you live together. She's going to ask."

"None of her business."

"Who's going to make the lunches and drive your three kids to school?"

"I'll drop them off and tell her I'm leaving. We agreed we'd start dating other people. It was her idea. I'm only here for the kids."

"And to save on rent."

Adrian owned his own business renovating houses. It paid well enough when he had a project, but he also spent a good amount of time looking for work or taking on charity cases for neighbors in need.

"Yeah, money's tight," he admitted. "It's easier to stay in the downstairs bedroom for now."

I tugged on Bishop's leash again to keep him moving. "Book the flight and let me know when to pick you up. I'm nervous but I really want to see you."

"I'll rent a car. I might fly in tomorrow early. It'd be nice to catch up with my sister while I'm in town."

"So that's what you'll tell your wife."

"Please don't call her that. She's my ex. I'm not telling her anything."

I could feel the heat rise in my neck. "I'm not going to change my mind about anything, so don't come if you have expectations of sex or anything like that. Only a few hours, in public."

"I just want to see you."

"Good. I'll call you in the morning." I smiled again. He always knew what to say.

CHAPTER 5

...

TUESDAY, OCTOBER 11, 2016
Night

IT WAS ADRIAN'S words that had ultimately lured me in. As I walked along Sunset Cliffs with Bishop's leash firmly in hand, my gaze drifting toward the twisting narrow path ahead, I allowed myself to reminisce about how we got to this point.

I had reconnected with Adrian on Facebook years ago, but over the past several months we'd been private chatting a few times a week, nothing serious, all light banter. He said he was going to read a recent op-ed article I'd submitted to a local lifestyle magazine. I was flattered.

A man I once loved was interested enough in me to bother reading what I wrote. But after that conversation, Adrian stopped messaging me. I didn't hear from him for weeks.

I unfriended him, convinced it was dumb to converse with him anyway, that I'd read too much into his flattery and I was simply desperate for the attention.

Of course, I checked nearly every day to see if he noticed I'd unfriended him.

Then, nearly a month later, he sent me a private message.

Adrian: *Why'd you remove me from FB?*

Exactly the question I hoped he would ask.

After his note came through, I sat on my neatly made bed, in my enviable home, with my supposedly perfect life, and debated what to write. Like a petulant teenager, I messaged him back, my fingers tapping against the screen.

Me: *You just now noticed? Never mind, it doesn't matter.*

Adrian: *It matters to me... very much.*

An obvious hint of flirtation in his words. He cared. He noticed.

I wanted more.

Me: *You haven't written in three weeks.*

Adrian: *I've been very busy with work.*

I didn't believe him. He probably hadn't thought about me until that moment.

Adrian: *Will you add me back?*

Me: *It's not a good idea.*

Adrian: *Why?*

I bit my lip hard. I'd fantasized about him asking me this very question for the past twenty-two days. I'd tell him he hurt me, or say I didn't care, or maybe I would pretend it was an accident. The growing tension as I waited for his reaction these past several weeks had pushed me past reason. I typed the truth.

Me: *Because I'm still attracted to you.*

Hitting the send button, I bounced my knees up and down. Back in my journalism days, my co-workers joked that I liked to play my cards close. In the past, I'd made it a point to keep my true thoughts, feelings, and motivations private. It was safer. These days, with my sense-of-self diminished, the reckless need for Adrian to see me as a desirable woman took charge.

I hurried to the kitchen to wash the dishes, anything to distract myself from what I'd done. Before the faucet water could even warm, the phone chimed. I had a new message.

Adrian: *Do you really mean that?*

I typed back, beginning to pace in anxiety.

Me: *Yes.*

Adrian: *Is this a joke?*

Me: *No.*

Adrian: *Are you sure?*

Me: *Um yeah, why would I joke?*

Adrian: *I don't know. Maybe you're going to write an article soon on your ex-boyfriends and you want to gauge my reaction.*

Me: *Not a bad idea, actually.*

Adrian: *So you were kidding.*

Me: *No, I wasn't. I meant it. Why is that so hard to believe? Can we forget about it now? I'm embarrassed I said anything.*

Digital green minutes ticked forward on the microwave clock while I waited for a response. My boys were at school for another two hours. I had grocery shopping to do and the floors needed vacuuming.

What if he didn't say anything back? That would be that. I was a sad, neglected stay-at-home mom and I had made a gigantic fool of myself. He would tell our mutual high school friends. They would laugh about it together. I had gone from a respectable career woman to a pathetic cliché. Hope Rains Sullivan, Desperate Housewife.

He finally messaged me.

Adrian: *You know back when we were young?*

Me: *Yeah?*

Adrian: *I loved you hard.*

Me: *That's supposed to make me feel better?*

Adrian: *You made a confession, now I have.*

I bit the inside of my cheek in frustration.

Me: *Well that was a long time ago. I was talking about now.*

My mind flashed back to our first kiss. His cinnamon breath smelled like Wrigley's Big Red chewing gum.

Adrian: *Do you really think those kind of feelings go away?*

Me: *Yes.*

Adrian: *Not for me.*

Dusty butterfly wings flapped in my belly, the ones I never expected to feel again. He still cared about me after all this time.

I bounced back over to the kitchen sink and squeezed soap on the sponge. Turning on the faucet, I picked up a plate. The butterfly wings in my belly beat harder. The water turned hot and burned my hands. Adrian still cared about me after all this time, and I had told him I was attracted to him. This was a dangerous game.

I plunked down the plastic plate, shut off the faucet and texted him back.

Me: *I think it's best we don't talk anymore.*

Adrian: *Why?*

Me: *Because I'm married. You're married. We have children. This is completely inappropriate.*

Adrian: *So that's it, we never speak again?*

Me: *Yes.*

Adrian: *Are you sure?*

Me: *Positive.*

Adrian: *If we're never going to talk again, we should tell each other everything.*

The doorbell rang and I raced to check who it was through the peephole. A delivery man set a package on my doorstep. I decided the mail could wait, and walked back toward the kitchen as I texted.

Me: *I did tell you everything.*

Adrian: *I didn't.*

Curiosity got me.

Me: *OK. Go ahead.*

Adrian: *Not now. I'm at work. Tonight?*

Me: *What time?*

The anticipation made my heart pound.

Adrian: *Late.*

Me: *How about 11?*

Adrian: *Okay, I'll send you a message on Facebook at 11.*

Me: *Perfect. Have a good day* ☺

Adrian: *I already am.*

The butterflies twisted to knots inside my belly.

CHAPTER 6

...

THE PAST – ABOUT THREE MONTHS AGO
Night

IT WAS AROUND midnight by the time I was ready to sneak online and chat with Adrian. I'd spent the day folding laundry, organizing toys, doing homework with Michael and Zach, and making myself sick with worry.

Kevin and the boys were in bed asleep when I finally huddled at the breakfast nook with a blanket, vibrating with nerves and anticipation. I would hear what he had to say, I reasoned with myself, revel in it, and never speak to him again.

We started off making small talk. Then Adrian got serious.

Adrian: *Do you remember the last time we talked when we were teenagers?*

I was seventeen to his eighteen. We'd had a huge blow up a few months prior and, in the interim, I'd met Kevin.

Me: *Yeah, you hung up on me and never called back.*

Adrian: *Kevin was at your house and when he asked you who you were talking to, you told him it was nobody.*

Me: *Because I was mad at you.*

Adrian: *Why? You were the one who stood me up.*

Nestled on the soft built-in breakfast bench in my gleaming Tiffany blue kitchen, I bristled at the memory of the fight I'd had with Adrian before our final phone call.

Me: *Here's how I remember that night. It was close to ten o-clock and you called to demand I meet you at some eighteen-and-under dance club.*

I could still picture myself dressed in a baggy nightshirt, standing in Mom's oversized kitchen. She had a hairdresser's cape wrapped around my stepdad as she trimmed his hair. I was trapped by the short old-school telephone cord with the two of them listening to every word of my conversation.

Adrian: *I begged you to meet me and you said 'no.'*

Me: *Exactly. I was tired of being used. You called me at the very last minute because you had no one else, and you didn't want to be alone. I was finished, Adrian. I deserved better than that.*

Adrian: *You are dead wrong. I never used you.*

Me: *You loved me when you were fourteen. But when we reconnected my senior year of high school, I became your buddy when you had nothing better to do. You were the bad boy, and I wasn't cool enough for you to date anymore. Your friends all thought I was a prude. They never liked me.*

Adrian: *When you were seventeen, I spent at least one night a week at your house for a year... I sat there and watched you while you did homework. Why do you think I did all that?*

Me: *Maybe because you had a crush on my best friend...or you were bored. I don't know. My mom always fed you when you* came over and you usually ended up passed out on my bed. I honestly thought you were on drugs and my room was one of your places to crash.

Do you remember the time I told you, you could kiss me once, and you started to and then you stopped? Right before you made contact with my lips. You were repulsed by me.

I pouted, my bottom lip protruding in my lonely kitchen.

Adrian: I was in love with you, Hope. When you broke up with me in middle school, it nearly killed me. I had you back in my life again, and I was afraid to lose your friendship. If I kissed you and you didn't like it, I risked losing you completely.

Me: I had no idea.

Adrian: How is that even possible?

Me: I'm not a mind reader.

Adrian: I practically lived at your house. I worshipped the ground you walked on. I didn't make a move on you because I didn't want to risk losing you.

I blew some dust off my keyboard as I played this new scenario over in my mind. A door creaked open. Before I had time to react, Kevin was standing in front of me in his boxers.

"Hey," he said, rubbing at the sleep in his eyes.

"Hi." I slammed the computer shut as my breath caught in my throat.

Kevin's blue eyes searched mine. "What are you doing?"

"Nothing." I ran an index finger along my computer top. "I couldn't sleep. What are you doing awake?"

"I thought I heard you typing." He smoothed his large hand over his blond hair, still trying to orientate himself in his haze of sleep.

"You need to get a haircut, babe," I said, trying to change the subject.

"Yeah." His eyes drifted around our surroundings. All the lights were off. I shivered in my blanket in the corner of the breakfast nook.

"Anyway," I said. "I was online reading about some old *Dateline* episodes. I'll be in bed in a little bit."

His brows knitted together in a frown. "You sure?"

"Yeah, it was a long day and I need a little alone time to unwind. That's all. I'll be in bed soon."

He stood there, rubbing a hand over his stubble, awareness seemingly seeping in.

"Goodnight." I yawned, stretching my arms over my head and clasping my hands together. "I'll be quiet when I come back in so I don't wake you."

He titled his head to the side, edging closer to me.

"Is something else wrong?"

"No." I shot him a lackluster smile, pressing the palms of my hands harder onto my laptop as if to keep him out. "Don't be silly. Go to bed, you're tired."

He nodded, looking around the room once again. "Night," he said, slowly turning away and walking toward the bedroom. "I love you, Hope."

"Love you, too," I murmured, fighting a near paralyzing wave of guilt.

I waited until the door creaked shut and the floorboards groaned as he lumbered back into bed. Tapping my fingers across the glass table, I debated whether to reopen my computer. This was my whisper from the universe to stop before I got caught.

I didn't listen.

Reopening my laptop and typing in my password, I responded to Adrian.

Me: *So then why did you really call me that night to go dancing, so late and last minute?*

Adrian: *Where did you go?*

Me: *Kevin walked in. He's gone now. Why did you call me that night?*

Adrian: *I had flowers for you. I spent my last fifteen dollars buying you a dozen roses. It wasn't even enough, but the lady felt sorry for me and sold them to me at a discount.*

Me: *You bought me flowers?*

Adrian: *And a card.*

Me: *What did it say?*

Adrian: *Hope, don't pretend like you didn't know.*

I yanked my hair back in a bun.

Me: *How was I supposed to know you bought me flowers? Why didn't you just come over to my house and give them to me?*

Adrian: *Because your mom and stepdad and all your brothers and sisters were home. I was embarrassed. What if you turned me down?*

Me: *So you thought it was better to call me up all frantic and demand that I come to you? That wasn't very smart.*

Adrian: *My car was out of gas. I used my last dollar to buy you those flowers.*

My shoulders relaxed. The visual was beyond romantic, something straight out of one of my favorite 80's movies.

Me: *And I thought you were being rude and bossy. I was so proud of myself for taking a stand, for finally giving up on you and realizing I deserved to be treated better.*

Adrian: *I still have the card.*

37

Me: *Really?*

Adrian: *I saved it.*

I looked around the darkened kitchen as I let his words settle in. Moonlight filtered in from the window above the kitchen sink.

He messaged back.

Adrian: *I thought you knew what I was going to tell you and you weren't interested so you blew me off.*

Me: *I swear, I thought you were looking for a last-minute friend to hang out with. How could I know you were standing there with flowers and no gas in your car?*

Adrian: *It was getting late, and I was afraid they would wilt if I didn't give them to you soon. I was so sure you knew. That's why I pressured you so hard.*

I slid my hand across my collarbone.

Me: *What did the card say?*

Adrian: *It's embarrassing.*

Me: *Tell me.*

Adrian: *Why, what does it matter now?*

Me: *Because we're talking about it. You said you would tell me everything.*

The Facebook chat sat empty. He'd gone quiet. I released my hair from its tight bun and contemplated what to do next. The bubbles on the screen moved. He was typing.

Adrian: *The card said, 'I'm still in love with you. Can we try again?'*

My eyes stung with tears.

Me: *I wish I would've known.*

Adrian: *Would it have changed anything?*

When we first met, Adrian had been so good to me. He loved me with such tenderness it felt suffocating. I was a thirteen-year-old girl whose mother threw hot buttered corn at her father across the dinner table. A girl whose dad called her mom a fat slut and barked at his children like a drill sergeant every time he got high on methamphetamines. Adrian's attentive kindness made me nervous. Real men didn't behave that way.

When I turned seventeen and Adrian no longer seemed romantically interested in me, I felt torn between hurt that he didn't want me any longer and fear of trying to change his mind. I worried if I won him back and something went wrong in the relationship, he wouldn't forgive me. I, too, was afraid of losing his friendship. But I knew I would have taken the risk if he'd made the first move.

Me: *Of course it would have changed things. I wanted you to want me.*

Adrian: *Then why didn't you come that night? Why did you say I was nobody when I called you on the phone?*

Me: *When you finally called me all those months later, I was furious. The fact that you blew me off for so long, just because I didn't want to go dancing at the last minute, was confirmation you didn't care about me. I'd met Kevin and he was there the day you called. I'd finally found someone who truly appreciated me.*

I shrugged off my blanket and stood to pour myself a glass of water.

Adrian took his time typing a reply. I sipped from my cup and watched the little bubbles bouncing, waiting for what he would say next.

Adrian: *I spent those six and a half months completely straightening my life out to make myself worthy for you. I dropped my old friends, found a real job, enrolled in college.*

I eventually got my education because of you. When I called you that day it was because I was ready for you. Ready to be the man you deserved.

My chest tightened with sorrow and an overwhelming feeling of honor.

Me: *I didn't know.*

Adrian: *And you said I was nobody.*

I couldn't believe he was telling me all of this, couldn't believe it was real. I pulled my blanket tighter and typed my response.

Me: *I'm so sorry.*

Adrian: *What are you thinking right now?*

Me: *I'm thinking I feel like the tragic heroine in a star-crossed romance movie.*

If Adrian had told me what was on his mind all those years ago, our lives would have taken a different path. I wouldn't have met Kevin. I wouldn't have had my same children.

Me: *I can't believe I might have gone a lifetime without knowing how you felt about me if I hadn't contacted you on Facebook. We wouldn't be talking to each other right now.*

Adrian: *I've thought about you constantly, but I wouldn't have ever reached out again. You made it clear how you felt.*

Me: *I should go to bed now.*

I needed to be alone with my thoughts. I wanted to revel in his words and hold them close.

Adrian: *Are we ever going to talk again?*

I drew in a deep breath and exhaled slowly.

Me: *Maybe. I don't know. I need to think. Whatever happens, I won't regret finding you again. Thank you for sharing with me.*

Adrian: *That's it?*

Me: *For now.*

CHAPTER 7

...

WEDNESDAY, OCTOBER 12, 2016
Morning

THAT CHAT ON Facebook wasn't our goodbye. It was the moment my heart broke open to the possibility of something else. So many beautiful conversations had led me toward agreeing to meet Adrian the following day. I needed to look him in the eyes and see if my feelings were real. I hoped they weren't, it would be so much easier to let him go.

I checked my text messages from bed before I dressed to visit Mom at the hospital. My stomach fluttered with anticipation. One was from him.

Adrian: *Good morning, beautiful.*

Me: *Morning.*

Adrian: *I'm flying in tonight at 6. Want to meet for dinner?*

Me: *No. I told you I would see you tomorrow.*

I turned my phone to silent to avoid getting tempted into a debate with him over my plans.

* * *

At the hospital, family drama took charge. Despite all of Mom's protests for privacy, my older brother, Pete, rolled into town from Los Angeles, his illegitimate daughter in tow.

Dressed in a stylish by Alan Thicke sweater and the latest Adidas high tops, Pete sauntered into the room, holding Maya's plump little hand. He smiled at us as if he had just stolen another man's parking space, or better yet, pulled someone else's clothes out of the dryer at the Laundromat before the timer went off. He did things like that.

"Hi, Trouble." I grinned.

"Hey, little sister. Hey, Sharon," he said to our mom. She frowned back at him.

"After you spend a few minutes with Mom, why don't we hit up Costco?" I asked. "I told Curtis I'd get some food in the house for when she comes home. You could keep me company."

I watched Mom's face soften from the corner of my eye. I was positive I'd earned some brownie points with her by finding an excuse to drag her trouble-making son out of the room.

"Sounds like an adventure." Pete smirked.

"For sure," I said, ready to break free of everyone and check my texts. Even family drama couldn't keep me from thinking about Adrian.

* * *

"You want me to drive?" I asked Pete as we walked down the hospital's chilly corridors toward the elevators.

"Sure, you know your way around better."

"True." I scooped Maya up into my arms so we could walk faster. "We'll go to the one I'm most familiar with. It's out of the way, but I have a few other errands I need to run near my old neighborhood." I wanted to stop by my former beauty salon to pick up a small bottle of my favorite jasmine and freesia scented perfume for my non-date with Adrian. "Are you in any hurry?"

"Not really. As long as we make time for lunch."

"They have pizza and hotdogs for sale outside of Costco."

"Candy." Maya looked at me with a crooked, mischievous grin. I set her back down, surprised at how heavy she was for a four-year-old. "That's up to your daddy."

Pete smirked. "So I hear your favorite stepsister is coming into town for a visit."

"Don't start with me."

"Heh. Heh. Heh," he laughed, sounding like our dad. "Is she staying at Sharon's place with you?"

"Probably."

"That should be interesting."

The elevator dinged, and we stepped inside. I guided Maya's finger so she could push the button for the parking structure level. Pete grinned at me, waiting for a reaction on his comment about Tawny. When he didn't get one, he continued. "Skye said Tawny lost most of her baby weight, and she's looking great."

"I have no idea," I said, refusing to take the bait.

"I kind of liked her gigantic ass the way it was." The elevator bounced to a stop on the wrong floor. When the doors slid open, a non-descript man in his late forties stepped inside. I inched backward, hating the way my brother talked about women in front of his own daughter. We all waited in momentary silence for the doors to close again.

"Last time I saw her walk through that narrow entryway into Sharon's kitchen, I thought for sure she was going to get stuck," Pete said, not even bothering to lower his voice.

"Nice. You're such a gentleman." *How would he like it if someone said that about Maya?*

"What? I was giving her a compliment. I like fat asses." He chuckled. "Not really. But maybe now that she's slimmed down, I'll ask her out on a date."

"You're disgusting."

"It's not like we're really related."

I sagged against the back wall. Mom and Dad had Pete back when they were teenagers. When Grandma Sue figured out her sixteen-year-old daughter was pregnant, she sent Mom away to a home for *girls who had gotten in trouble.* As soon as Mom gave birth, the nurses took away her baby and placed him up for adoption.

My younger sister and I always knew about Pete, the mysterious brother our parents hadn't been allowed to keep. Pete reunited with us when he turned eighteen and was legally allowed to look at his adoption files. Mom's persistence in making sure the files held our current address had finally paid off.

"That's gross, Pete. Tawny's still your legal stepsister."

He shrugged.

"What about the fact that she's happily married with two children. That's not an issue for you, either?"

"Whatever."

The elevator doors slung open on the parking level with a whoosh, and we stepped out. I dug around in my purse for my keys. "I think the car is this way." I pointed beyond the first two rows of cars.

Pete took Maya's hand. "Seriously though, you think you two will ever bury the hatchet?"

I walked faster to get ahead of him. "It's in the past, okay? I don't want to talk about it."

I spotted what appeared to be my car and hit the lock button to hear it beep. "It's over here." I motioned. "Zach's booster seat is in the trunk. Will that work for Maya?"

"Oh, shit."

"What?" I asked.

"I have Roxy in my car."

"Are you kidding me?"

"No. What was I supposed to do, leave her alone in my apartment in L.A.?"

"Don't you have any friends?"

"Very funny. We have to get her."

"I don't want her in my car."

"Why? She's not going to do anything."

I leaned against the trunk of my Audi rubbing my hand across my forehead. "Pete, you're such a pain in the ass." Popping open the back, I yanked out the booster seat and marched to the backseat to set it up for Maya.

After strapping her in and settling into the driver's side, I got directions to Pete's car to collect his terrorist Puggle. "She better not destroy my car."

"Roxy is perfectly well behaved," he said without an ounce of honesty in his voice.

I was a pushover and a fool allowing his ill-mannered dog in my car. I needed to learn how to say no. "So I heard from Dad you have some news."

Pete lifted his left eyebrow. "Yeah? What'd he say?"

"He said to ask you."

My phone rang and I slid the button to answer it. "Hang on," I said to Pete. "Hello?"

"Hey, Mama." My son's voice poured from the car speaker.

"Hi, Michael, aren't you supposed to be in school right now?"

"I am. The teacher said I could go to the principal's office to call you. I miss you, Mama."

"I miss you, too, Bubalah. I'm also in the car. You're on speaker phone with Uncle Pete and Cousin Maya."

"Hi," Michael said, the enthusiasm dropping from his voice. "What are you guys doing?"

"Driving to Costco. You having fun with Daddy?"

"Not really. He yells a lot."

"What good things are happening?" I knew kids on the autism spectrum tended to focus on the negative. It was my job to redirect him toward positive thinking.

"I don't know," he said.

"Something good had to have happened."

"We ordered pizza for dinner and he gave us lots of screen time." I cringed at the thought of all that unhealthy food. My boy knew exactly what to say to get his mama upset.

"Hold on, hon. Pete, is that your car?"

He nodded.

"Put Roxy in the back and let's go. Make sure you bring her food and water bowl, or whatever it is she's been using."

"You're letting Roxy in our car?" Michael shrieked. "Don't let her on my side. She's gross, Mama. She'll pee all over everything."

"She's potty trained," I told him.

"Last time Roxy was at Auntie Skye's house, she pooped on the floor and bit Zach when he wouldn't give her his green bean casserole."

"It'll be fine. Don't worry. If anything happens, I'll get the car cleaned."

"I hate that dog."

"Michael! I told you, we're on speaker phone."

"I'm sorry, but you need to learn to set boundaries," Michael replied with the bluntness of a typical non-neurotypical.

Pete ignored Michael's concerns and got out of the car. When he returned with Roxy, she snorted and squiggled to break free like an underdeveloped rodeo bull. Pete tossed her chunky body into the backseat of my car.

Maya giggled. "That's my sister."

"Gross, Mom, I can hear Roxy breathing," Michael whined over the speaker phone. "Maya, she's not your sister."

"Enough, Michael," I told him. "Change the subject."

"She's going to get my seat all dirty."

"Don't insult Maya's sister." I giggled, thinking of Adrian's advice to me recently, about enjoying my son's quirkiness. He was right. I had to stop obsessing about Michael's future happiness every time he said something I worried would offend people. Adrian volunteered with kids on the spectrum, and he gave me such a comforting perspective. It was easy to imagine having a partner who was more involved in my life.

"We're driving to the store to get some food and wine for when people come over."

Michael sighed dramatically. "Are you leaving Roxy in the car alone while you go in the stores?"

"No," I lied.

"Promise?"

"Michael!"

"What?" he argued.

"Oy." Emotionally exhausted and in need of some sunshine after arguing with my brother and then my son, I decided I didn't want to wait until tomorrow to meet up with Adrian. I was going to text him as soon as I was alone. I wanted to see him. Tonight.

CHAPTER 8

...

WEDNESDAY, OCTOBER 12, 2016
Night

"PETE, I'M TAKING the dog on a walk. See you in a little."
It was exactly 9:14 pm. Adrian was supposed to meet me
around the corner in one minute.

"Want to take Maya?" Pete sauntered out of the kitchen,
his wild curls in need of a cut and the smell of pot wafting
all around him.

"No, I'm walking near the cliffs. It's not safe. See you
soon." I swept out the door before he could argue.

The clouds had rolled in off the coast, their extra layer
of warmth hugging my arms. A little painted sign Mom had
hung on the old wooden chair on her porch pronounced, *If
you're lucky enough to live at the Beach, you're lucky
enough.*

It was dark outside, besides some porch lights and a hazy half-moon. I looked left and then right down the street and didn't see him.

Full of nervous anticipation, I sent him a text.

Me: *Where are you?*

After twenty long years, I was going to see my first love in person all over again.

Adrian: *On the corner*

Me: *Of what streets?*

Adrian: *I don't know.*

Me: *Stay there.*

I turned to my right, searching for him in the darkness.

Me: *I don't see you.*

Adrian: *I'm here.*

A shadow of a man moved, a man I should not be following. A stronger woman would turn around.

"Adrian?"

"Hope?" He stopped.

"Yes. Go by the street light." I waved him in the right direction, watching him walk with uncertainty. At about five foot ten, he wore light gray jeans that fit him just right. A black t-shirt highlighted his taut muscles. Under the lamppost, I could see his dark hair sported streaks of gray and his cheekbones had grown more prominent with age.

My heart raced. He looked better than he did in his pictures on Facebook. The insecure boy had been replaced by a man.

Adrian dropped his keys and reached down to retrieve them, revealing his nervousness. I smiled as I stepped closer to him, heat burning in my cheeks. Within touching distance, I leaned in for a light hug and felt his heart thumping as fast as mine. I rested my head on his chest to steady my nerves. "Thanks for coming."

"Thank *you*." He kissed the top of my head taking in a long inhale through his nose. "You're even more beautiful than I remember."

I let out a tiny burst of air. "Thanks. I'm nervous."

"I'm a total wreck." He laced his fingers through mine.

"I know. I could tell by the way you dropped your keys."

"I've always been such a complete mess around you. Whenever you put your hands on me, it made me insane. I have missed you so much. I feel like I'm fourteen again."

"Me, too," I said, feeling slightly more at ease after he took hold of my hand. So much for my rule about no touching.

His warmth comforted me. I hoped he wouldn't let go.

"It's being near you, I completely lose my cool."

"Like you ever had any." I rolled my eyes skyward and flashed him a shy smile.

"I never did around you."

Leaning down, I untangled Bishop's leash caught under his front leg. "I can't believe you came all the way here to see me."

"People don't get these kinds of second chances." He rubbed his free hand on his thigh. "I had to."

The idea of taking things further ruffled me. "You said you'd come, but I didn't think you actually meant it."

"I mean everything I say to you," he said squeezing my hand tighter in his.

"Follow me," I nudged.

I guided him toward the ocean. We had one street left to cross - Sunset Cliffs. I bit my lip and, as soon as the silver headlights of cars cleared, we ran.

"Hurry," I said.

Wild energy pulsed through me. He was better looking than I expected. His hand wrapped over mine felt better than I imagined. Being in his presence exhilarated me. This wasn't going the way I hoped. Adrian, in the light of reality, was far from the letdown I'd planned for.

The dirt path meandering along the jagged cliffs crunched under our feet. Moonlight guided our way as we walked. "I love it here," I said, filling the silence. "You know, these cliffs turn gold when the sun goes down. Ocean Beach has the most beautiful sunsets in all of Southern California."

A couple had already claimed a spot at the first bench we passed. "I wanted to sit with you." I tugged Adrian forward. "Come on. There's another one up ahead."

The next bench remained free, waiting for us. He sat first while I tied Bishop's leash to the bench's base and then took the space next to Adrian, placing my legs over his legs. He rubbed my bare thigh while looking at me, the ocean rolling before us. Waves broke and the tide pulled back in retreat.

"You look even more beautiful than you did when we were kids."

"No, I don't." Feeling shy, I tucked a loose strand of hair behind my ear. The kelp-scented mist from the ocean soothed my concerns.

"With age comes beauty. You're a woman now. You're not a girl anymore."

"Thank you."

"I have to tell you some things, in case you never agree to see me again," he said, his voice catching in his throat.

"Okay." I played with the fringe of my purple cotton mini-skirt, waiting for what would come next.

Adrian looked out at the resilient star-lit waves, the tips curled with white foam before breaking against the cliffs. His lips parted and then shut again. I watched him, wondering what he was thinking. "Hope?"

"Yes?"

"For the past twenty plus years, I've measured every woman against you, always thinking of what I could have done differently to be with you. What I could have tweaked. What I should have said. If I just had a little more fight in me back then." His words spilled out with an emotion I could feel, heavy in the air between us. "You've always been my perfect. The girl I would do anything to be with. And now, here you are. I can't let you slip away again."

I studied him, trying to find words. He'd told me so many times how he felt about me, but never in person, not when I could touch him and watch him speak. His eyes conveyed his conviction deep into my bones.

"I wish I were a more literary person," he continued. "I wish I had a better grasp on words. There's probably some French phrase or some Swahili proverb that means a thousand things I can't say."

Waves tumbled and thrashed against the shoreline, mimicking my emotions.

"I didn't miss you all these years, it was bigger than that. You were missing *from* me. Being here with you now, all these feelings are flooding back. It's like right where we left off. Your sweet smell. Your legs pressed on mine." He inhaled as his brows creased. "I have to see you tomorrow."

The amber lights to our north shimmered across the ocean waves. My resolve to maintain boundaries melted. It felt better than it should, to feel appreciated, desired.

My fingers trembled. I wasn't going to think, just let go and feel. I leaned closer and put my forehead against his. "I'm going to count to three, and then I'm going to kiss you. Ready?"

He nodded.

"One. Two..." I held my breath for a beat and tilted my head to press my lips against his. Our mouths parted, fitting softly together at first, until he kissed me harder.

He tasted so good, my body pushed closer. Our lips knew each other. I moved on top of his lap, my legs on either side. His warmth, his crisp citrus scent. This was what kissing someone should feel like.

Hormones, pheromones, love, whatever it was, washed over me. I needed this man. I wanted to feel this way every hour of every single day.

My hand found its way up the back of his shirt. His skin ran hot. The ocean roared. I heard voices talking low, a couple walking by us.

His hand pressed into the small of my back. His other hand grabbed at the nape of my neck. He whispered, "I love you, Hope."

I froze. He tried to kiss to me again. He couldn't, not with my lower lip firmly entrenched in my teeth. I bit down with such force, I worried I'd draw blood. Why was he doing this to me? Why was I allowing it to happen?

His amber-green eyes held onto mine.

Tears pooled against my lashes.

"I wish you could feel what I'm feeling," he said, "so you'd know it's true."

I slid my body off of his, sidled beside him, and rested my head on his already familiar shoulder. "This wasn't supposed to happen."

"Can I tell you something?" he asked, leaning his head low to face mine.

"What more is there to say?"

"When you looked at me for the first time when we were in middle school, something in my soul clicked. I was never the same. I have always loved you, from the moment I set eyes on you. This kiss reconfirms what I've always known."

"I just look good for my age." A tear slipped from my eye. "You were pleasantly surprised, and now you're feeling a false sense of affection."

"You could have been four by four squared, and I'd still feel this way. Don't get me wrong, you're gorgeous, the most beautiful woman I've ever laid eyes on. But it's so much more than that. It's the way I feel when I'm next to you."

My heart ached for my loss. I couldn't keep him. "Why me? Of all the women, why do you feel this way about me?"

"You were my first love. I've never let it go."

"I need to get back to the house." I scooched my bottom halfway off the bench.

"Are you still going to meet me tomorrow?"

I stared at the ground, kicking at the gravel and refusing to make eye contact. As shameful as it was to admit, I wanted to see him again. We'd already crossed the line. What more harm could be done?

Once again, without giving myself the space to resist temptation, I tilted my head toward him and allowed desire to take the lead. "Of course." I reached for his hand as I stood, nudging him forward, every yes bringing us closer to a place I'd promised myself I wouldn't go. "Come on, walk me back." Bishop stayed put on the ground. Nobody was making it easy for me to leave.

Adrian leaned in, wrapping one arm around my waist and lifting my eyes to his. "Let me kiss you one more time."

I barely whispered, *yes*, as my lips met his.

I was in so much trouble.

CHAPTER 9

...

THURSDAY, OCTOBER 13, 2016
Evening

I'D SPENT MY day secretly texting back and forth with Adrian while I sat in Mom's room at the hospital. Rather than meeting up at a restaurant or bar as we'd originally discussed, I decided I wanted to meet him somewhere more private. Somewhere we could be alone, so I could kiss him again if I wanted.

Pulling up to the curb directly in front of Coronado's Hotel Maribel, Adrian waved at me through the lobby's arched glass windows. He stepped through their front doors up to my car, wearing dark blue jeans and another great fitting t-shirt.

"Hey, you made it," he said through my rolled-down passenger side window.

"Help me find parking." I waved him in. "We can walk back together."

"Anything for you." He opened the door and climbed inside, leaning over to kiss my right cheek.

I rubbed at his lip print with growing anxiety. Splintering pieces of me wanted to drop Adrian back off and race home. Instead, I drove with trembling hands toward the end of the short block and turned a tight corner, scanning the crowded narrow streets for an open spot.

Coronado Island, a popular resort town connected to the mainland by the Silver Strand, lay across and around the spectacular San Diego Bay. Even on a Thursday night, it was brimming with street life and prying eyes.

"Don't get too excited." I shot him a warning look, trying not to notice his intoxicating citrus scent. "We're only here to hang out. I didn't ask you to get a room so we could have sex."

"A guy can hope."

I whipped my head around to glare at him.

"Oh, relax. I'm kidding."

"Good." I saw a space up ahead and flicked on my blinker. A tight squeeze, but I excelled at parallel parking. After a little maneuvering, we were in.

As soon as I turned off the motor, I reached in my purse and slipped out a Xanax. Twisting open the cap on a half-empty water bottle, I took a sip and swallowed the pill.

"What was that?" he asked.

"Something for my nerves." I screwed the top back on and placed the water bottle back in my cup holder. "You ready?"

"Yes. Stay there." He hopped out of the car and rushed around to open my door.

"Such a gentleman." I smiled as the sounds of nightlife filled my ears. "Thank you." I snapped off my seatbelt and took a deep breath, catching a glimpse of my face in the rearview mirror. *This was it. I was meeting a man at a hotel room behind my husband's back. I barely recognized myself.*

"I'm upset you took something. I wanted all of you here," he said, reaching for my hand.

"Sorry, I'm really nervous. Hopefully the pill kicks in fast." I could feel my ankles wobble as my heels hit the pavement.

"I wish you wouldn't have done that."

"I wouldn't be able to function if I didn't take something." I was sliding into a panic attack.

"Why? You're with me. You're safe."

"This isn't fun or exciting for me, Adrian. I feel like a horrible human being." I pulled at a lock of my hair, twisting it vigorously around my index finger. "We're just going to hang out? Right?"

"Whatever you want. I just want to be with you."

I squeezed his hand to stop mine from shaking, and we walked toward the hotel. My new high heels pinched at my toes, and I felt my freshly purchased form-fitting green dress inching up my thighs. I was a harlot on the prowl.

"Thanks for coming, Hope. I was afraid you weren't going to show up."

I nodded and tried to let the touch of his hand on a warm cloudless night soothe my guilty conscience. The tangy smell of tomatoes and garlic drifted from an Italian restaurant lit with twinkling lights. Smiling couples and groups of families crossed paths with us on the sidewalk. I checked their faces to make sure I didn't know any of them.

"You okay?" he asked. "Are you hungry?"

"No, I'm good. Let's get there." I wanted to escape the crowd and shut the door behind us. We walked through an ornate iron gate into the old-world hotel's lobby and headed left toward our room. Adrian waved to the receptionist. He'd already checked in and asked for the key. *Did she notice we didn't have any luggage?*

The curved corridor, paved in elegant Spanish tiles, gave way to an open-air restaurant to the right of us. We were exposed once again to strangers living morally correct lives, dining with their friends, family, and significant others.

"You sure this is the right one?" I asked him when he stopped in front of room number twelve hundred. "It's directly across the hall from the restaurant."

He slid the key card through twice and the red light blinked, telling us we couldn't enter. My vision blurred and my pulse raced, sure signs of a full-blown panic attack taking hold. It hadn't happened in years, but it was possible I might stumble or even black out if we didn't get inside the room.

"It's not like I do this, either," Adrian said. He flipped the card over and slid it again, the light blinking green.

He opened the door and held it for me. I surveyed the large, outdated space. A small straight-backed beige couch faced faded pictures fastened to the wall, set up like a living room under hazy yellow lighting with what looked like a separate room for sleeping.

"Do you like it?" he laughed, acknowledging the decor was a disaster. "I upgraded to a one bedroom suite."

It was awful. The kitchenette screamed 1970's. I nodded and stepped toward the couch.

"Can I get you some water?" he offered.

"Yes, please." I kept my purse on my lap and imagined all the people dining in the restaurant on the other side of the hallway. I could hear their soft chatter and the clink of silverware. The sensory overload was overwhelming. "I can't do this here," I called out to Adrian as he filled a glass in the kitchen sink.

He walked back toward the sofa and handed me my water. "You want to leave?" His brow furrowed. "We can go. I'm so sorry, I got the upgraded room, because I wanted it to be nice for you. It's not that nice, though, is it?"

I inhaled and took a sip of water. "It's fine. The room is great, I just don't feel well. The meds should kick in soon." I took another sip from the glass. "Can we go into the bedroom? I know it sounds strange, but it's further away from the front door and it's dark in there."

I felt like I was on stage in that living room, the audience watching with x-ray vision from the other side of the door, judging my shameful behavior. The bedroom seemed like a sanctuary, tucked away from their conversations and their goodness.

Adrian's eyebrows lifted in surprise, but the grin that followed told me he wasn't disappointed. "Sure." He held out his hand to help me up.

I set the cool water glass on the side of the couch and stood, once again feeling the pinch of new shoes. "We can sit on the bed in the dark and talk."

"Would you like me to turn on the TV?" he asked as we walked into the darkened room.

"No, thank you." The Xanax begin to loosen the grip on my nerves. A soft rush of release. I slipped off my heels and propped some pillows against the headboard of the bed. Sitting closest to the slightly open door, I leaned back and made myself more at home.

Adrian took the spot beside me. "Are you comfortable now?" he asked.

I wanted our situation to feel more natural. I also wanted to admire what lay beneath his contoured t-shirt.

"Will you take off your shirt?" I asked without thinking. Xanax courage.

His eyes locked with mine while his lips curled into a dare. "You first."

The glorious relief from anxiety left me feeling reckless. I looked at him as I stood up and lifted my dress over my head. "That's it though," I said, opting to stay in my bra and underwear.

I froze while he gazed at me. "Now you take your shirt off."

"Okay," he said. "But I'm not going to measure up to you. There's going to be a level of disappointment."

"Not possible." I wanted to feel him, skin to skin.

"Whatever you like." He leaned forward and shook his head at me.

Dim light filtered through the partially closed door. I watched him as he lifted his shirt over his head and exposed his muscular chest and well-defined stomach. His skin was the perfect tanned brown.

He was everything my husband wasn't, a man who worked with his hands, and was even willing to use them in a fight. A man who preferred time with his kids versus earning another luxury vacation to impress the neighbors. Maybe this was the kind of relationship I was supposed to have.

Adrian leaned back against the headboard as I stepped closer to him, climbing back onto the bed and snuggling under his arm, resting my head on his chest. "Can we stay this way?"

"I couldn't ask for anything more."

I traced my finger across his chest and over a fading scar. "What's this from?"

"Just another one of my war wounds."

"This one stands out," I said, melting into him.

"It's so faded, I'm surprised you can see it at all."

I knew what I was looking for. "It's an old one."

"It is." He hugged me closer.

"Adrian?" I whispered, my ears luxuriating in the quiet. "Do you remember the second time we started hanging out… when I was a senior in high school?"

"I remember everything," he said. "You showed up on my doorstep one afternoon, wearing jean shorts with a big sew-on flower patch along with a red sweatshirt. You said you wanted to make sure I was alright."

I nodded. "A friend of yours told me you'd been stabbed and almost died in the hospital."

"He was exaggerating. I lost a lot of blood, that's all."

"He said you were in a gang, and they were jumping you out. When I asked you about it, you said it was all nonsense and you were fine."

"I was better than I'd ever been. Hope Sullivan was standing on my doorstep." He grinned at the memory.

"You told me you wouldn't do something stupid like that. It was true though, wasn't it?"

His posture stiffened. "Let's talk about something else."

"No." I touched his scar again. "I want to know the truth."

He cleared his throat and rubbed my bare thigh. "When we were kids, you were the single good thing in my life. And when you dumped me, I was desperate to find family and belong somewhere."

"So at fourteen you joined a gang and stayed in it until you graduated high school?"

"Do we really have to talk about this?"

The air-conditioning rattled on, and I cuddled in even closer. "Yes. Please, I want to know."

He sighed with reluctance, smoothing back his long bangs. "For years after you dumped me, I was desperate to belong to something. I wanted to have a bond to someone. I wanted to have a family. You have no idea what it's like to feel completely alone in this world. You had a great mom who looked out for you. I wanted to feel like someone would have my back and I'd have theirs."

"And it didn't work out?" I asked.

"I joined the beginning of my senior year of high school. But when the shit hit the fan, those assholes took off and left me to die. I did almost die. It was bad. It was really fucking bad."

"What happened?" I folded the top of the comforter over my body for extra warmth.

"It was a long time ago. Back then, I didn't have anyone who really loved me. My dad beat on all us kids and my mom didn't do a thing to protect us. Whenever a neighbor would call because they heard fighting, my mom would cover for my dad. She was embarrassed for anyone to know. That was her priority. Keeping his secrets."

I rubbed my hand across his chest to comfort him.

"I lost count of how many times she lied and told the police I fell down the stairs or tripped and fell. It was bullshit."

"I'm so sorry."

"It was a very dark period in my life that I'd like to forget about."

"Tell me once what happened the night you were stabbed." I draped my arm around his waist. "We won't ever talk about it again."

He cleared his throat and looked away from me as he spoke. "There were only four of us. We went downtown. We were in the wrong territory. One of my friends kind of broke off from our group. Guys from a rival gang started to rush him, so I went to his defense and I got pounced on. I don't remember how many guys it was. It was a lot. There had to be at least ten, eleven, maybe a dozen."

"You must have been terrified."

"I remember black jackets everywhere. I stood my ground as long as I could until I felt something hot come across my chest. It felt like someone burned me with something. I looked down and everything from the bottom of the left side of my chest to my waist was turning red. My shirt was soaked in blood. I remember looking at them, and they drew back. I think they saw what they had done and got scared."

"Then, what?"

He shrugged. "They turned around and scattered in different directions. I didn't know if they were going to come back, so I made it to the curb. I started to walk down the street. It felt like the city was empty. I was getting weaker and weaker, so I sat down on the curb. I don't know if I passed out. Someone woke me up and said the police were coming and the ambulance was coming and I was going to be ok. I don't remember much else. I think I lost so much blood, I blacked out."

"What happened to your friends?"

"They ran. They left me there to die. So much for family."

I wanted to slip back in time and save him. "I'm so sorry."

"I was in the hospital for an entire week. My parents never once came to visit. It was fucking awful."

"Did they let you leave the gang after that?"

"When I got better, I went to our leader and told him exactly what had happened. 'I want out. This is not what I signed up for. Your boys left me to die. I'm not getting jumped out. I paid my dues.' He nodded at me and that was it. I never saw any of them again." He brushed his hands over his hair. "One of them died two years later in the same park. I remember reading about it in the paper."

"Why did you pretend like it was nothing when I came to your apartment that day to check on you?"

"Are you kidding, Hope? I was in love with you. You were too good for me and I already felt unworthy. I felt so lucky we reconnected your senior year. When you showed up that day after all those years of me missing you, I panicked. I would have done anything not to scare you away.

Do you remember? You said since you could see I was fine, you were going to leave. I convinced you to come inside and hang out with me for a few minutes. I parlayed that into visiting you at your house the next day. I made up every excuse in the book to be near you. I wasn't going to blow it by telling you I was a dumb jerk who had joined a gang. You wouldn't have gone near me if you knew that."

"I would have understood."

"No, you wouldn't have. You would have judged me instantly. You would have been scared, and I would have never seen you again."

"So you lied."

"You were the one thing that was good for me. My life was so fucked up without you. You were seventeen and I had just turned eighteen. If I could manage to stay in your life that second time around, we were old enough that I could marry you. Just being in your home again with your mom. I used to love it when she would answer that door, motion me inside and ask if I'd eaten before I went up to your room. It made me feel so special. Cared for. You were like food for my soul. I was so hollow. I had no idea how it felt to be loved and cared for. I always felt like family with you. I was so comforted being in your home and being next to you." He laughed at a memory. "I was this big gang banger guy, and I felt safe around this little five foot three girl."

Tears formed in his eyes. "Hope, that wasn't me back then. I did wrong, I hurt people. I will spend the rest of my life doing good and helping people to make amends. I strayed from who I was and I paid for it. I'll never be that person again. I'm a good man now."

"What about being here with me tonight, do you think either of us are being good people? Doing whatever it is we are doing, knowing I'm a married woman and you still live in the same house as your wife? Doesn't that make you feel bad?"

"Not at all." He shook his head. "You and I were supposed to be together. I have no remorse and no regrets for whatever happens from this point on. You were stolen from me." His hands clenched into fists. "My only regret is not fighting harder for you back when I had the chance. We would have been together for twenty years now. I was such an idiot."

"Adrian," I whispered as I leaned over to touch his shoulder. "You were an eighteen-year-old boy scared of getting hurt. You can't blame yourself for being young."

"But I knew better. I knew you were the one for me and I let you go. I knew when we were kids you were the one. I knew better then. The stories you've told me about your husband, how he's pushed you and screamed at you. It makes me sick. He should have never had the chance to get near you, let alone marry you. He stole you from me. I hate him for that."

"That's not fair. You and I weren't together when I met Kevin. He didn't steal me."

"I should have been the one. You should have had *my* babies." Adrian kissed the back of my wrist and held it pressed to his lips for a beat, seemingly lost in his memories. "It would have been so different. I would have worshipped the ground you walked on."

I rolled atop him, straddling his waist between my knees, meeting his gaze. I kissed his cheeks, his forehead, and his lips. "I'm so, so sorry for everything you've been through." My body ached for him. I wanted to make love to him and give us both back what we'd lost.

"If you stay with me, Hope, I will make you so happy. I'll work like a damn slave, hold down three different jobs if I have to, anything to give you everything you deserve."

He kissed me, and I wrapped my legs tighter around his naked torso, gripping his chest as he rolled to tuck me beneath him. His long bangs fell around my face like a cocoon. "I love you, Hope, more than any man has loved any woman."

His scent, the warmth and care of his touch, the dim light shining through the crevice of the slightly ajar bedroom door. I could feel the memory forming, marking this moment before I plunged into the dark waters of infidelity.

I breathed in when he breathed out. This was it. I could end it. I could say no.

But the taste of him, the smell of his skin. The feel of his rough cheek against my ear, of his bare chest against the top of my breasts. How could I walk away?

He reached behind my back and, with one hand, unclasped my bra. I told myself to remember this. No matter what happened from here, if I got caught and branded a cheater, if I ended up with an angry husband and children who resented me, if the man I married left me and I faced a life on my own, this moment mattered. This was about being fully alive.

His hands reached down my panties.

"Adrian."

"Yes?"

"We can't go that far. I promised myself."

He started to withdraw his hand, and I stopped him. "Stay there, we just can't make love completely."

"Are you sure?"

"Yes."

He touched me with his hands, and eventually slid low enough to use his mouth. "What are you doing to me?" This was not something I had truly appreciated before tonight.

"Just enjoy," he replied in a hushed voice.

With a deep breath, I lifted my head. "Seriously Adrian, what exactly are you doing?"

"I'll never tell, unless you marry me."

"I might have to. Oh my God." I squirmed in pleasure. The gentle slip of his tongue over the exact right place got me close within minutes. Then his hand slid along my thigh, seemingly unsure but wanting to go inside. I couldn't hold back. How could I have lived thirty-eight years and not felt this way before? How could I ever give him up? I gasped, my back arching as the release of pleasure took over my body.

My breath came heavy and relaxed. "Holy shit, where did you learn to do all that?"

"I want you so bad right now."

"I'm sorry. I should have stopped you."

"No. I'd do it again every time, it's just…you're hard to resist."

"Maybe I could return the favor?" I smiled, putting my mouth on his and kissing him, allowing the rough stubble of his goatee to scratch across my face. Sliding past his chest, my nipples lightly touched the surface of his skin as I went down.

I used delicate fingers at first before grasping him more firmly. His breath caught, and I watched as his tongue slid along the seam of his lips, catching the full lower curve between his teeth.

My tongue slipped around the head with each thrust as my mouth moved rhythmically. I looked up at him, into his eyes, starting and stopping, going slow and then fast. I wanted to see his face, to know that I had him.

Adrian ran his fingers through my hair, watching me move. His hips lifted and my belly tightened in anticipation. He was ready. I told him to give in. His final thrust, and the low, thick hum of his voice as he came, left me every bit as satisfied.

"Feel better now?" I asked with a smirk.

"Oh my God, yes."

I stretched out my free arm to check the time on my cell. "I should leave soon."

"Can't you stay another hour? I flew all the way here to see you."

"I shouldn't."

I didn't want to leave either, but one of us had to be responsible. It was close to midnight, and my brother was a night owl. He'd ask questions about where I'd been so late at night, and if in a sour mood, he'd give me a hard time and rat me out to Mom. I wished Pete had stayed in Los Angeles so I could spend the night with Adrian.

I tucked one of his strands of stray hair behind his ear and looked into his amber-green eyes. His lashes were so thick, it looked like he had applied eyeliner. "I have to go now."

"I want to see you again."

I wondered if it were possible for reality not to ruin what we had. "Isn't it better we remember each other this way?"

"Hmmm." He smirked.

"What?" I asked. "See? I knew it. You're thinking about it. You don't really want to taint this perfect memory, see all my bad habits, discover all the not-so-hidden flaws."

"You couldn't be more wrong. I want to know everything." He looked me in the eyes. "I want the whole package, all your idiosyncrasies, your whole life."

"Promise me you won't contact me again after this," I asked, even though it's not what I really wanted.

His eyes dropped. "If that's what you want."

CHAPTER 10

...

FRIDAY, OCTOBER 14, 2016
Morning

THE NEUROLOGIST AND hospitalist exhausted all of their medical arguments, but to no one's surprise, they failed to convince Mom to stay. She signed out against medical advice on her fourth morning at La Jolla General Hospital, and Curtis drove her home.

I met them back at the beach house where she stumbled out of Curtis's sedan without assistance. "Mom, you're going to fall." I rushed down the front steps to help her.

She waved me away with her right hand, her face twisted in frustration.

"Sharon, give me a minute." Curtis came around from the driver's side of the car to help her.

"I'm fine," Mom said, showing no further signs of resistance as Curtis put his arm around her waist and guided her.

"I'll get your stuff from the trunk." I worrying about if she could make it to her bedroom. Mom had insisted we not move her to the downstairs guestroom while she recovered. She didn't want anything in her home rearranged.

We all figured we'd wait and see if she changed her mind once she faced the reality of dozens of steps to tackle each time she wanted to go in or out of her second story bedroom. Mom stumbled and nearly fell down the stairs twice on her way to her room. When she finally made it into her bed, her eyelids drooped and she shooed us out.

About two hours later, I tapped on her door, taking a deep breath and composing myself before she noticed something off about my behavior. I'd woken up that morning in pain from an ongoing condition I'd had since my college days, vulvodynia. When I experienced extreme stress, it triggered the nerve endings in my bladder, which for unknown reasons made my vagina feel like it'd been lit on fire.

The guilt and stress of the previous night with Adrian had taken its toll. Each careful step I took triggered flashes of pain.

"Mama, I've got food. You hungry?" I nudged the door open with my foot and hobbled in with a wooden tray in my hands. "I've got scrambled eggs, orange juice, and toast. Curtis made everything. It smells delicious." Tucked in the corner of the tray, under her cup, rested a sealed envelope I'd discovered in the mailbox.

Mom frowned. "I'm not hungry." Her feistiness made my stomach tighten a notch. After a long nap, she was still resisting help.

"Well, you need to eat to get your strength back. Before you know it, it'll be dinner time. The doctor said—"

"I don't care what she said."

"I know. Can you take a few bites, though? If you don't, your body will get used to not eating and the lack of nourishment will make it harder to recover. All your grandchildren have been asking to see you."

"They don't need me."

"No, but they want you, and that's important, too, isn't it?" I set the tray down beside her and studied her.

To my relief, she sat up and gathered the blankets around her waist. A stack of news and gossip magazines rested on the nightstand.

"You want me to open the sliding glass doors so you can hear the ocean?"

"No." She stared straight ahead.

I let out a long breath of air. Mom was used to being in charge. She wasn't going to accept my help without a fight, and I wasn't sure I had it in me. "Alright, well I'll leave your food here for you."

"Don't."

"Okay, Mama."

"Next time, maybe you'll listen to me."

I nodded as I picked up the envelope on her tray, considering a different approach to cheering her up. "You got something in the mail."

She looked over at me with a raised eyebrow.

"It's probably nothing," I continued. "But, it's from the Department of Children & Family Services in Illinois."

"Can I see it?" She reached out for the letter, her features softening.

I placed it in her hand. "Do you think it might be from Lucy?" Lucy was the mediator the Illinois court had assigned to Mom's case to find her second-born son.

My brother Pete wasn't the only child my parents gave up. Two years after Pete was born, Mom got pregnant again. Determined to keep the baby, she and Dad drove from Chicago to San Francisco to elope and give birth in secret.

I wasn't the only one who in my family who had made mistakes. Mom told me as soon as they arrived at their rundown apartment in Haight-Ashbury, she grew frightened. There were people strung out on drugs, nobody held a steady job, and she realized she couldn't bring her child into that seedy world.

My parents moved back to Chicago. Dad enrolled in college, and Mom worked as a telephone operator for the original Playboy mansion. She hid her pregnancy under baggie hippie clothes and when the nine months passed, they gave their second baby up in secret to the same Jewish adoption agency that had placed Pete.

Near the beginning of the year, Mom initiated the request to find my long lost brother. She filled out a bunch of paperwork and paid the court's three-hundred-dollar fee to get the process started.

The court granted a mediator access to my mystery brother's birth certificate and all of his official adoption paperwork. It'd been nearly three months and as far as I knew, Mom hadn't heard anything.

I'd wondered about my mystery brother since Mom first told me about him when I turned thirteen. What did he look like? What kind of personality did he have? Pete had so many of my dad's traits, but maybe this brother was more like me. "I hope it's good news."

"We'll see," she mumbled. Mom pulled the letter from the envelope and smoothed it out on her lap. "Why don't you take the food downstairs now?"

My jaw fell open in disappointment. "I want to know what it says."

"Okay, come sit with me." She cleared her throat as she began to read.

I moved the tray of food to her end table and sat on the edge of the bed, peering over to try and read the letter with her. As she read the words, a tiny smile crept across her lips. "She found him."

"No way."

"Lucy called him to find out if he was interested in speaking with me. He said yes, so she told him what paperwork he needed to fill out in order to get our phone number."

"Is he going to do it?" My mind drifted to my own, often times unstable childhood. Dad hadn't set the best example on how men should treat women. Would I have turned differently if I'd grown up in a more traditional family? Would I have still made the same choice in a husband?

Mom placed the letter on her lap face down and stared at it. "He said he would fill out the paperwork."

"Did he tell her anything else?"

"Just that he was surprised anyone wanted to find him. Both his ex-wife and his sister were adopted, and when they tried to find their biological parents, they didn't have any luck. He figured it would be the same for him."

A motorcycle roared down the street and we paused until we could hear each other again. "He needs to file the paperwork and reach out to us."

"Maybe he already did."

"Maybe," she said in a measured voice.

Not knowing how something so important would turn out was scary. I knew how she felt.

"Do you mind taking down the tray?" Mom fiddled with the edge of the letter.

"Sure. I'll take Bishop on a walk. This is great news Mom, everything is going to work out for the best. Don't worry." I stood up to leave, unsure how I would manage that much movement with the pain shooting from my bladder.

I reminded myself, however, I had bigger concerns. Even though I'd told Adrian goodbye the previous night and that we could never see each other again, I already longed for him to try and change my mind.

CHAPTER 11

...

FRIDAY, OCTOBER 14, 2016
Morning

GATHERING THE ENERGY to push past the searing pain to take Bishop on a walk, I stopped in Mom's guest room to grab a protein bar and my phone. As I glanced at my cell, the notice board read "one text message." I couldn't help myself, I swiped left to read it.

Adrian: *Hey, Beautiful. How's your mom? How are you doing?*

He'd given me exactly what I wanted. Knowing he cared boosted my confidence, but I needed to put on a tough front.

Me: *I told you we can't talk anymore.*

A few minutes later, when he didn't respond, anxiety blinded my ability to reason. What if he gave up? The thought of never hearing from him again made me desperate to hold him.

I sat on the hard bed and texted him again.

Me: *I miss you.*

Adrian: *Last night was the best night of my life.*

I flopped on my back with the love-drunk smile of a silly teenager and pictured the two of us together in last night's hotel room. Even though I stopped him before we fully consummated our relationship, Adrian was the best lover I'd ever been with.

Me: *Thank you.*

Adrian: *Do you regret seeing me?*

I bit my lip, feeling the piercing guilt of my pleasure.

Me: *Yes*

Adrian: *Ouch.*

Me: *I'm sorry, but it was wrong. We have to stop now.*

Adrian: *Can we talk on the phone one more time?*

He called my cell. I sent it to voicemail. I could hear my brother and niece rummaging around in the kitchen. Even though I'd left Mom upstairs in her bedroom, she had ears sharper than any FBI informant. I couldn't have this conversation with my family around.

I debated what to do. If I stuck to my guns and ignored Adrian, it would be easier to put him behind me. Communicating would make me want him more.

I wandered into the empty living room and picked some dog toys off the oriental carpet, tossing them in Bishop's doggie basket. Pete and Maya were arguing about hairbands when my phone chimed with a text. I had no doubt who it was.

Adrian: *Our night together wasn't a spur of the moment happening. It's something I've hoped for ever since I lost you. What if it was fate? It hurts me that you regret what happened.*

Me: *Give me five minutes.*

I reasoned I was still in San Diego and on a hiatus of sorts. I could cut Adrian off after I drove back home to my husband and children.

Me: *I'll take the dog out for walk.*

I hooked the leash on Bishop and headed for the front door. Creaking it open, my bare arms shivered with goosebumps. October was a fickle month. Yesterday's warmer weather had passed, leaving a chill in its wake. I grabbed one of Curtis' dark hoodies off the coat rack and stepped outside.

Heavy grey clouds had rolled in overnight, shrouding Ocean Beach's morning sun. A damp mist cooled my cheeks, and I wondered what I would say to Adrian when he answered my call.

"Hey," I said, taking small, careful steps, and crossing the street toward the ocean.

"Hi." His deep scratchy voice lulled me back to the previous night. "Are you sure you don't want to talk to me anymore?"

The sky closed in on the surf, mingling and intimate. "I need some time to think," I said, breathing in a gulp of salted ocean air.

"So that's a maybe?" His voice sounded hopeful.

"Can we please change the subject? I've got so much going on."

"What do you want to talk about?"

I kicked at a pebble and watched it roll toward the edge of the cliff. "My mom may have found the second son she put up for adoption."

"That's great news!"

"I know. Talking to him would make her so happy. I brought up the subject with Pete the other day, and he said Mom already had a son, she didn't need another one. He acted like he would be replaced if we liked the other brother better. But I think if we get to meet him, it'd be good for all of us."

"I agree."

I swept my hand through my hair. "Oh and my stepsister Tawny is flying in tomorrow, the one I told you about. She had some work already scheduled here, so now I guess she's going to stay a few extra days."

"How do you feel about that?"

"Not great." *Why was he so easy to talk to? He actually listened to me instead of tuning me out.* I found the bench where we'd kissed two nights ago, and eased down on its edge.

"How are you feeling besides seeing her?" He turned the subject back to us.

Being here, looking out at the same deep ocean we gazed at together, made me feel closer to him. It also reminded me of the potential consequences. "I'm hurting, actually. Too much stress."

"What do you mean?"

"It's nothing really, just not feeling good."

"Was it something I did?"

"No, not physically."

"Are you sure?" he asked. I could hear the guilt and concern in his voice. "I would never do anything to intentionally hurt you."

"It's all the stress of what we're doing, that's all. Karma isn't a big fan of adultery. It's kind of funny though."

"If you say so."

"Who needs a scarlet letter when your own body rebels against you?" I leaned my back against the bench's wooden slats.

"Stop. I don't want to hear you talk about yourself like that anymore."

"I'm having an affair."

"It's not an affair."

"What is it then?" I asked.

"It's something that was meant to be. We're supposed to be together."

I watched an ocean liner slip off the edge of the horizon. "You know a lot of people would say you're a home wrecker. Don't you feel a little guilty about trying to talk me into seeing you?"

"No."

"Not at all?"

"The only thing I feel bad about is that I didn't fight harder for you in the past. That won't happen this time."

"You're so dramatic."

"Really? Am I? Or maybe it's that you choose to forget the way that man treats you. Whether you end up with me or not, you deserve better."

"I guess."

"Remember the family pictures?"

"I should have never told you about that."

That is what Adrian did, he took something small that bothered me, that I should have kept to myself in the first place, and he blew it into a massacre story.

It was early afternoon about two years ago. Family photos had been an issue since Michael and Zach were born. Kevin didn't like them. I did.

I'd arranged to have one of Skye's friends, a photographer, meet us at the beach in Coronado to take our holiday pictures. I had specifically chosen a special spot behind the Hotel Del Coronado. The sprawling Victorian boasted a stunning red-shingled rooftop that backed up to a pristine stretch of ocean and sand. It was the ideal backdrop for our holiday cards.

For two weeks, I'd reminded Kevin about the arrangements. I bought new color coordinated clothes for all of us to wear. The previous day my neighbor glued extensions into my hair to make it look fuller, and just that morning, I spent more than an hour dressing and grooming the boys, blow-drying my hair straight, applying my make-up, and stuffing myself into a pair of tight blue jeans. All the while Kevin did nothing to prepare, despite my hints to get ready.

When it came time to leave, I marched into the living room and asked my husband, dressed in his normal weekend attire of shorts and a faded t-shirt, if he was ready to go. He looked up from his spot on the couch and ran a hand through his dirty-blond locks. "Can't we go later?"

"Yeah, Mommy, let's cancel," Michael piped in. He and his brother sat coiffed and adorable on the couch next to their daddy. I couldn't wait to capture this stage of their lives in a family photo.

"I told Heather we'd meet her at noon."

Kevin cocked his head to the side in agitation. "Can't you reschedule it for another day?"

"I already straightened my curls the way you like it and got Michael and Zach their haircuts." I waved my hand at the boys to make my point. "Everybody's dressed. Heather worked us into her busy calendar."

Kevin rolled his eyes at me.

I crossed my arms and tapped my booted toe on the travertine tile. Tears pierced my eyes. "I knew you were going to do this."

"Do what?"

"Make me feel bad. I've been reminding you about these pictures for weeks. You said it was fine. Now you're acting like I'm forcing you."

He stood up and tossed the clicker on the couch. The boys stayed seated without complaint. "I was just asking if we could reschedule. I'll get dressed."

I took a deep breath in relief. I was angry, but I needed to let it go. He was coming. That's what mattered.

Kevin pounded toward the stairs leading to our second-story bedroom, and then he stopped. "Where are we going, anyway?"

"The beach."

"Which one?" He turned around to face me.

My heartbeat quickened. The Hotel Del wasn't close. It was a good thirty-minute drive depending on traffic and parking.

I bit my lip before responding to his question. "Coronado."

Kevin went dark.

"Heather lives right by there," I said, defending my decision. "She thought it would be nice."

"Why can't we do it in our front yard?"

I crossed my arms across my chest. "Because I already made plans for us to go to the beach. It's too late to change."

He titled his head and squinted his accusing eyes at me. "Why do you have to make everything so difficult?"

"I'm sorry," I said, feeling a moment of genuine guilt for upsetting him.

"What time are we supposed to be there?" he asked, his face still pinched in frustration.

"Twelve."

"It's 11:15. I don't have time."

The boys shifted closer toward each other on the couch. I kept my focus trained on Kevin. "That's why I've been asking you all morning to get ready."

"It's too far. We'll never make it in time."

"Fine!" I stamped my foot, my own resentment boiling beyond the point of containment. "You always do this. You know what? We'll go without you. You don't ever have to be in another family picture ever again."

"What?" His lips curled into a snarl.

"From now on, just me and the boys. It'll be easier that way."

He grabbed the back of his head and rubbed his neck, glaring at me as if I'd murdered his grandmother. "You are such a bitch."

The laugh track sounded off on the television, mindless giggles from an invisible audience. I stared back at Kevin in shock. Zach and Michael were sitting right there.

Before I could respond, he burst toward me. Kevin picked up a chair from the breakfast table and hoisted it over his head. "I'm going to throw this chair right out the window," he threatened.

Poison bloomed in my belly. I wanted to egg him on, tell him to go ahead and throw it, but I feared he actually would.

He slammed the chair back onto the floor and came at me. Instinctively, I took a step backward. My body expected it, anticipated it, and in the moments before his hand made contact with my arm, I braced for it.

This had happened before. But never in front of our children. Like some terrible after-school special, I was seeing it through their eyes. Domestic abuse.

He squeezed my bare arm tighter and yanked me forward. "We're going upstairs."

I balled my right hand into a fist and punched him in the chest. He didn't flinch. I dropped my weight like a dead woman and tried to wrench free of his grip. He strengthened his grasp.

"Let go of me." I could feel the tears rolling down my cheeks and dripping into the crevices of my neck. "No," I shrieked.

Kevin pulled harder, dragging me past our boys.

Daddy was hurting Mommy. Mommy was crying.

Zach and Michael stared straight ahead at the television screen as if frozen. I stood up and punched Kevin in the chest once again. My knuckles ached. The hit hurt me more than him. We rounded the staircase.

Never let them take you to the second location. I learned that on an Oprah Winfrey show. Whatever a man wants to do to you in private is far worse than what he will do to you in public. I had to stay downstairs. It was safer.

I tried not to sob. My tears were probably ruining my makeup. He could rip my top if he pulled me too hard.

Even worse, our children were watching. They heard their father call their mother a bitch. They saw from the corners of their eyes as he dragged her against her will toward the stairs.

I'd witnessed many fight scenes between my own parents. My mother dominated. She hurled the insults. Dad, no stranger to callous words, never touched her. Yet I picked a man who could hurt me.

I wouldn't allow this for my boys. This was not who we were. I dropped to my knees and tried to wrench my arm free. "Let me goooooo," I wailed.

He wouldn't give in. Kevin tugged harder and dragged me up the carpeted stairs, my knees bumping and my toes flexing against the inside of my boots for traction. He ignored or was perhaps invigorated by my wails for him to stop.

Acid churned in my stomach, creeping up my throat. When he got me to the second floor, I stood up and he shoved me into the laundry room. My back hit the wall.

A sharp exhale. Tears. Disbelief. Rubbing my arm in the spot where he had grabbed me, I recoiled as he thrust his face into mine. "What is wrong with you?"

"You left bruises." I sniffed, eying him with fear. "I can see your fingerprints."

He relented, pulling his head out of my face and crossing his arms. "You bruise easily, it doesn't mean anything." There might have been an edge of regret for what he had done in his voice, I wasn't sure.

"Why are you doing this to me?" he asked.

I took a defensive step sideways in case his temper flared.

"Why do you have to push all my buttons?" he put his hands up in frustration. "Why?"

"I just wanted to take a family picture."

Our fight cooled from there, the worst of it over. My resentment and hurt, however, lingered. That year our holiday card featured two pictures, one with me and the boys, and a separate one, taken on a different day, of Kevin with the boys.

My husband forever maintained the incident was my fault, that I had provoked him. For me, it was the silent line of demarcation. There was a before, and then, there was an after.

I peered off Sunset Cliffs looking again at the ocean, calmer on this day, less angry. Glistening tentacles of seaweed floated in clumps, rising and falling with the tender waves. "It honestly wasn't that big a deal, Adrian."

"Really? Physical violence is acceptable?"

"No. He was wrong to do it, and I told him so."

"How many other times has that happened?"

"I don't know. Maybe five, I can't remember." I pushed up from the bench and prepared to hobble back toward Mom's.

"The way you repress things, if you say five, it was at least double that. Besides, once is too many. You should have left him the first time he did it."

"That was the only time in front of the boys. And when I finally put my foot down and said I would leave him, he stopped. It's been two years. He hasn't touched me since."

"Does your mother know?"

Panic rose in my chest. "No. And don't go telling anyone either."

"Why don't you tell her if it's no big deal?"

A small dog on a leash barked at Bishop. He ignored its yapping. "I didn't say it's no big deal; I'm saying this kind of thing happens in relationships. Kevin never punched me. He never actually hurt me. He just scared me."

"And the bruises?"

"I do bruise easily. You look at me the wrong way and I bruise. It was wrong. Okay? I know that. Still, it isn't worth obsessing over."

"Then why don't you tell your mom? Does Sydney know?"

I hadn't mentioned anything to Mom or my best friend. If I had, it would have made it real. I would have had to confront the issue long ago. "Adrian, drop it. I don't want to talk about this anymore."

"You never even told your best friend?"

"Stop."

"Doesn't that tell you something, Hope? What about the rough sex, bet you never mentioned that to them either."

I had told him once, that in the past, Kevin hadn't always been gentle enough in bed. Adrian wielded that information like a weapon against me. "I'm finished now. I've had enough."

"Why? So you can push it to the back of your head and forget about it? Like you do with everything unpleasant. That guy is a fucking asshole. It's never alright for a man to put his hands on a woman. Especially not you. You're so small and delicate. I would love to spend five minutes alone in a room with that piece of shit."

"You're feeling overprotective."

"Damn right, I am. You need to stop defending that bullshit. Do you know how many times my ex has gotten in my face, screamed at me, even punched me? How would you feel if I ever dragged her up the stairs on her knees or fucked her like a whore in bed?"

"I wouldn't like you."

"Why not?"

"Because it would make you a bad husband." I unzipped my jacket, feeling a flush of heat.

"What does that say about him?"

"I admit it was wrong. New conversation, please." I couldn't take the emotional upset any longer.

"Always changing the topic."

"Yeah, well, I'm going to see Sydney this afternoon. She's in town, and she wanted to stop by and see my mom and hang out."

"Are you going to tell her about us?"

"About seeing you last night? Probably."

"She's going to tell you to stay away from me. Great."

"She already has."

"I want you to tell Sydney what he did to you when you see her this afternoon."

"Why? It's embarrassing. Why can't you let me forget about it, Adrian? I'm so sick of reliving this."

"Because I want you to see her reaction. I want you to start talking about the things he does to see what other people think. You don't take me seriously. You think everything I say is only because I love you. But it's more than that, Hope. You tell Sydney, or I will."

Anger boiled to the surface. "Fuck you."

"How come you have no problem saying that to me?"

My hobbling stroll morphed into a full stride blaze toward Mom's. Anger numbed my physical pain. "Because I'm not afraid of you."

"Why not, I'm much more dangerous than him."

"You don't scare me."

"He shouldn't, either. Don't you think that's a problem?"

"Enough."

"Okay, Hope, I'm done for right now. But I want you to think about how your mother would feel, knowing her daughter is being treated this way."

We hung up, our relationship on an undetermined status. I scolded myself for calling Adrian in the first place. I should have ignored his texts. I was breaking my promise to myself. That never landed me anywhere good.

My phone buzzed. I knew it was a follow-up text from Adrian. He was relentless. I shoved the phone deeper into my back pocket wanting to possess the strength to ignore him.

A surfer parked his car on the curb beside me and smiled. His bare chest and sun-kissed tan matched his loose brown hair and sparkling green eyes. Maybe I could run away with him and forget about everything and everyone else. We could live in Mexico. I could sit on the warm white sand and watch him take the waves, cheering him on while I sipped tart lemonade and read a juicy novel.

Digging into my back pocket, I pulled out my phone.

Adrian: *I hate that love is making me feel this way. Love should fill you up...bring you joy. All I feel is hurt. It feels like I'm losing you all over again...I'm hurt that you're suffering...hurt that I can't fix it. I feel so much regret that I didn't pursue you relentlessly long ago. Regret for the things*

I may never experience with you. Regret for the time we will not spend together. You are an amazing woman. You are my one....even if I'm not yours. I love you, Hope Sullivan.

CHAPTER 12

...

FRIDAY, OCTOBER 14, 2016
Afternoon

I WOKE IN a haze, my cell phone ringing its Spanish banjo tune, while a dream from my accidental nap still floated in my mind as if it were real.

"Hello," I said, trying to remember what city I was in.

"Hey, it's almost noon, did I wake you up?" Kevin asked.

"No." I rubbed at my eyes. If I were sleeping, that would mean I was taking it easy while he carried the heavy load of watching the children and working. "I was only laying here for a moment. My mom had me up late last night."

"No problem. Well, I booked a flight for the boys and me to come down tonight. I got us a room at the La Jolla Shores hotel."

My brain searched for traction. This was my safety zone. Kevin's unexpected trip felt like the latch had been broken open on my war bunker, and I still didn't know whose side I was fighting for. "But I'm driving home this weekend."

"Maybe the boys can drive back with you and keep you company."

"Nothing like an eight-hour car drive with your mom and brother to make some lasting memories." I rolled my eyes to the ceiling. "Sounds like a blast. What time does your flight arrive?"

"Right around eleven. It's the earliest one they had last minute. I'll text you the details."

"Do the boys know what's happening with my mom?"

"Yeah. We talked about it last night while I was putting them to bed. They miss you."

"I miss them, too. All of you. But it's not like I'm on vacation. I need to help their bubby until I leave. That's why I'm here."

"You can take some time with us. We'll have a nice lunch. Michael and Zach can swim in the pool there. I want to talk with you, Hope. Alone. I thought maybe we could leave the boys at your mom's and we could spend a night together."

"Babe, I'm here helping my mom recover from a stroke. My brother is staying in the second guest room with Maya and his obnoxious dog. I can't dump our kids with my mom and Curtis for the night."

"What about your sister's?"

My wind pipe began to squeeze shut. I cleared my throat. "My sister lives in a tiny little house with two children, an oversized dog, three cats, and a husband. There's no space for the boys."

"We'll figure it out when we get there. You'll be able to pick us up?"

"Of course," I said, relieved to drop the subject.

"Great. See you soon, then."

A child's hand rapped on my bedroom door. "Yes?" I asked, hanging up the phone.

"Aunt Hope."

"Yes, Maya?"

"Aunt Hope."

I decided it was best to answer the door. "What's up, kiddo?"

"Bubby wants you."

That was a first since my arrival. I hoped everything was alright.

CHAPTER 13

...

FRIDAY, OCTOBER 14, 2016
Afternoon

I WAS LOUNGING upstairs with my mom, relaxing on her bed, gazing out at the ocean view through her French glass doors. The doorbell rang downstairs and the front door creaked open. I heard Sydney's high-pitched laughter as she said hello to Curtis and stepped inside.

"I better get down there. I'm so glad you called for me to bring you food. It's such a relief you finally ate something, Mama." I checked my cell for the time. Twelve-thirty. I had scheduled a last-minute doctor's appointment for a vulvodynia treatment in forty minutes, and I felt on edge about talking to Sydney. "I gotta go."

"You're not even dressed."

"What do you mean? Yoga pants are clothes." I looked down at my stained tank top and purple stretchy pants covered in dog fur. "I'll change." Springing off the bed, I prepared to sprint downstairs.

"Where's Pete?" Mom asked. "I haven't heard a peep from your brother or Maya all day."

I stopped at the top of the stairs to answer her question. "He borrowed my car to run some errands."

"I was hoping he went home," she said.

"Yeah, that's not going to happen for a couple of days, at least."

"Why?"

"His car got towed."

"From where?"

I put one toe down the first stair. Sydney was going to have a fit. She hated running late, even if it wasn't her appointment. More importantly, I wanted to get our "talk" over with before I lost my nerve. I needed to move along this conversation with Mom.

"Shocking news, Pete got into an altercation yesterday. He parked his car in front of the next-door neighbor's house yesterday. This big dude came outside with his wife and told Pete not to park in front of his mother-in-law's house. Pete told him it was a public street, he could park wherever he wanted. The guy got in Pete's face and was about to punch him when the guy's wife pulled him away."

"God forbid your brother move his car."

"I don't blame him for not moving it. But, of course, he managed to turn it into a shit storm. When we woke up this morning, poof. His car was gone. Pete said the tags were expired. They must have called the police."

"So why is he out running errands, instead of getting his car back?"

"He plans on making the old lady pay for it."

"Does he have an ounce of sense in his head?"

"Apparently not." I heard Sydney nervously chatting away downstairs with Curtis. "I gotta run. Sydney's here to see me."

I shuffled into the living room, feeling slightly frazzled. "Hey, Syd," I leaned in to wrap my arms around her slim frame and thick mane of curly brown hair.

Sydney and I had been best friends since middle school. She grabbed my hand all those years ago, as I tried to run past her in our seventh grade PE class. She told me she had a cramp and I needed to slow down and walk with her.

Back then, Sydney was the tough Italian girl who talked back to the teachers and had a reputation for decking anyone who pissed her off. Ever since that day we walked the mile together, she'd become my protector and trusted confidant.

We gave each other a tight hug. "Took you long enough." She glared at me with mock anger.

"Sorry. I'm so glad you're here." I could feel tears of relief welling in my eyes. It'd been five months since I'd seen Sydney in person. I would confess my sins to her and my best friend would make everything better.

"What's the matter?" she asked, cocking her head to the side in concern. "Don't worry, your mom's gonna be fine. She's a tough lady." Sydney laughed. "You're not going to wear those dirty clothes out in public, are you?"

I threw my hands up in the air. "I was going to change. I didn't want to be late."

"Go. I'll run upstairs and say hi to Mom-Number-Two while you put on something presentable." She pointed her index finger at me with great seriousness. "We leave in ten minutes."

"Perfect," I agreed.

Close to twenty minutes later, we climbed into Sydney's rental car.

"So, explain to me again what the fuck we are doing today?" she asked, clicking on her seatbelt and pushing the key into the ignition.

I loved her frankness. "I'm getting a bladder installation. I had a really bad flare up and I don't want to wait until I get home to take care of it. Luckily my old doctor's office had a last minute appointment."

"Because your vagina hurts?"

"Yep. A nurse practitioner inserts a little tube up my urethra and injects medicine into my bladder."

"That's so weird."

"No kidding."

"Ha! Only you," she laughed. Looking in the rearview mirror, she backed the car from the curb. "And you're under a lot of stress with your mom. Right? That's why it's all the sudden acting up again after all these years?"

"Uh, huh," I said in a shy, restrained response.

"Is there something else you're not telling me?" she asked. The car shot off like a bullet.

"Kevin and the boys are flying in tonight."

"That's nice."

"I guess."

"*I guess.* Why would you say that?"

"I don't want to talk about it."

"Why not?"

"Because I don't want to think about it."

"Fine. But I'm not going to let it go, so be prepared to talk after your doctor's appointment."

Waiting through the doctor's appointment to talk would only stress me out more. I'd rather spit it out and get it over with. "I never told you how it first started."

"How what started?"

"My vulvodynia."

"Yes, you did. Your vagina hurt during sex when you were in college, and you went to the doctor and found out that you have this V thing."

I took a deep breath and rolled down the window. Jagged palm fronds flashed by as she weaved her way along Sunset Cliffs. "I never told you exactly how it started back in college."

"So, it wasn't stress? It was something else?"

It was time to see what Sydney thought. Maybe the whole thing wasn't as bad as I imagined.

"I'm going to tell you."

"Okay. I am waiting."

I wrapped my hair back into a bun and rubbed my hands on my thighs. "It was my last year of school. Kevin had been pressuring me for more sex. It seemed like however much we had, it wasn't enough."

"I remember that."

"Yeah, it's like he was a sex addict or, you know, he always needed something over-the-top, whether it was alcohol, drugs, sex or spending stupid amounts of money."

I bit the top of my thumb nail, suddenly nervous. What was the point in telling her any of this? "I changed my mind. Can we talk about something else?"

"No. Repressing shit isn't helping you." She patted her hand on my thigh while simultaneously switching lanes. "Get it out, you will feel better about it."

I nodded my head to encourage myself to continue. "It's when Kevin worked on the East Coast for that big-time marketing firm, and they were flying him back to LA on the weekends. He would come home and make me feel like a jerk if I didn't want to have sex with him multiple times a day. Anyway, I wanted him to know what it felt like, so one night after the cab dropped him off at our apartment in Westwood, I attacked him. Every time he came, I pretended I was dying to do it again. We must have had sex at least seven times over the course of the night."

"Holy Shit!"

"I know! He complained his penis was chafing. I gave him a real hard time then, saying things like 'Okay, if that's all you can do. I guess I'll be fine.' I wanted him to know how shitty it felt to be pressured into sex and then be told it wasn't enough. It was never fucking enough. The next morning I woke up in so much pain. I broke my vagina. For about seven months, it hurt to wear pants or even wipe after peeing."

"Bet he was thrilled about that. No more sex for him."

"We still did it. I told him how much it hurt. He would mope and make me feel bad, so I would eventually give in and let him do it. Inside my head I would be thinking, 'I fucking hate you, you piece of fucking shit.' After a while he started to notice and get irritated, so then I kept quiet and pretended I liked it. If it was bad sex, it didn't count, and he'd want to do it all over again." I rubbed at the back of my neck. "Looking back, it was probably the coke or some other drug he was doing at the time. He didn't realize he was hurting me."

Sydney looked at me wide-eyed. Her voice hitched when she spoke. "You never told me he was doing cocaine."

"It was only for a little while. I forgot about that until now."

"The whole fucking thing is awful. Why didn't you tell me?"

"I guess I didn't want to think about it. And then I mostly forgot." I bit the edge of my lip. "He told me I was frigid and I felt ashamed. We would get in these big fights if I wasn't in the mood, and he'd scream and sometimes push me to calm me down. He said I was hysterical and he needed to snap me out of it."

"Push you?!" Tears welled in her eyes.

I felt the car jerk faster in her anger. "It was my fault for going along with it. I could have said no."

She swiped away angry tears. "That's bullshit. Listen to yourself. You sound like some classic sexual abuse victim. Does he still do shit like that?"

"No. It hasn't been an issue since we got married. We have an unspoken rule. He lets me initiate sex so I don't feel pressured, and I make it a point to pursue him at least twice a week. Three times when I'm good. Although some weeks I can't do it at all and he gets a little mopey. But, he hardly ever complains."

"What the fuck? I would have fucking left his ass. That's bullshit, Hope."

I fidgeted with my hands, working up the nerve for my next confession. "I have something else to tell you."

"It gets worse?"

"Well…"

"We're getting closer to the doctor's office. Maybe we should wait until after your appointment so you have enough time to tell me."

I looked at the time. With Sydney driving like a New York taxi driver high on crack cocaine, we were no longer in danger of being late. "I need to tell you now. I don't want to wait."

"What is it?"

I told her what had happened with Adrian since arriving in San Diego.

"The last time we talked about this, I thought you were going to end it with him."

"I know. I didn't."

"Okay. I think I understand." She scratched her head as she squinted into the sunlight. "Not that what you told me wasn't awful, but has Kevin maybe done more stuff that you haven't told me about?"

"Yes."

"What?" she asked.

I reluctantly filled her in about our last big fight, the one during which Kevin grabbed me in front of the boys and dragged me upstairs.

She clenched the steering wheel, her cheeks flushed red. "I can't believe he would do that to you. He should know how delicate of a person you are and that you should not be treated that way." Sydney swerved lanes and flipped the guy off for honking. "I fucking hate him. I wish you had told me earlier so I could have been there to help you."

I felt like a jerk for upsetting her. "I'm sorry. It was two years ago. I was ashamed. I didn't want anybody to know."

"He's the one who should be ashamed. Fucking jerk. There's never any shame in telling me anything. Why don't you leave him? Anyway, you've always cared for Adrian, and he's always cared for you. He seems to always be popping into your life. Maybe this is happening for a reason."

"I don't know."

"Well, I do. Which way do I turn here? Fuck, I wasn't paying attention to the road."

"Go left. Then straight for about 2 miles." I picked at a piece of lint on my new pair of clean rainbow-colored yoga pants. "Can we stop by Jamba Juice on the way back? My mom keeps craving their Orange Dream Machines. It's like the single thing she actually wants to eat besides peanut butter and jelly sandwiches."

Sydney lifted an eyebrow at me. "Is that you changing the subject?"

"Yes."

"Fine," she said.

I rested my skull against the headrest as we pulled into the medical complex's parking lot, mentally preparing myself for the poke of the catheter.

The tires screeched as she swerved her car around the ramp to the next floor. "I can't believe you didn't fuck Adrian when you saw him. You have some serious self-control."

"I'm a saint." I gave her a wry half-smile, sincerely hoping the nurse's numbing medicine would do its job. Each step I took felt like walking in silky underpants filled with shards of broken glass.

I didn't care what Sydney said. My body was giving me a message. Be faithful. Stay the course. Stick to what you know.

CHAPTER 14

...

FRIDAY, OCTOBER 14, 2016
Evening

DAD'S HUNTER-GREEN, sport Mini Cooper clunked onto the curb and jumped the sidewalk before backing up and landing in place with a jolt.

It was close to five o'clock. The bladder treatment wiped out most of my pain, and Sydney had dropped me off at Mom's. After three full days in town, I was finally going to see my dad.

"Come on, Maya, hold my hand. Grandpa's here." I motioned my niece toward me, holding the spare booster seat tight in my right hand.

Maya grabbed her stuffed purple penguin and ran toward the door, the plastic hair clip in her crooked braid swinging with each step. Roxy protested with yapping barks from the backyard as we nudged Bishop out of our way and closed the squeaky front door behind us.

"Ready for some dinner?" I asked Maya. She nodded a yes.

Dad climbed out of his cluttered car and watched us cross the street, his arms folded over his big belly. He sported his standard layers of colorful Grateful Dead t-shirts under an ever-present beige fishing tackle vest. As if his outfit wasn't enough to grab someone's attention, Dad had a new do.

"What did you do to your hair?" I asked, feeling my jaw drop in surprise as we approached him. Dad's shoulder-length curly white hair was done up in cornrows. "You look like a homeless hippie Santa Claus."

"Heh. Heh. Heh." He laughed. "You like it?" Dad smiled and patted his hand over his head.

"Not really."

"The Jamaican lady who does our hair at Barely Living styled it special for me." The name Barely Living was our inside joke. Most of the men and women who resided at Dad's assisted living facility were either out of their minds or completely falling apart. "I think it's fan-flaming-tastic."

"It's delightful." I kissed him on the cheek.

"Hey, squirt." Dad ruffled Maya's hair. "Where's your daddy?"

Maya wrapped her arms around my leg as she surveyed Grandpa Dan with her big brown eyes.

"Pete took my car," I answered on her behalf. "He went out to run some errands earlier today. Then he decided last minute to go down to the DMV and pay off his tags so he can get his car out of impound."

"Wasn't he going to have that old bag next-door pay for it?"

"Yeah, right." I hugged Maya with my free arm.

"I'm surprised he gave in so easily," Dad said.

"Maya's mom called and insisted Pete bring her home sometime this century, like before the weekend ends, so Pete gave in and went to take care of his car. He should have been home by now, but he said to go without him if he wasn't back in time."

"Running late, per usual." Dad shook his head.

"Exactly. Anywhoo, this little one's hangin' solo with us for dinner."

My phone rang. I reached in my purse and glanced at the screen. Adrian. I hadn't heard from him since our argument earlier that morning. I was afraid he might have decided to let me go. "Dad, take Maya's car-seat and get her loaded in your car. I forgot the coloring book I was going to bring for her. I'll be right back." I tried to hand him the seat.

Dad waved his arms in protest, desperately trying to shoo it away. "I don't know what to do with that cockamamie thing."

"Set it in the seat and have her sit down. I'll strap her in when I get back." I shoved it in his hand and took off for the house before he could argue. Dialing Adrian as I speed walked, I prayed Mom's medication had knocked her out cold.

"Hey gorgeous." His sexy voice rumbled in my ear giving me chill bumps. He still loved me.

"What's up? I'm going out to Balboa Park to have dinner with my dad."

"I'm thinking about taking a fight."

My stomach flip-flopped. Adrian had raved about his glory days in MMA fighting, how he'd spent several years after college moonlighting on the side as an amateur mixed martial arts fighter.

"What fight?" I pushed open the front door, lowering my voice in case Mom could hear me. "I thought you gave all that up years ago."

"I've been sparring to get back into shape. My old coach came into town. He needs a second alternate for a fight that's coming up in five weeks down in Sacramento. He wants to see if I'm in any kind of fighting shape and where my weight is."

"How is he going to find that out?" I went into my room where I'd stored a bag of activity books and crayons I had bought for Maya.

"He wants me to come into the old gym and see what I've got left. It's going to be tough, though, because it's a massive weight drop."

"But you just got home. Did you run into him today?"

"No, it was before I came to see you. He called me today though to see what I wanted to do."

I bit the inside of my cheek. My hippie, drug abusing dad used to teach martial arts. I grew up around professional fighting. The thought of Adrian beating another man turned me on more than I would ever admit. It was barbaric and dangerous, but it was also incredibly sexy to know a guy could protect you with his hands. "What if you get hit?"

"I don't plan on it, but it's not like it hasn't happened before."

"I'm worried you'll get a concussion. Your hand already has a tremor. I want you around when we're older."

"So you plan on keeping me?"

I lifted up some dirty clothes and searched for the plastic bag full of books. "Even though it can't work out now, we could still be together when our kids are all grown."

"That's not soon enough."

"Please tell your coach 'no.'"

"Hope, you're pushing me away, and you and fighting are the two things that I can zone my life out with. Your senior year of high school, when you let me hang out with you in your room while you did your homework, it was the only place I could shut the wheels off, unpack all those racing thoughts in my head. It was the one place I could be at peace."

"What's your point?" I asked.

"You gave me a level of comfort I never had anywhere else. Only thing that comes close is fighting. Right now, I have nothing to do, nothing to look forward to. This fight would give me some sort of direction. Focus."

"I understand that." I found the bag. "But you're too old for this, Adrian. One bad hit and the rest of your future is erased. At the very least, you owe it to your kids to stay healthy. Your doctor said if you ever got another concussion it could cause permanent brain damage."

"I'd like to prove to myself I still have something left in the tank. It's the only healthy way I can get out all this aggression."

I sat down on the bed. I wasn't even sure if I was going to keep him around, so who was I to tell him what to do? Either way, I cared about Adrian. I didn't want him to get hurt. Knowing he could fight was enough excitement for me. I wasn't willing to accept the actual consequences of him getting punched in the back of the head.

"Does it really bother you?" he asked.

"Yes."

"Would you come watch me?"

"Absolutely not. I won't encourage any of this."

"So you really don't want me to?"

I stood, ready to charge back out to my dad, who was no doubt having a meltdown trying to figure out the booster seat. "Yes. Promise me you won't."

"If it means that much to you. But you owe me something. You owe me another chance to see you."

"Fine. I was planning on it anyway." I hesitated at my unplanned announcement. I'd already decided I *wouldn't* see him again until the boys left for college. Why did I tell him otherwise?

"Really?"

"Yes. I mean, no. I don't know. We'll talk more later. I need to go. Thank you for not fighting. Remember your promise, Adrian. Tell the coach 'no.'" I hustled out the front door, a wide nervous smile spreading across my face. Adrian's sacrifice made me want him more. On the heels of confessing my adultery to Sydney and gaining her approval, I doubted I could resist seeing him again. He was becoming my addiction. I was losing control.

CHAPTER 15

...

FRIDAY, OCTOBER 14, 2016
Evening

A HANDSOME WAITER with ratty blond hair tied in a man bun seated us on The Prado's stunning back patio. A red umbrella shaded our table from the early evening's golden light. I laid my cloth napkin across my lap and took in the view of the fountained courtyard below, with the seemingly endless tree-lined canyon beyond.

My thoughts drifted. I imagined myself walking down The Prado's curved concrete staircase in a strapless white dress, my friends and family gathered to watch. I drifted toward the man I loved. It was our wedding day, and this was the spot where we'd take our vows.

"Yo, Hope. Earth to Hope." Dad waved his red napkin at me. "You in there?"

"Huh?" I focused back in on my dad. "Sorry, I was thinking. Balboa Park is my favorite place on earth."

"Move home. We can have lunch here every Sunday."

I took a sip of my water. "Kevin did promise when we left we could move back in two years. It's been two years exactly." Maybe that was what Kevin wanted to talk about alone with me tonight. I doubted it, but anything was possible.

"Your mother and I aren't getting any younger." Dad had been reminding me of this fact since as far back as I could remember. It was one of his favorite lines.

"None of us are." I picked up the menu as the waiter approached. Dad and I decided to share a Kobe cheeseburger with truffle fries. Maya wanted the kid's corkscrew pasta with a fruit melody and a Shirley Temple.

"So how's it going, Papa?" I asked, pulling out the coloring book and crayons for Maya.

"Great. Happiest I've ever been in my life."

I felt my smile lengthen as I leaned back in my chair, enjoying the company as well as the view. "And to think you fought so hard against moving to Barely Living."

Dad laughed. "I was a fool."

"No kidding." I shook my head at him. Dad's life had taken a dramatic turn in the past seven years. Shortly after retiring from a life-long career as a middle-school English teacher, Dad had gone on an epic prescription painkiller bender.

He saved up at least a month's worth of Vicodins and right before it was time for a refill, he crushed them all up in one big powdery pile and snorted them like cocaine. The party crashed. Dad spent two full days paralyzed on his loveseat without food, water, or a visit to the bathroom.

When he finally gave in and was able to dial my number, he called for help.

Seven months pregnant with Zach, I raced over to his condo with Michael strapped into the car-seat. I somehow managed to roll Dad in his office chair out the front door and push his stinking, shivering body into my car's front seat.

On the drive to the emergency room, he yelled nonsense about dead presidents and his favorite childhood cat. He scratched at himself and waved his arms around in the air. Blood spurt from a vein in his bruised hand, splattering fragmented droplets across the fabric ceiling of my car. Michael screamed from the backseat, begging for me to kick Grandpa Dan to the curb. When we finally pulled into the ER drop-off lane, I watched in frozen horror as Dad slapped enough oxycontin patches onto his bloated belly to annihilate an extended family of T-rexes.

His body caved. Dad fell into a drug-induced mania. After he stabilized, the hospital transferred him to a psychiatric facility to ride out the high. He stayed there for nearly six weeks.

Then came Fine Living. We forced Dad into the assisted living home where a staff of professionals would make his meals, regulate his medications, and wash his laundry. He shouted vile epitaphs at Skye and me, accusing us of parental abandonment and made us feel like we had shipped him off to a Benghazi torture camp.

"You put Skye and me through hell and look at you." I waved my hand at him with a gentle smile. "These past seven years have been your renaissance. You have a girlfriend, you're the reigning king of bingo night, and best of all, you're the only man there with a bonafide sports car and your own private balcony to smoke weed."

"You bet your ass I am," he agreed, puffing with pride. "Shoulda done it sooner."

The scruffy waiter placed our food before us on the table. Maya reached her little hand forward to grab a piece of pasta. "Use your fork, my love," I advised, pushing the plate closer to her.

"I don't know why your fookin' brother couldn't be bothered to join us." Dad wrapped his hand around his mug of coffee.

"I told you he had to go to the DMV. He's probably at the impound place by now. I'm not sure how late those places stay open."

"He couldn't have handled that earlier in the day and been back by now? How often does he spend time with his sister and old man?" Dad stabbed his fork at a piece of fruit. "Maya, you dropped your napkin. Pick it up."

Maya slid her back down the chair and disappeared under the table.

Dad leaned forward and spoke in a lowered voice. "Did Casanova tell you he knocked up his girlfriend?"

"You mean Maya's Baby Mama?"

"Same hoe-bag." He nodded. "Your brother needs another kid like he needs another hole in his head."

"How's he going to support a second child?"

"He's got some scheme worked out. On his off hours, he's been snagging Prada shoe boxes from the dumpsters behind those glitzy stores in Beverly Hills."

My brother, a man with a master's degree in finance and a formerly lucrative career in contract negotiation with Los

Angeles's largest hospital, got himself fired for harassing his boss's personal assistant and was currently working part-time as an Uber driver.

"What's he going to do with the shoe boxes, sell designer organic marijuana kits to hipsters on the Westside?"

"Heh, heh, heh, now you're thinking, Princess."

"I'm serious."

"So is he. Your brother calls himself a high-end recycler. He claims when women sell their shoes on Ebay, they rake in a better price if it comes in the original box."

Maya popped her head back up and settled onto her chair. I handed her a French fry from my plate.

Dad took a bite of her fruit and picked up his half of the cheeseburger. "He's gonna sell his boxes for five dollars a pop."

I put my hand over my mouth and tried not to laugh out loud.

"Hey, it's worth a shot," Dad said. "Five dollars, ten dollars, pretty soon you've got a hundred dollars."

"Yeah, that should definitely cover the cost of diapers, formula, and daycare." I shook my head in disbelief. Pete's life was like an episode of The Jerry Springer Show. He made my affair with Adrian seem almost quaint in comparison.

"What can I tell you?" Dad attempted to wipe at the ketchup stuck in his beard, the huge droplet smearing as he continued to wipe. "The men in this family are *mashugana*." He reached for another piece of fruit off Maya's plate. "So, what's up with your mother?"

"She acts like she's fine, but I'm worried. The doctors said if she doesn't take her medication correctly, she could have a brain hemorrhage and bleed to death."

"Holy Christ." Dad's eyes bugged open wide.

"I know, it's awful to even think about."

"That's no way to go."

"No kidding."

"When I die, I want my ashes spread over the ocean in Hawaii."

"Jesus, Dad, can we not be so morbid?"

"I'm just telling you. That's what I want."

"I'll make a mental note of it."

"Thank you. I'd appreciate that."

Maya's Shirley Temple toppled over and the plastic lid broke free. Pink soda poured onto her pants. "Oh, no," she said, pushing back in her chair. "I'm wet." Tears filled her eyes.

I patted my linen napkin across her pants. "Don't worry, kiddo, it's a small spill. I have a change of clothes in the car." I looked at my dad. "Want to take a quick walk around the park after we get her cleaned up?"

Dad shook his head. "My knees are killing me."

"Since when?" Dad and I had been going on hikes since I was Maya's age. We'd climbed the trails of Mount Tamalpais together when I was four years old, and we'd discovered new trails each week when Kevin and I moved back to San Diego before Michael's birth.

"I haven't had my oldest daughter and grandkids around to drag me outdoors. My joints are stiffening up. I told you, Princess, I ain't getting any younger."

A lump of disappointment filled my belly, destroying my appetite. I picked Maya off her seat and set her in my lap, wiping her little hands and cheeks.

My dad couldn't go on a simple walk after dinner. My mother had survived a stroke. The boys and I had missed two years' worth of birthday parties and holidays with their cousins. Living an eight-hour drive away from our true home with a man who avoided spending time with us meant lost memories with the rest of our family.

"When will I see you again after this?" Dad asked.

I shrugged, "I'm really not sure." The answer would all depend on the choices I was about to make.

CHAPTER 16

...

FRIDAY, OCTOBER 14, 2016
Night

I CREPT UP Mom's staircase. Hazy stars and a half moon illuminated her picture windows in the late evening darkness. Dinner with Dad had been a great distraction. But it was time to get real.

Kevin and the boys would arrive in San Diego in another hour or so, and I needed to talk to Mom before I saw them. I'd been intimate with Adrian and I

still wanted him, but I couldn't go back and forth between two men.

I needed to choose.

"Mama?" I said as I slipped through her door. "You up?"

Her sheets shuffled as her body stirred. Mom cleared her throat and coughed. I walked closer to her bedside. "Ma?"

"What? Who's there?" she asked in a groggy, disorientated voice.

"It's Hope. I wanted to talk to you. But if it's not a good time, I can come back later."

My eyes adjusted. Dim silhouettes cast long shapes against sand colored walls. I could see her push herself up into a sitting position, leaning her back against some pillows. "Where's Curtis?"

"Downstairs watching TV. Pete and Maya left. You were sleeping and he needed to drop her back off to the baby mama. He said to say bye."

"That's good." She cleared her throat. "You didn't bring food, did you? I'm not hungry."

"No. It's not that." I wasn't sure I could tell her. Sydney might have condoned my behavior, but Mom wouldn't be so easy.

"What is it?"

I hesitated, my nerves taking control.

"Tell me."

Shame washed over me. I couldn't choke out the words. "I can't. Never mind, I can't do it." I turned to walk away.

"Why? Is someone hurt?" she asked.

"No, nothing like that." I faced her again, pushing through the sickening hot flashes of guilt. This was not a conversation I ever thought I would need to have. "It's about me. I did something really bad," I said, my voice cracking.

"Did you murder somebody?"

Here in Mom's presence, the magnitude of what I'd done settled on top of me. I felt exactly as if I had killed another human being. "No dead bodies." I let out a fake laugh.

"Then it's not that bad."

"It is. I'm a horrible person." I flopped down Indian style on the cold wood floor beside her. Tears broke free from my bottom lids and slid down my cheeks. I wiped at them with the cuff of my sweater and buried my head in my lap. "I'm so ashamed."

"What did you do?" I could hear the rise of concern in her voice. I was upsetting her. She didn't need this.

"I was going to tell you before you had your stroke. I shouldn't have brought it up."

"Did you have an affair?"

Relief surged through my body. She had said those shameful words out loud for me, I didn't have to. "Yes." I wiped at my running nose.

"With whom?"

Thick salty air washed through Mom's opened French-doors. Tears dried against my cheeks. "Someone from middle school and high school. Adrian Sicario. He used to come over to our house all the time."

"I don't remember him."

"You would always ask him if he had eaten. When he said 'no', you would make him lunch or warm up dinner."

"I was raising five kids at one time in that house. We had a lot of teenagers over."

"He really liked you," I said, hoping that would endear him to her.

"Are you still seeing this guy?"

"Yes."

"For how long?" she asked.

I sniffled and swiped again at my running nose. "We've been talking for a couple of months. But I've only met up with him in person twice, and that was while I was here."

"You've been sneaking around?"

"You were in the hospital. I went on a walk with him once, and then one real date."

"Do you love him?" she asked.

The tears fell harder. "I don't know." I breathed in for composure. "Maybe."

"Does Kevin know?"

"No."

"Does anyone know?"

I could feel her looking at me, even though I refused to make eye contact. "Sydney. And now you."

"Stop telling people." She coughed. "It makes it more complicated."

"I don't know what to do."

"Cut it off."

I looked up to her for a moment. "I tried to."

"Then you didn't try hard enough. Is he married? Does he have children?"

Her questions about his life-story continued. I answered them all. Her response was simple. Everyone makes mistakes. Can't you forget about this guy?

"I'm so lonely at home." I decided to focus on what really bothered me in my marriage, the pushing and other issues were in the past. "Kevin never wants to be with us. Do you know he switched his work days? He stays home on Friday's when the kids are at school and I'm running errands, and then he goes into the office on Sundays.

He says it's because he can get more work done without interruptions, but I think it's an excuse to escape." That was the root of my problem. I missed his companionship, and I wanted his support with the boys. I wanted a family that did things together and enjoyed each other's company. "And then there's the therapy with Michael."

I took Michael to his appointments once a week with Zach in tow. His therapist taught me how to guide our son in social situations. Then Michael and I would go out to public places like the Stanford Mall to practice. I forced him to make eye contact with strangers, pay for things himself at the register, say thank you.

Every time, he had breakdowns, red-faced and screaming, crying, telling me how much he hated me. We played personalized charade games at home. I would act out an emotion, and Michael would have to guess which one it was. It took weeks for him to recognize my mad face, sad face, happy face. That was just the beginning.

In real life, people often express their emotions in more subtle ways. I went to school with him three times a week to guide him on what people were thinking as he interacted with his peers. For all I put him through, he often despised me.

"The days are grueling and then at dinner when I look to Kevin for compassion or sympathy, he criticizes me. The other night, he told me right in front of the boys that Michael was fine, and I needed to find my own problems to worry about. He thinks Michael is rude to me because I'm weak and I allow it, not because he struggles with autism."

Mom kept quiet. I ripped at the edge of a dry cuticle, listing to the soft hum of her air purifier and the rumble of a motorcycle somewhere in the distance.

"Have you sat down in a calm moment and explained to Kevin how you feel about everything?"

"I try to. It's hard, though. He gets agitated and he yells. He makes me feel like a jerk. Adrian has been in love with me his whole life, he puts his kids first and all he wants is to make me happy."

I scooted a little closer to her and rested my forehead on the cool iron bed frame. The familiar scent of her jasmine lotion comforted me. I wished I could crawl into bed with her like I had as a child. "I think about what it'll be like when Michael and Zach leave home. Adrian is my chance to grow old with someone who actually likes spending time with me."

"He's courting you, Hope. What he says doesn't mean anything."

My jaw tightened. "I want someone who takes my side. Adrian believes I'm a great mom. He thinks the struggles I go through with Michael are admirable."

Mom kicked off her blanket. "Easy for him to say when you live so far away. You should never leave your husband for someone else. You have no idea if this other relationship will work out. What are you going to do, take Michael and Zach and move to Oregon? Maybe this new guy'll change his mind. He hasn't actually moved out of his wife's home. If you leave Kevin, do it because you don't want Kevin. Not because you are counting on some other man."

"Adrian could move here," I said. Mom had no idea how much he loved me, what he would sacrifice to be with me.

He wasn't some guy I'd bumped into at the grocery store or met at one of Zach's soccer games. Adrian had wanted me since we were kids.

Mom pulled the blanket back over her feet. "You know all too well what it's like to blend families. Remember how many problems it caused? You and Tawny still don't speak."

It was one of the many things about a life with a new man that scared me. If I left Kevin and married Adrian, I would be combining families the way Mom had. I would be generation 2.0, repeating history.

Skye and I barely spoke for years after our stepbrother and sisters moved in with us. Skye took their side in disagreements. I felt abandoned. My older stepsister, Tawny, stole my innocence, my belief that all people were inherently kind.

We lived in a house divided, led by a clever, outspoken, tireless woman. I wasn't nearly as strong as Mom, and I certainly didn't want to push a similar fate onto my own children, to put them in a situation where they would feel alienated and more like a number than a beloved child.

To keep our large household humming, Mom went military. Every tag on every item of clothing I owned boasted a tiny light green peridot, my assigned color, to mark the item as mine. Chores were employed with precision. Mom assigned each sibling one major room in the house to clean, in addition to our bedrooms. No one was allowed outdoors on Sundays until *everyone* had scrubbed and tidied his or her appointed spaces.

Mom's system came with its own built-in task force. If one kid deserted their duties, the rest of us would bully the slacker into getting his or her work done so the others could take leave.

Thinking about reliving all that made my stomach hurt. Yet, I wanted Mom's approval. "But you're happy you left. You have a great marriage now."

"It nearly broke me." She smoothed the sheets with her hands. "I had no choice but to leave your father. We were both miserable. I knew if either of us had any chance at finding happiness, it was worth a try. Kevin loves you. I know he does."

"He does. We've been together since I was eighteen."

"Twenty years." Mom patted my hand.

I looked at my mother in the quiet intimate space between us, desperate for her to tell me it was okay to run to Adrian, or somehow make me magically fall back in love with my husband.

"Kevin tells me every day he loves me and that I'm beautiful. He's a good husband." Again, I chose not to mention the pushing. It had been two years and he'd promised never to do it again. I trusted him to keep his word.

"Would you leave Kevin if Adrian weren't around?"

"Never. I'd rather have a partial husband than be completely alone."

The tears started all over again, I shouldn't have spent time alone with Adrian. I'd made a huge mistake. "Kevin makes dinner most nights, he rough houses with the boys before they go to bed, and when he does come to sleep, he's a great cuddler. Plus, I can't stand the thought of not having the boys full-time. Michael is killing me slowly each day with his accusations and temper tantrums. There are so many times I've wanted to throw myself off a bridge. But they are my world. I couldn't survive without my children full-time."

"Have you considered couples' therapy?"

"I've begged Kevin for the last twenty years to quit smoking pot every night in the bathroom after work. Whenever he tries and fails, he says it's my fault for being a nag, for making it impossible for him to succeed. Imagine what it would be like if I asked him to work on other, harder stuff? I can't do it, Mom. I can't be the bad guy anymore."

"Life's not easy, no one ever promised it would be." She shook her head.

"What should I do?"

"I can't tell you that."

"You always know what to say. I've been counting on you to make this decision for me. I need you."

"I can't help you with this one. You have to figure it out on your own." The crease in her brow deepened. Her lips narrowed into a tight line. "And you need to start toughening up and speaking your mind. Acting helpless may have worked in your twenties, but it's not cute anymore. You are an adult, a mother. Whether you try to work on your marriage, or build a new one, you have your work cut out for you. There's no easy answer."

CHAPTER 17

...

FRIDAY, OCTOBER 14, 2016
Night

KEVIN STRIPPED OFF his clothes in a heap on the hotel floor and climbed into the small second bed as soon as the boys fell asleep. I'd picked him up at the airport as promised, and, around midnight, we'd checked ourselves in to the La Jolla Shores Hotel for the next two days.

He patted the spot beside him on the bed as he yawned. "Come to bed, Baby."

Eager to avoid Kevin in this cramped single room until I was ready to tell him my truth, I searched for an excuse to keep my distance. "I was actually thinking about going to the hot tub."

"Can't you do that later?" he asked, eyeing me like a midnight treat.

"No, I'm not tired yet." I turned to my canvas overnight bag on top of the squat wooden bureau and dug through it, looking for my bikini. If I stayed outside long enough, he would crash as quickly as the boys had.

"I'll go with you." He half smiled.

I could tell by the desire in his eyes, he wasn't tagging along because he wanted to talk or spend time together. He definitely wanted sex.

"Sure," I agreed with a shrug. "We'll be able to see the front door from the Jacuzzi so the boys should be fine."

Kevin sat up in bed. "Will you give me a little kiss first?" He watched as I changed into my suit.

I glanced over at him. *I'm not in love with you anymore.* The thought struck me, clear and precise. I wasn't interested in him as a wife to a husband anymore. "No, I want to go in the hot tub. I'll see you out there."

Outside, the night was warm and balmy, the stars sparkled with unusual brilliance. They say God laughs while you're busy making plans. I released the bulky hotel towel wrapped tight around my body and dipped my legs into the warm swirling water, remembering the better days, the days when Kevin was my center.

I'd first met him at a seedy night club set along the main drag in Mission Beach, a party town in San Diego that attracted college kids, surfers, and an eclectic group of vagrants and high school drop-outs.

The Red Onion, a hot spot known for raking in more city violations than any other bar in town, was referred to by locals as The Spread Onion. It'd earned its sobriquet based on the night club's reputation for sloppy drinking and easy hookups. Sydney and I went to take advantage of eighteen and up night with dollar shots. We had free passes, courtesy of the bouncer she made friends with the previous weekend.

Kevin was hanging out in one of the booths with a handful of buddies. His blue eyes cut across the crowd and met my gaze at the bar. I stopped at the sight of him. He smiled subtly with curved, sensual lips, and let our unspoken connection linger between us until I looked away.

I tried not to stare, but allowed myself to glance briefly in his direction once more, hoping he wouldn't notice. He stood with rigid confidence, a girl hanging on his sculpted arm. Like a star-struck teenager, she gaped at his wavy blond hair, tanned skin, and squared jawline. I'd watched him too long. I took a breath and forced myself to look away.

In the darker recesses of my mind, I sized up my competition with confidence. He didn't seem too interested in his gangly female companion. Perhaps she was a groupie.

Inhaling the lingering currents of heavy cologne and spilled beer, I coasted toward him on autopilot. Sydney found me and yelled in my ear, "Did you see that guy over there?"

"Yes," I said. "I think he smiled at me."

"He's a total babe, Hope. You should go talk to him."

We fell in love fast. Kevin was twenty-three, five years older than me. He served as a Green Beret in the Army's Special Operations Unit, stationed on a military airfield north of Seal Beach. In my impassioned teenage eyes, Kevin was a real man, not a boy, with a crazy sexy job. Just like Adrian, he told me he knew the moment he first spoke to me, he would marry me. He was sure we were meant to be.

I believed him then. At that moment, I was no longer so sure.

Kevin met me on the edge of the Jacuzzi, my legs dangling inside the hot bubbling water. The rest of my body enjoyed the soothing warmth of the ocean air at night.

"It gets so cold in Northern California after the sun goes down, no matter how warm it is during the day," I said, making nervous small talk.

He nodded and took a seat next to me.

"I like it so much better here," I said.

"I don't. It's greener in Northern California."

"It's lonelier there."

"You have so many friends," he said.

I popped a foaming bubble with my toe. "It's not the same as family."

"Your mom visits all the time." He edged closer to me.

"She used to, now she might not as much. My dad hasn't come up once. With his diabetes, there's no one to help him with his insulin shots, unless I did it." I recoiled at the thought of stabbing Dad with a needle. "When we lived here, he used to come over at least once a week and hang out with me and the boys. He kept us company."

I glanced over at my husband and moved my hand away from his, working up my courage to tell him how I felt. Our children were asleep, Kevin was angling for sex, and I'd spent time with another man. This was the time to come clean. "You never even want to go out with the boys and I on the weekends."

"That's not true."

"It is. On our way to the last hike, after we took a wrong turn getting there and you had to pull over so the boys could pee in the woods, you said you never wanted to go anywhere with us again. You walked ten feet ahead of us during the hike up into the mountains. You got so far ahead of us that I had to carry Zach on my back because he was exhausted. By the time we caught up with you, you were already at the top of the hill waiting for us."

His jaw tightened and a muscle pulsed. Clearly, this wasn't the conversation he had in mind when he joined me outside. "What's your point?"

He'd asked me directly. I could do this, I could be strong like Mom advised and tell him the truth. No more acting like a scared little girl.

"I don't think I'm in love with you anymore." I said it so fast, I wondered if it was real. Waves collapsed in the distance and exploded against the shoreline. A stray hotel guest crept by toward the lobby.

Kevin narrowed his eyes at me in hurt and confusion. I bit the inside of my lip and wondered if I could dissolve in my own anxiety.

He leaned in so close I could feel the heat of his anger. "What does that mean?" he hissed.

"I don't feel the same." I spoke so quietly, I could barely hear myself. "You never want to spend time with the boys and me anymore. I'm lonely."

I didn't know what I expected when I told him. Maybe some tears and a declaration of his love. A promise to make me and the boys his priority? Or maybe I wanted him to get angry. That way I could feel justified in leaving.

He took a deep breath and pursed his lips in thought. Kevin was not guilt stricken or begging for a second chance.

A cold shiver of terror shot through me. With my words laying thick in the air, I felt defenseless. How could I make it without Kevin? Adrian wasn't nearly as intelligent or accomplished as my husband, and I had never stood completely on my own. Most of the time, Kevin treated me better than any man I'd ever met. He'd made my life better.

Only six months into our whirlwind relationship, we got engaged. When I wrapped up my second year at Mesa Community College, Kevin requested an honorable discharge from of the Green Berets after he injured his knee in a parachuting accident. He could have stayed at the job he loved and accepted a desk position. Instead, he decided to start his own marketing consultant company so he could follow me to UCLA.

Kevin paid the rent on our spacious sun-filled apartment in the heart of Westwood. He prepared gourmet meals for us at dinnertime and treated me to weekend shopping excursions at the Westside Pavilion, selecting and paying for whatever clothes suited my figure and style.

He custom-ordered straight from Italy one of the first Ferrari 360 Spiders to ride the streets of North America. Electric blue exterior on blue leather interior, with all the upgrades. We took exhilarating rides crisscrossing Malibu's hills. Rocketing along perilous mountain roads with the windows rolled down and wind exploding through the car, Kevin took sharp turns around staggering unguarded cliffs.

We traveled across Europe, dined at the best restaurants, and paid the bills without stress.

After my college graduation, and a short stint as a weekend reporter in Palm Springs, Kevin followed me to Portland after *The Oregonian* hired me as a general assignment reporter. When the boys were born, I was one of the lucky moms who had the luxury to stay home and care for our children on my own.

Kevin was my universe.

"Why are you doing this?" His voice softened. "Is it because you're upset about your mom?"

"Maybe." I eased off from a fight. "Everyone's acting like she's fine, but she still doesn't have full use of her right side, and she's terrible about taking her medications when she's supposed to. Seeing her like this reminds me of how little time we all have here, that none of us will be around forever."

He sat back down next to me. Taking my hand into his, he said, "We need to go home on Sunday. Your mom's one of the toughest ladies I know. She's going to be fine. Curtis will take great care of her, like he always does. You're just feeling disorientated."

"My car's here. I'll have to drive."

"Why don't you leave in the morning, and we'll meet you there?" he asked.

"I'd like to stay a few more days to make sure everything's good. Also, my dad's birthday is next week. It'd be great to take him out to dinner at that Italian restaurant in Hillcrest, the one he likes so much."

"You can do that on your next visit. You've been gone a week now, Hope. It's time to come home."

"My dad has hardly seen his daughter in nearly two years. Do you know how hard that's been for him?"

"He's a drug addict who threatened to kill you when you were a kid. I'm sure he'll be fine until he can see you next time you're back in town."

Pulling my hand back from his, my anger flared all over again. "Reminds me of someone else I know."

Kevin's eyebrows knit tightly together. "You're not comparing him to me, are you?"

I felt brave in the cloudless October night. There were people behind most of the closed doors surrounding the pool. Kevin wouldn't cause a scene in public. This was my turn to vent. "Who do you think?"

"I'm nothing like your father," he seethed under a furious glare.

"Really?" I shot back, equally outraged. Old hurts needed to be spoken. "Who comes home every single day after work to drink a six pack and hide in the bathroom to smoke dope? You pushed me around and told me it was my fault."

"I have a good job. I'm not a hoarder. Children don't cross the street to get away from me. My kids aren't scared of me."

"Your wife is," I whispered, feeling fear creep back in.

"What?"

"Nothing."

"No. What did you say?" His jaw pulsed.

Sliding half my body into the hot tub, I walked across to the opposite side, putting space between us. I turned to face him again, my arms folded across my chest. "I said your wife is."

"I've never hurt you, Hope. Don't make a bigger deal out of everything than it is."

"I wish you could acknowledge that you've done wrong."

"It was wrong." He looked at me, his face tight with anger. "I'm sorry."

"Thank you." I nodded, my crossed arms loosened, relieved he had finally apologized.

"Why don't you try remembering all the things I've done right? I've supported you since you graduated college so you could take your dream jobs where you made no money. I pay the bills so you can stay home and live in our million plus dollar home and take naps. You do whatever you please while the kids are at school."

His point cut to the heart of my deepest fear. What if I couldn't make it without him? What if I left Kevin and Adrian dropped dead, or equally worse, what if the years of mixed martial arts fighting took its toll on Adrian's brain and he was overtaken by dementia.

My freelance writing for magazines wouldn't cover the bills. Soon enough, our children would be grown and leave me, and I would end up homeless living under a bridge, possibly getting raped by filthy deranged men. My anxiety took over and plunged me into all the what-if's, whether they were rational or not.

My sunken posture and tear-stained cheeks only seemed to fuel Kevin's anger. "Your father was a failure as a husband and a dad. I'm not. I cook dinners, take you on nice vacations. I help you clean the house. Do you understand?"

"Yes."

"Then don't ever say that again." He jumped up from the hot tub and began to pace. "I'll put in my notice, and we'll move back to San Diego. Okay? We'll sell the house and move over Christmas break. Does that make you happy?"

His unexpected offer to move back to San Diego was

a good one. If Kevin and I lived close to my family again, they might be enough to fill the emotional void in our marriage. Perhaps we could fall back in love and return to the way things were before we moved. "I would like that."

He forked his hand through his thick mop of hair. "I'll call my boss on Monday. Tell him they either need to let me work remotely or I will quit. That proves how much I love you."

"Okay." I looked at the hot water gurgling around my waist, exhaling dense threads of steam into the darkness.

"Will you come home on Sunday?" he asked.

I nodded.

His nostrils flared in nervous triumph. "Let's go to bed."

I stepped out of the hot tub and followed him back to our room, feeling defeated but also relieved. This was a good thing. We were moving home. Everything would be fine.

CHAPTER 18

...

SATURDAY, OCTOBER 15, 2016
Afternoon

MY PHONE CHIMED. Sydney had sent me a text.

Sydney: *Iacobelli's closes at three. I'm leaving now with Brooklyn and Nicole to pick you up.*

It was already 1:30. The boys and I had woken up early and driven to Mom's so Kevin could sleep in. Sydney and I had made plans the day before to meet up with her sister and her sister's daughter for lunch.

Me: *I'm at my mom's house. Let me text Kevin at the hotel and see if he still wants to go.*

Sydney: *Leave his ass in bed and come with the boys, because I really don't want to see him. There's not enough room in the car for all of us anyway.*

Me: *I already told him about it, and he wants to come. Can you please be nice if he does?*

Sydney: *Sure. For you, I will be nice. I'll put on my happy face. But you need to hurry.*

The whole thing put me on edge. Kevin and I had a terrible night. No matter how hard she tried, Sydney wasn't going to be sweet. On top of that, Kevin didn't like to be rushed. If he joined us, I would need to play mediator.

I texted Sydney back after speaking with Kevin.

Me: *He wants to go. I will pick him up and meet you there.*

Sydney: *That's stupid. You two always end up getting lost and taking forever to get anywhere. The hotel is on our way. We'll meet you in La Jolla so you can follow us.*

Me: *Okay.*

I sighed in resignation, knowing Sydney would make this suggestion. Arguing with her would only make it worse.

Waiting for Kevin to get inside the car felt like watching a big-rig creep slowly toward my favorite rose bush. I had tried to convince him to stay at the hotel and let me bring him take-out, but he insisted he wanted to join us. I hoped after our conversation last night, he wanted to try harder to socialize and spend time with his family. The look on his face and his slow saunter to the car told me otherwise.

"Why didn't we meet them there?" He frowned.

"I told you," I said as I scooted over to the passenger side so he could drive. "Sydney's afraid we'll get lost if we don't follow them there. She called ahead. The restaurant said they lock the doors at three. If we don't get there by then, they might not let us inside."

"It's 2:15 already. Can't we go somewhere else? There's a hundred restaurants right here in La Jolla."

Wringing my hands, I slid my wedding ring on and off in nervousness. "Little Italy's only fifteen minutes away."

"I don't want to feel rushed through our meal."

"They said as long as we get there by three, it's fine. They just lock the doors and stop taking orders by then. There's no rush to get out at any particular time. I think they just need some down time before they reopen their doors for dinner."

Sydney pulled in behind us, honked her horn and waved her hand to get us going. Kevin put the car in first gear. Sydney darted away from the curb, gaining speed to lead the way, and headed toward the 5 South.

Kevin's whole body tensed. "What's her problem?"

"They used to eat at this place with their mother when she was alive. It's special to them. Sydney only flies in from Maui every few months and going there is important to her." I patted his hand. "You won't find a more authentic Italian restaurant in San Diego."

"In San Diego." He smirked. Kevin didn't come to San Diego for good food. We lived near San Francisco after all.

Sydney's rental car slithered along the cramped La Jolla streets. I could feel her agitation at not being able to move faster. If she had her way, she would blow every other vehicle off the road.

Kevin pointed to all the great places we passed by. "Look, La Romantica, we ate there last time. Can't you text her and tell her you will see her afterward? We can eat here with the boys and then you can drop me back at the hotel and go meet up with them for a few hours."

I bit my lip in anxiety. If I was going to stay with Kevin, I needed him to do things my way every once in a while, it couldn't always be me catering to his needs. I wanted to keep my plans with Sydney. She would be angry if I cancelled on her after she'd gone out of her way to drive to the hotel to get us. Kevin didn't have to be here, I'd encouraged him not to come.

I tugged at my wedding ring again, gathering my courage. For once, I wasn't going to cave. If nothing else, it was a test to see if Kevin could operate on my terms. "We told her we were going to lunch with her. I don't want to bail out at the last minute. Can you please have a good attitude?"

He ran a hand across his chin, his jaw line tensing.

"I'm hungry," Zach spoke from the back seat.

"We'll be there soon," I assured him.

"I don't like Italian food. It makes me throw up," Michael threw in for good measure.

Kevin scowled at me. "See? This isn't a good idea."

Sydney swung her SUV around a black corvette slowing us up at a yellow light. She made it into the left lane and hit the accelerator, speeding through the light as Kevin came to an abrupt stop.

"You could have followed her," I said, placing my hands on the dashboard.

"There are too many cops around here. I don't need another ticket."

My cell phone chimed.

Sydney: *Sorry. But there was enough time for him to have made the light!*

"What did she say?" he asked.

"She said she's sorry," I only halfway fibbed, desperate to break the building tension. I couldn't help but think how much nicer this would be if I were with Adrian instead of my husband.

Kevin's full lips formed a tense line. The light turned green again. He drove forward. Sydney, who had pulled over to wait for us, shot away from the curb and back into the intersection in front of us. We followed her onto the freeway entrance and Kevin accelerated to eighty miles an hour to keep up.

"This is ridiculous!" he shouted, punching the steering wheel. Kevin turned to me in a sudden rage, his arm lifted. "Why are you ruining our Saturday?"

"I'm not," I spoke back in a whisper, scooting as far from him as I could.

"Text her we aren't going."

"No," I said, standing my ground. There was nothing wrong with joining my best friend and her family for lunch while we were all in town.

"You are so fucking selfish."

I could feel the blood drain from my face.

"Daddy," Michael spoke up from the back seat. "Why are you yelling at Mommy? We want to go out with Auntie Syd."

"Shut up, Michael. Stay out of this. It's none of your business." He looked over at me, his eyes narrowed in angry slits. "Are you happy with yourself? Do you like ruining everybody's day so we can all do exactly what you want?"

Tears welled in my eyes. I gave up. "Let's go back to La Jolla. I've lost my appetite."

"No. You wanted to go here so bad. It means so much to you. We're going."

I spent the rest of the car ride with my stomach in knots, my forehead pressed against the passenger window, tears trailing down my cheeks. As soon we exited the parked car, Sydney pulled me aside and hissed in my ear. "Are you okay? Brooklyn and I could see him yelling at you."

Kevin would know what she was saying. I didn't want to make him any angrier. "It's fine. We'll talk later."

"He's an asshole." She glared in his direction.

"Let's go inside before they close."

Her sister went to pull the glass door open and it didn't budge. "Shit!" She yanked harder before looking over at Sydney, her hands flailing in front of her for emphasis. "They're fucking closed."

I felt the full strength of a panic attack wash over me. The tingling had already begun in the car ride, along with the buzzing in my ears. My hands began to shake. My eyesight blurred. There was nothing that embarrassed Kevin more than a public scene and Brooklyn was quite possibly the loudest woman I knew.

"This is fucking bullshit." Brooklyn, a carbon copy of her little sister minus a few inches and some added curves, stomped her high-heeled foot. "It's not even close to three o'clock. They fucking closed the doors early."

"Let's go somewhere else." Kevin walked back toward our Audi. "Boys, get in the car. We're leaving."

Zach looked over to me while Michael clung to my arm. "We want to eat with Auntie Syd," Michael told his dad.

"Don't worry." Sydney rubbed Michael's back. "They'll let us in. Brooklyn," she said to her sister. "Calm down and knock on the door."

"I'm leaving." Kevin climbed into the driver's seat, the vein in his neck pulsing. "Boys, get in the car."

A tear rolled down Zach's cheek. This kind of prolonged tension between his dad and I was unusual. I normally went out of my way to appease Kevin and put out the flames before they flared. Michael and Zach looked toward me for guidance.

"We'll catch a ride back to the hotel with Sydney," I said to Kevin. "Go ahead and grab something there."

His left eyebrow arched in shock. "You're staying?"

"Yes, the boys and I are starving. It'll be quicker to stay here. You go back to the hotel."

He grimaced hard and shook his head, slamming his car door shut behind him. A young woman inside the restaurant, dressed in a crisp burgundy apron, walked toward the glass entrance. She turned the key in the lock and opened the door. "Sorry about that, ladies. The new guy got a little ahead of himself." She waved us in.

Sydney wrapped her arm around my shoulder and pressed her body close to mine as the waitress led us into a wood paneled dining room lined with rows of red pleather booths. "What was his deal?" she asked.

"I need a drink first. Let's get settled."

The rich aroma of garlic and tomatoes tempted back my appetite. I surveyed the medium-sized table the waitress had led us to, counting the seats to see if there was enough room for all of us.

"Boys," Sydney motioned to the empty table next to ours. "I want you to sit here with Nicole. This is going to be the kids table."

"But we want to sit together." Nicole popped out her plump lower lip and batted long lashes.

"Too bad." Sydney pulled out a seat for Nicole. "You guys are sitting here, because we need to have an adult conversation."

To my surprise, all the kids listened to her. Brooklyn and I followed suit, taking our seats at the Big Girl table and ordering wine and food.

I placed my napkin across my lap as I replayed the scene from the drive over in my head. I'd set Kevin up to fail. He didn't do well with chaos or loud anxious women.

When Sydney moved to Maui several years ago, an island where Kevin and I used to vacation, I switched our holiday destination to different locations so that we could be alone. At family gatherings, I made excuses to Mom as to why Kevin stayed behind. All these years of doing my best to shield him from social distress, and the night after telling him I wasn't in love with him, I threw him in to the fire.

Sydney wasn't feeling as sympathetic. "Okay, so tell me what happened, what went wrong in the car? I saw his arms moving in angry motions. We all thought it looked like he was yelling at you."

I filled her in on our argument, including what I told him last night about not feeling in love with him anymore and his offer to move back home to San Diego.

"So does that mean you're going to give him a second chance?" She leaned in closer to me from across the table. "Is that what you want after everything he's done?"

"I don't know." I pushed the palm of my hand into my throbbing forehead, attempting to drown out my frustration and confusion. "I thought it was. But, that bladder installation I had yesterday helped so we had sex last night and it sucked, and the way he treated me in the car ride over here, I'm thinking maybe I really don't love him anymore. I don't know if I want to give him a second chance. I'm so conflicted. It's all becoming too much." The nervous shake in my hands intensified. "Where's my wine?"

"She's coming right now," Sydney said. "I see her behind you."

I twisted my neck around and zeroed in on the smiling redhead carrying our drinks from the far end of the room. An aggravated diner held up his hand to ask her a question. I turned back to Sydney, knowing full well I'd have to wait another painful couple of seconds before my relief arrived. "I shouldn't have forced myself to have sex with him last night. It only made me like him less."

The memory of our intimacy made me cringe. Monogamous by nature, my body had already made the shift to a new man, a new body. It didn't matter that Adrian and I hadn't gone all the way. My husband's touch already felt heavy and awkward.

"Why did you fucking do it? Especially with your vagina on fire all day long! I know the installation you had helped but sex could have aggravated it again." Sydney slammed her hand on the table. Brooklyn who sat beside her, flipped her dark mane of hair over her shoulder and gave me a conspiratorial raise of the eyebrows.

"Because it calms him," I said.

"Why the fuck do you care? I thought you didn't do that kind of thing for him anymore. Disregard your feelings. Why do you always give in to his demands and what makes him happy?" Sydney's hands waved in short bursts as she spoke, underscoring her indignation. "Why don't you ever stick up for yourself and do what makes *you* happy once in a while? You're always trying to appease him. It's annoying."

I tore at my paper napkin as the waitress finally set down our much-needed glasses of merlot. Swirling the wine in its glass, I inhaled its rich aroma, allowing myself a long grateful sip. The liquid slid down my throat and warmed my belly, slowly beginning to release the suffocating tension.

After a few delicious moments of silence, Sydney stood to use the restroom while Brooklyn went over to the kids' table to give them an iPad so they could watch a movie.

Gazing into my glass, my mind drifted.

There was a reason I avoided conflict.

CHAPTER 19

...

SATURDAY, OCTOBER 15, 2016
Afternoon

FROM AN EARLY age, I'd learned not to argue with men when they're angry. It only makes things worse.

After nearly twenty years of marriage, my parents separated the autumn of '92. Dad was furious most of the time, his ranting scarier than usual. But he needed a friend, someone who would listen to him. I was first on his list.

He called me one afternoon and spoke before I had the chance to say *hello*. "I was called Yellow Number 2," Dad told me, apropos of nothing. "The dude who ran the place was Yellow Earl." His words came too fast. He wasn't making sense. I let the receiver slide down my ear. Dad was on another tear, and my thirteen-year-old rationality was to ignore him.

"We mostly drove around down in the town square of Sausalito. Yellow Earl would sit up in the hills, spying on me with binoculars. He'd say things like 'Yellow Number 2, get your feet off the seat' whenever he caught me relaxing in the taxicab. He was a total hillbilly, no one liked him as you can imagine." Dad's monologue about his days as a San Francisco taxi driver was sure to continue for another thirty to forty minutes.

On the weekends I visited him, he obsessively moved his stacks of junk mail from one cluttered surface space to another, or stood in his small, dimly lit kitchen, shaking clouds of Comet over piles of dirty dishes like it was pixie dust and the cups and plates would magically wash themselves. He took the occasional break from his work to duck into the only bathroom and smoke dope, a whirling overhead fan doing little to remove the choke of bong resin and burnt weed.

I was beginning to think that my father, an honor's English teacher, a man who could cite the date of any major event in history off the top of his head and discuss Shakespeare or Hemingway at length, was descending into madness.

After that particularly frustrating rant, my teenage hormones got the best of me. I slammed the phone down on him, leaving him alone to stew.

It was sometime after middle-school had let out, and I was home alone with my sister. Fifteen minutes after I hung up the phone, an angry fist pounded on our front door.

"Hope!" Dad screamed. "Hope. Answer the door!" I could tell by the sound of his voice he was already knee deep into one of his *Mashugana Meltdowns*, Yiddish for batshit crazy. I should have done what I always did with Dad when he was angry. I should have appeased him.

Only this time, for the very first time, we didn't live together. This wasn't his house anymore, and I didn't have to let him inside. I could block him out completely.

Full of bravado, I swung open the large peephole cutout in the front door. "What?" I peered into his methamphetamine eyes.

"Open the fuckin' door!" He grabbed the handle, frantically twisting it back and forth. Beads of sweat dripped from his forehead into his overgrown eyebrows.

"No. Tell me what you want."

"Hope, don't play your little games with me. Open the goddamned door!" The intensity of his rage seeped through the crevices of our entryway.

"No," I whispered, shrinking back.

"Open the door!"

My heart hammered. I shut the peephole and turned the second lock for safety. Dad pounded harder and raised his voice loud enough for the neighbors to hear. My stomach twisted itself into knots. I worried I might throw up if he didn't leave.

Skye, around eight years old at the time, tumbled out of her room to see what all the commotion was about.

"Is that Dad yelling out there?"

"Yes. Don't let him in," I snapped.

She scrunched her freckled nose. "Why not?"

Delirious and afraid, I felt like biting her button nose right off her face. "Because I said so. Do you hear me? Do *not* open that door!"

She stood there, in our sunlit entryway, twisting a lock of her dark brown hair, contemplating her next move. Dad screamed out my name once more like it was a dirty word. I turned to creep away, to escape his violent shouting.

That's when Skye brushed past me and turned the locks. The door flew open and whacked the interior wall. Terror grabbed me by the throat.

With a shot of adrenaline, I raced toward one of the only rooms with a lock on it, my mother's master bathroom. Dad chased after me, steps behind. I smashed the door shut within seconds of him grabbing the handle, squeezing the doorknob while I locked it, desperate to keep him out.

He punched the door. "You open this goddamned door, you little bitch!"

I eyed the small window over Mom's bathtub, which sat close to the ceiling. If I could pull myself up high enough, I could wiggle out.

Bang. A hard kick rattled the door. "I'm going to break this door down. Do you hear me? You fat little whore. You're just like your fucking mother!"

The door buckled inward as I tried to pull myself up to the small window with sweaty hands. I slipped. It was no use. I was either too panicked or not strong enough.

"When I get in there, I'm going to kill you!" Dad shouted.

I tilted my head toward the open window and screamed for help. No answer. I was on my own. My heart raced. It became difficult to breathe. Tears flooded my eyes until I couldn't see clearly.

I gave up, resigned to my fate, and sat on the closed toilet seat, sobbing, waiting with dread for whatever would happen next.

Dad's voice disappeared. The room went silent. I quietly pressed my ear to the door, unsure if he'd left or if this was a trick to lure me from safety. There was no way to know for sure, not without opening the door. I definitely wasn't going to do that. Instead, I lay myself on the floor and let the cool white linoleum comfort my overheated skin. A thick, heavy sleep enveloped my strained body.

The next week Dad called to apologize. He mailed me a long, beautifully written letter, explaining how he'd had a bad trip and he would never use hard drugs again. Dad bought me a gold ring encrusted with diamond and ruby chips from an upscale jewelry store. When I slammed the phone down on him like that, he said, he couldn't help himself, he flew out of control.

Perhaps it wasn't my fault. But, the lesson stuck. Don't argue with angry men, appease them.

CHAPTER 20

...

SATURDAY, OCTOBER 15, 2016
Afternoon

"HOPE." SYDNEY'S VOICE carried me back to the present. We were waiting for our lunch at Iacobelli's. My boys sat at the kids' table with Sydney's niece. The pizza, three cheese ravioli's in meat sauce, along with a family sized antipasto salad would be brought out any minute.

"Huh?"

"How much longer are you going to let Kevin treat you badly?" she asked.

"I shouldn't have let him come today." I took another sip of wine. "After telling him I didn't love him last night, he was probably overwhelmed."

"All you keep doing is making excuses for how he treats you and the kids. Going out to lunch with us should not have caused him to act like an ass. That is complete bullshit!"

"You know he doesn't like any kind of chaos."

"He should know better when he is going out with my sister and me. It's not like he hasn't known us for twenty years or what he was getting himself into when he agreed to eat lunch with us." She flung her long hair behind her back and threw it up in a ponytail. "If he was not up to the task, he shouldn't have come. It's as simple as that."

"I know," I agreed with her, wanting to end the conversation. "I still feel bad, though."

"You shouldn't feel bad. He should feel bad for putting you in this position and acting like a fucking pussy."

The waitress placed our pepperoni and pineapple pizza on a metal stand and then came back with our salad and pasta.

A text came through from Adrian as we set the kids up with their food.

Adrian: *I will wait until you are ready even if that means it doesn't happen. I'm always... always going to be here for you. You don't have to reciprocate.*

A grateful smile tugged into my cheeks. Adrian was my hero.

"Who was that?" Sydney asked, sitting back down and taking a bite of her ravioli.

I showed her his text.

"What's that about?" she asked.

"I had to tell him it was over for now. I'm not going to see him again or talk to him until I've given Kevin a chance."

"Okay, if you want to give it a shot." She dabbed her napkin on her lips. "But, remember the golden rule. People have to want to change in order for change to occur."

I took a bite of my pizza slice, relishing the sweet tangy sauce, and trying to block out Sydney's unwanted advice.

"How long do you want to try for when he's been acting this way for twenty years now?" she continued. "You just told him how you felt last night, so you'd think he'd be making an effort today. He didn't. He's still acting exactly the same."

"He was thrown into an uncomfortable situation, Sydney. It's not fair to judge him on this one car ride."

She set down her napkin and stared into my eyes. "Again, all I hear is excuses form you for his horrible behavior. How long do you want to give him to change before enough is enough?"

"I've built this great life for my boys and me. I don't want to ruin my family."

"You mean like your life was awesome when you got pregnant with Michael and Kevin drank and smoked pot the entire pregnancy and ignored you. Or when Michael was born and had colic and Kevin blamed you for wanting a baby in the first place? That's your perfect life?"

I squeezed my crumpled paper napkin into a ball. Sydney didn't have children, she didn't understand. "My boys don't know those things. All they see is a stable nuclear family with two parents who love them."

"But they don't." She leaned closer toward me from across the table. "Michael sees what Kevin does. He even told me his dad is always working and never spends time with you guys. He sees you're not a family unit. Besides that, do you want them to treat a woman the way Kevin treats you? The older they get the more they will see the truth you keep repressing."

My throat constricted. Another panic attack was ramping up again. "No."

"Why don't you each move into your own apartment when you get back here to San Diego? If he really wants to make it work and change, then he won't have a problem with that plan."

"I was texting with Adrian this morning and he said the same thing."

"He's right."

I looked over to Brooklyn for support. She nodded in agreement with her sister.

"Adrian said whether I end up with him or not, this is my chance to get away from Kevin." I glanced over at the boys to make sure they weren't listening. "That kind of feels like tricking Kevin into selling our house so we can move back here."

"So?" Sydney lifted her eyebrow at me.

"I don't like that." I took a sip of wine. "But then, maybe it's the only way to take some time away from both him and Adrian so I can see who I miss more and what I really want. A separation would give me space to think."

"It would," Sydney said, trying to assuage my guilt.

She wasn't successful. My lies and betrayal felt like a fatal swig of poison. It was only a matter of time before I felt the effects. The only thing I knew for sure was I needed to make a choice between the two men in my life. The indecision was brutally unfair to my loved ones.

* * *

When the boys and I returned to the hotel, we found Kevin packing his toiletries. "Hey," I said, standing in the doorway with Michael and Zach, peering into the dimly lit room.

"Hey." He continued folding clothes into his suitcase. "It's only Saturday."

The boys broke free of my grip and climbed atop their bed. They started jumping. "We don't want to leave yet, Daddy. We just got here."

He ignored them and fixed his blue eyes on me. "I called the airport and got an earlier flight."

"What about Michael and Zach?"

"They can drive home with you tomorrow."

"Yay," Zach shouted. "The arrow plane hurts my ears."

"How will you get to the airport?"

"I'll take an Uber."

"So, you're not going to stay for dinner tonight with the family? I told them you were coming. Curtis is making his cheesy meat tacos everyone loves." My words were barely audible over the bedsprings squeaking in protest under the boys' feet.

"Michael. Zach," Kevin said. "Enough. Get down and find something quiet to do."

"Dad," they moaned in near unison. Michael cocked his head, no doubt ready with a new tactic. "We're on the bottom floor and it's a crappy hotel bed. No one cares."

"Michael Alexander," Kevin said.

"What?" He continued jumping.

Kevin frowned at Michael. "Get down before I remove you myself."

"Make us, Daddy." Zach smiled. "Push us off."

Kevin moved toward the bed and playfully pushed Zach. My youngest son laughed, his blond curls bouncing in the wake of his fall. "Do it again." He jumped up to his feet.

Kevin smirked at me. "I better not. Mommy doesn't like it when I push. She thinks it's mean."

I could feel the heat rise in my cheeks.

"No, it's not." Zach was back on his feet. "I like it."

"It makes your mommy cry," Kevin said, his smile curling into a dimple.

I crossed my arms across my chest. "That's hilarious. Teach your boys it's okay to push a woman." I felt safer making a snide remark in front of my children. He was less likely to retaliate.

Michael froze. "Don't start fighting. If you keep yelling at each other, you two are going to get a divorce."

I held my breath. Michael's intuition scared me.

His little lips tightened in anxiety. "You aren't, are you?"

"No, Michael," I said. "Please get down from the bed."

"Why are you leaving early, Daddy?" he asked as he stood his ground atop the sunken mattress.

"I got a call from work. There are some things I need to take care of tomorrow before Monday."

"I don't believe you."

"Michael," I lowered my voice into serious mommy mode. "You and your brother need to get off the bed right now and go take a bath. We're leaving in forty minutes to go to Bubby's."

I was furious Kevin planned to take off early, especially since he was leaving the boys with me. They had school on Monday, so I had no choice but to drive home tomorrow, whether I wanted to or not.

Sydney's instincts seemed to be on target. Kevin hadn't gone out of his way to be kind to me, nor did he put my needs first. Wanting to avoid another fight, I let it go.

While Michael and Zach bathed and dressed, I gathered up our belongings to take them to Mom's to spend the night. If I had known what would happen next, I would have done things differently. As it stood, I had no idea just how much I was about to lose.

CHAPTER 21

...

SUNDAY, OCTOBER 16, 2016
Morning

SUNDAY MORNING BROUGHT on a heat wave, mirroring my own internal storm. Santa Ana winds, formally referred to as Santana winds, or Satan's winds, had blown in from the east overnight. Temperatures were predicted to rise to the high nineties.

Outside the living room windows, palm trees stood naked, stripped of their fronds. Power lines must have been knocked out. Mom's clocks were blinking and the ceiling fans no longer spun. Sensitive to the change in air pressure and the myriad of allergens blown in with the hot desert winds, the boys and I would suffer wicked sinus headaches by the end of the day.

I quietly dragged our overnight bags to the front door and planned what I would prepare Michael and Zach for breakfast before I woke them. It was going to be a long drive. At least we would have air conditioning.

I heard Mom clomp down the stairs and drag herself into her office. I peeked inside to check on her. Mom's face looked red and tight.

"Mama, let me pull out the chair for you."

"I've got it."

"You look stressed. Why are you up so early?"

"I just got off the phone with Jonas."

My stepbrother wasn't one for calling home, not at seven-thirty in the morning.

"You should sit down." Mom motioned her head toward her chair at the desk.

"No," I said, feeling my throat tighten.

"I have some bad news."

"No," I said again. "Don't tell me." Whatever it was, I didn't want to hear it. I'd had enough bad news. Nothing else was allowed to go wrong.

"Your father passed away last night."

Tears stung my eyes. My lips quivered in rebellion. "No, he didn't."

"Jonas' fire station was called to the scene. He's there with your dad now. He died in his sleep, honey. Jonas said he looked peaceful. Usually they don't look like that."

"No!" I shook my head violently, feeling my heart crash against my chest. Why was she lying to me? My dad was fine. Mom was the one who was fragile from her stroke. She was the one I needed to worry about.

Mom reached out to hug me as I dropped to the ground and curled into a fetal position, tears fighting against my closed lids. "Jonas is wrong."

After a lifetime of chronic anxiety, my body knew exactly how to shut down. The world went black. I couldn't think. Each broken heartbeat deepened the pain in my chest.

My dad had come close to death so many times. For years, I dreaded every early or late-night phone call. I'd been prepared.

But then I let my guard down. He'd been doing so much better. He had a girlfriend. He led the homeowner's association at his assisted living home. I had just spoken with him yesterday and cancelled our plans for his birthday. I asked Mom to call Jonas back and make sure she had the correct information.

Dad and I had a complicated relationship. Previous therapists labeled it troubling, and in my younger years, extremely dysfunctional.

Dad taught me how to grow marijuana in our suburban garage in Atlanta, Georgia when I was five. He took hard drugs and called me terrible names. There was that time he threatened to kill me.

But he also danced with me in our living room when I was a kid, dressed up with me in funny outfits, and scouted out our nature walks. As I matured, he scanned the newspapers and internet for local art shows and made sure we visited all my favorites together. Picasso, Degas, and Gauguin.

Sometimes we'd even drive to The Getty in Los Angeles. Once we went as far as The Palace of Fine Arts in San Francisco for a special exhibit. We made it a tradition to eat lunch together first at a nearby café and then buy at least one memento from the gift shop afterward.

After Michael's birth, Dad came to my apartment a minimum of three times a week to hold his grandson so I could nap. He took my side when anyone hurt my feelings, and made time for me even if it was last minute or in the early morning hours.

We gossiped. He spilled his coffee on my countertops and in my car and sported questionable hairstyles. Dad made inappropriate jokes and thrived on watching *The Jerry Springer Show*. I didn't want to say goodbye. I wasn't ready.

My body turned against me, heavy and numb. I wanted to disappear. Anger, black and endless, stirred up the worst parts of me, tempting me to break things, or give up completely, abandoning everything for a year of sleep.

I pushed aside the chair and crawled underneath Mom's desk, sobbing. She kneeled on her good leg to rub my back. I nudged her hand away. "Leave me alone, please. Please go."

The floorboards leading to the office squeaked and Michael poked his head inside. I looked away as Mom ushered him out.

Minutes or hours passed. Details stumbled in. No signs of foul play. Probably a heart attack. No suffering. Dad had led a full life and he went in his sleep, the way most of us hope for.

Jonas stayed with Dad's body to make sure he was treated with dignity. We could go visit him at Fine Living before they took away his body if we wanted. I didn't. I didn't want to see my dad dead.

Knowing Jonas was there was a comfort. We were lucky my stepbrother was the one who found him.

Dad didn't suffer. He never had to go through that tragic decline where he lost his mind or faculties before his body set him free. His passing was for the best. That's what I tried to tell myself, but the pain of loss doesn't listen to reason.

Mom said my brother, Pete, back in Los Angeles, was launching a clunky investigation into Dad's death. He'd already interrogated Jonas as well as a friend of his who was a doctor. Pete was going to call the hospital next and ask questions about height and weight to medication ratio. This was someone's fault. Pete would find the person to blame and then, no doubt, sue.

Skye came over and busied herself with arrangements - where to take the body, how to dispose of Dad – cremation versus burial, which friends and family should be called and notified, what type of services would take place to commemorate our dad.

But I was a drifting, aimless ghost.

Curtis and my stepsister, Tawny, who had arrived the previous night, cooked breakfast.

I left Michael and Zach with Mom and drove to my old neighborhood in Cardiff. There was a spot at a large grassy park near the top of a hill with a steep slope of concrete stairs. One hundred and eight. I'd counted them once as I raced to the top, trying to work out some issue or another.

Flashbacks played out before me. Times of intense pain. When I was in college, my Uncle Dave had been killed on his way to work by a drunk driver. Shortly after Zach was born, my favorite aunt found out her husband was cheating on her with a co-worker. Aunt Sher shot herself in the head. Two years later, my twenty-seven-year-old cousin was murdered. Days after breaking up with her abusive boyfriend, he had stabbed her to death on the quiet Hawaiian street in front of her home.

Pushing against wind and dust, after climbing and descending those one hundred and eight stairs three times straight, my legs shook like reverberating strings on a weeping violin.

Getting older meant loss. We must learn to live without the people who have become integral pieces of our existence. My dad was not only my parent and friend. I didn't just love him. He was the ever-present background of my daily routine, the man I called to tell a funny story to about the boys. The person I cried to when someone hurt my feelings. The guy who updated me on the daily headlines when I was too busy to watch the news. Of all the loved ones I'd lost, Dad's absence would cut the deepest.

The Santa Ana heat was more brutal than I'd expected. I could feel my hair sticking to my neck and my tank top clinging to my skin. Two years in Northern California had weakened my ability to tolerate the beating sun. I regretted not bringing a water bottle to quench my thirst, or sunglasses to protect my eyes.

Joan Didion once wrote that Southern California's indigenous Indians would throw themselves into the sea when the bad wind blew. I imagined cutting the world loose and plummeting into the cold ocean.

Instead, I traversed the cemented walkway toward the place where it ended and continued hiking along a looping dirt trail near the edge of a canyon.

A helicopter flew overhead, the hum of its blades beating the air. I watched it circle. The pilot was searching for something. Brush fire? A missing senior citizen or a petty criminal taken off on foot? A molten ache scraped against my chest as I peered over the edge of the canyon and considered leaving the beaten path. My dad was dead. I felt like smashing things.

Crunching over dry patches of chaparral, I broke brittle sticks and stomped out clumps of dirt. Rocks rolled down the hill. The winds raged hot and wild, dredging up memories.

Like the time Dad drove to LA where I was living at the time, and then all the way to Palm Springs and back with me for a rumored job opening for the local newspaper. I got it in my head that if I personally turned in my resume, I had a better chance of getting hired.

Before Dad arrived, I straightened my hair, applied thick layers of makeup, and zipped up my best suit into a protective black plastic bag to keep it clean and wrinkle-free for the ride.

Dad knocked on my door right on time.

"Hey Papa."

"Hello, Princess. You look beau-ti-ful."

"Thanks, Dad. Do I look okay for real? My hairdresser made my hair a little darker brown. I thought it might make me look more mature."

"You look gorgeous. They're going to thank their lucky stars you walked through their doors."

I smiled at his compliment. "Oh, I hope they want to hire me, that's all."

"Well, they'd be *mashugana* not to," Dad said with a reassuring nod.

My dad's companionship and unwavering confidence gave me an edge. I got hired that day. From then on, he cut out every single story I covered and saved them all in a three-ring binder. Anyone who knew my dad had known his talented daughter was a reporter for *The Desert Sun*.

Death was selfish. Death did not share. I would never get to visit with my dad again. On my trek down the steep hill, I left footprints in my wake. Rosemary bushes snapped and scented the air.

I needed to do something to make meaning out of it all. Something good had to come from something so terrible. I promised my dad and myself I would honor his death by carrying out the second half of my own life differently. There was a famous speech by Steve Jobs. In it he said:

Remembering that you are going to die is the best way I know to avoid the trap of thinking you have something to lose. You are already naked. There is no reason not to follow your heart.

I decided I was going to live that way. Fuck fear. I was going to occupy this world with intention, as if each choice might be my last.

CHAPTER 22

...

SUNDAY, OCTOBER 16, 2016
Night

I FELT LIKE puking. Pulling my loose curls into a small bun at the nape of my neck, I shot my stepsister a nervous smile. "Ready?"

Mom sat on the couch dressed in sweatpants and an oversized t-shirt, trying to mask her glee. Despite the heaviness of watching her children lose their father, this was a moment she had long been hoping for.

After twenty-two years, I was finally going to break the silence between Tawny and me by confronting her. I'd made a promise to Dad to be brave. This was my first bold step.

"Ready." Tawny had changed from flip-flops to tennis shoes. Fitted black shorts complimented her trim new figure. Tawny, older than me by one year, had a tummy tuck recently and probably some lipo while she was at it. Thanks to the surgeries, she looked fantastic. I preferred her heavy.

"See ya'll soon," Curtis called out, poking his head around the kitchen door with a hopeful smile. Even as adults, our loving parents were micro-managing.

I pushed open the front door to a gust of warm night air. The devil's winds were still blowing.

"Just so you know," I said, stepping outside into the illuminated darkness. "I probably won't be able to look at you."

"She didn't mean she thinks you're ugly," Mom hollered from her perch on the couch. "Hope has a hard time making eye contact when she's uncomfortable."

"Thanks, Mom," I shouted back. Rolling my eyes, I shut the door behind us. "Let's go this way." I motioned Tawny toward the left. "We can walk around the neighborhood."

Hippie-free-love music flowed from someone's open window. Waves crashed in the distance. Neither of us spoke a word for an entire block.

Tawny cleared her throat. "How was it today at your dad's?"

"Pretty terrible," I said, inhaling the salty scent of the ocean. "My mom dropped the boys off at the airport before we went over to my dad's assisted living home. They've never flown alone." I wrung my hands together. "I was crying too much to make the drive back to Northern California without running off the road, and Michael and Zach have school tomorrow."

"How'd they do?"

"Kevin said they made it home fine." I bit the inside of my cheek. "So, my dad lived in this cramped kind of run down room with another guy he didn't really like. They barely had space for their two twin beds, matching armoires, and an easy chair. No kitchen or anything, only a bathroom. I know Dad loved living there, but it was super depressing."

Terrified to address the real reason for this walk, I rambled and didn't know how to stop. "Dad used to tell me how his roommate watched Spanish soap operas twenty-four seven, trying to learn the language. The guy barely ever talked, he just watched TV. When we got to my dad's, my mom asked his roommate if he was there when Dad died." I pictured the disheveled middle-aged man sitting on the edge of his recliner. He looked at us like we were robbing him with a water gun, all sorts of wild-eyed fear and paranoia.

"He said my dad sat up in his bed around three o-clock last night and stayed in a hunched over sitting position. He didn't move. The roommate asked him if he wanted him to call an ambulance and my dad said 'no' so the roommate went back to sleep."

I straightened the small diamond on my necklace, the one Dad had given me as a gift when I graduated from college.

Tawny shoved her hands into the shallow pockets of her black shorts.

"My dad had gotten sick in the middle of the night so many times before, and the paramedics saved him. He could be alive if his roommate had helped."

"He should have called 911."

"Yeah," I said.

This was the most Tawny and I had spoken in twenty plus years. I adjusted the electric blue bra strap slipping down my narrow shoulder, ready to change the subject. "It doesn't matter, though. We can't go back in time. It's too late."

Our footsteps thumped along the sidewalk. Original beach cottages stood proud beside newer, sprawling mansions wedged onto overwhelmed lots. Peeking through the windows of softly lit homes, other people's lives seemed so much simpler.

It was time to get to the point. "So, the reason I wanted to talk to you..." I re-wrapped my bun, prodding myself to speak. "I've always been nervous to ask you about Luke and Mauricio."

"I figured."

The shame and hurt of acknowledging I wasn't enough for my boyfriend had held me back from confronting Tawny sooner. While I despised her for what she did, I secretly blamed my own inadequacies for the betrayal.

I was sixteen when it had happened, during a time when Adrian and I were apart. I'd been dating a guy named Luke. His bad-boy attitude and natural sex appeal won my teenage heart.

The first time I saw Luke, he was lounging on the balcony of his resort beachside apartment. Sydney had met Luke's roommate at a Padre's baseball game that weekend, and she dragged me over to their place a few days later for an introduction. Luke was nineteen, a high school graduate, and a newly minted military man.

A transplant from the Bible Belt, Luke lay squinting his chocolate brown eyes in the brilliant California sunshine. His chestnut hair and the sprinkle of light freckles across the bridge of his nose drew me in. Sensual lips tugged on a cigarette, exhaling an elegant stream of smoke. If I could have him, my life would be perfect.

As I stood on that balcony watching him, our glorious future played out before me like a Kay Jewelers commercial. I saw myself looping his name on my notebooks in red sparkle nail polish. He would surprise me at my high school's senior lunch hour. Classmates would gossip about Hope Sullivan's gorgeous boyfriend.

Ten years down the road, we would marry and make love on our kitchen counter when he returned home from a long day at work.

Luke became the instant leading man in my make-believe blockbuster movie.

Tawny fidgeted with her hands and kept her head cast down, walking a step ahead of me in silence.

I quickened my pace. "So, what happened? Why did you do it?"

"I don't know," she spoke in monotone without emotion.

Anger replaced my apprehension. How could she not know why she fucked my boyfriend? And *then*, on top of it, fucked my best friend's boyfriend? That was not something that happened by accident. "Mauricio told me you slept with both him and Luke at the same time."

I waited for a reaction that didn't come. Clearing my throat, I tried a different tactic. "It kind of felt like you were giving Sydney and me the middle finger."

To be honest, Sydney hadn't cared one lick when I told her the news. She said she was breaking up with Mauricio anyway, and he could go fuck himself as far as she was concerned. I, on the other hand, cried so hard, I threw up. If only I were prettier, smarter, or more likable, Luke wouldn't have strayed.

"I thought Luke and Mauricio were cute," Tawny said. "That one night when we were all hanging out on the balcony, drinking, and you and Sydney went inside, the guys flirted with me. Luke offered me a cigarette, and they were both giving me the eye. Mauricio brought up having a threesome, and I thought it would be fun. It had nothing to do with you or Sydney."

A dog howled in protest in the distance. This conversation was complete bullshit. Tawny was either flat out lying or she needed a whole lot more therapy for her denial.

I held my breath for a beat to calm down. "If it was only a coincidence that the two guys asking you for a threesome happened to be your stepsister's boyfriend and her best friend's boyfriend, why didn't you say no? Didn't you think about Sydney and me?"

Staring at her while I waited for a response, memories flashed through my mind. I had walked into Luke's apartment unannounced that Sunday afternoon and found him watching a football game with his arm wrapped around Tawny. She smirked at me like she was a winner. The girl who got the most toys at Christmas.

It sliced me open. I felt myself plummet into a violent panic attack that annihilated my ability to think or react. I wanted to undo the scene. This wasn't happening. My heart unraveled in ribbons of pain and humiliation.

Later that week, Sydney got into a huge fight with Mauricio. Mauricio called me, and spat out the whole truth. Tawny had had sex with both him and Luke on the day I found them watching football. This time, I retaliated.

We waited until Tawny left the house for a weekend camping trip with Curtis and my stepsiblings. With Mom's permission, I called Sydney over to help carry out the attack.

I grabbed scotch tape from a drawer in the kitchen. One wall of Tawny's room consisted of floor-to-ceiling mirrored closet doors. Sydney and I ripped the wrappers off a stack of condoms we'd found hidden inside Tawny's sock drawer, and loosely inflated them. We taped them to her mirrored doors. I dug into my pocket for an old lipstick I'd set aside for this project. In large, waxy red letters, I scrawled the words *WHORE* and *SLUT* in the spaces between the condoms.

We dumped her tidy drawers onto the mint green shag-carpet and flung piles of her clothes across the room. Sydney discovered a diary in the rubble. I rifled through it first, frantic for damning details. What did Luke think was so great about Tawny? Why would they do this to me?

There was nothing on the threesome, but she'd written several entries on the most inane interactions between her and me. The time I beat her at basketball and supposedly rubbed her face in it. An evening she ate a second helping of mac and cheese at dinner and she was positive I rolled my eyes at her for overeating.

Tawny was psychotic and evil, and I was positive she had fucked two men simply to hurt me. I hated her for dragging my best friend into her pathetic drama and even more so for stealing what I coveted most.

Sydney and I shredded the pages and tossed them onto her bed so she could see we'd read them. Tawny would know we were keen to all the crazy crap in her lunatic brain. Her repulsive behavior was no secret.

I placed my hands on my hips in satisfaction and smiled at Sydney. Tawny's room looked like my broken heart, torn and desecrated.

The memory still stung.

My stepsister kept her focus on the road ahead as she spoke. "Luke and Mauricio were both charming guys, just like you and Sydney had described. I was flattered by their attention." She brushed a strand of loose blonde hair behind her ear. "I'm sorry."

There they were, the words I waited a good twenty years to hear. They felt completely empty.

"You were family, Tawny." My eyes widened in exasperation. Despite my instincts all those years ago, warning me something was off about her, I'd introduced her to Luke and his friends that summer to make her feel included, to show Mom and Curtis we could all get along. "I trusted you."

She nodded and walked faster.

I wanted to stomp home and forget this conversation. To hell with granting her forgiveness and understanding. All these years later, Tawny still didn't give a shit.

Clouds shifted and a rash of stars distributed shards of light. It was finally dawning on me that maybe this whole thing was about Tawny's insecurities and not some defect on my part. I dug deeper, determined to break her. "Why did you borrow one of my outfits the day you slept with them?"

"Because I didn't have anything I liked."

"That's it? You put on my clothes and slept with my boyfriend and my best friend's boyfriend at the same time and none of it meant anything? It was only for fun?"

"I didn't sleep with them at the same time." She braved a quick glance in my direction. "I changed my mind when I got to their apartment. I only saw one of them at a time."

I tweaked the movie I'd held in my head, the one with the three of them together in Luke's locked bedroom, Mauricio in front facing her, Luke from behind. Doing them both at once was dirty, but fucking them separately was worse.

A one-time thing could be played off as an accident. But separate, she had to make two deliberate choices to fuck us over. I blew out an indignant huff of air. This was her issue, not mine.

I looked over at Tawny and caught her eye. "You lied and told your dad and the other kids that Luke was your boyfriend, and I was the one who had slept with him. Skye took your side, and I'm sure Curtis felt the same way, too. I've been the bad guy all these years. Even though you were the one who set out to crush me, you managed to become the victim."

A large wave crashed against the shore. I imagined the spray let loose in the night air before returning to its thundering ocean.

Tawny mumbled, "I really am sorry."

She sounded sincere.

"I guess we were all doing the best we could," I said, trying to sort out my colliding emotions.

My love affair with Adrian certainly wasn't right, either. I was reaching out for the affection I desperately needed in a way that hurt others. I couldn't even allow myself to imagine the immense pain my infidelity would cause Kevin if he found out about Adrian.

Squeezing her arm in a gesture of understanding, I was ready to let it go. I still didn't like her, but that didn't matter anymore. I had spoken up for myself. Face to face and on my own, without any help from Mom or Sydney. I'd addressed a life-long grievance that scared the shit out of me. I was no longer Tawny's doormat.

This was my warm-up.

The battle ahead would be far more challenging.

CHAPTER 23

...

TUESDAY, OCTOBER 18, 2016

IN HONOR OF my dad and the promise I had made to him, I returned to Andalucía determined to maintain momentum. I had stood up to Tawny. The time had come to tackle my greatest fear and take charge of my marriage.

Tuesday morning, after I walked Michael and Zach to school, I tidied up our house in preparation for the meeting I'd scheduled with the realtor. Boots Benerman, a fierce, full-figured lioness of a woman, had helped me purchase our home two years ago.

Today, she assessed the nearly unchanged house in a studied ten-minute tour and formulated a plan. We needed to sell quick. The holiday season was fast approaching, and she anticipated a slight slow-down in the market.

By the time I'd cleaned up after dinner and put the boys to bed, there was no space for procrastination. After stopping off at a local U-Haul for packing materials that morning, I'd already arranged for movers to come the following week and load a pod I'd rented to store our life's belongings. Kevin knew I'd met with Boots, but he didn't know the details.

Chances were high he wasn't going to like our plan.

I found him in his usual spot, in the darkened office, sitting at the large walnut desk my dad had given us, playing an online video game with cyber friends. I could tell by the smell of skunk and the whir of the bathroom fan, he'd already smoked out and grabbed himself a beer. This was the most relaxed he was going to feel all night.

"You have a minute?" I stepped into his cave.

"Sure." The light from the computer illuminated his face. "What's up?" he asked without glancing away from the screen.

"I talked to Boots Benerman today about the house. She said if we're going to sell, we should do it now."

"Great. My boss is onboard with me flying home on Thursdays. They're even going to cover my plane tickets. The company is being really supportive."

"I'm not surprised." I maintained the physical distance between us. "You're a great asset to them. They need you."

He nodded.

"Boots said we need to make the house model-perfect. She wants everything but the essentials packed up by this weekend and for everything besides some of the furniture to be moved into storage. She's going to organize a painter, find someone to re-seal the floors, and hire a stager. In three weeks, we should be on target for pictures and showings."

Kevin's eyebrows knitted together in anxiety. "Is all that really necessary?"

"Yeah, she said if we want to get the best price, we need to hit it before the holidays and make the home look perfect."

Kevin jammed his fingers on the keyboard and spoke into a microphone to his online friends. "That's not a good idea, guys. Stay out of that room."

"I'll take care of everything," I continued. "You'll just need to be flexible with our living arrangements. We'll probably have to stay over at a hotel for a few days while they're painting and sealing the floors and stuff."

He looked over at me for a moment, his jaw tense. "My birthday's in two weeks."

"I know. Maybe you could stay here if you want, and I can take the boys to the hotel. They're the ones we have to worry about touching the walls and getting in people's way. Maybe you could just stay over at the hotel the one night while the floors dry."

He scratched the top of his blond head in frustration. "Stop," he spoke into the microphone. "Bad idea."

My stomached twisted. Fixing up the house would be a huge inconvenience for a move I knew Kevin would rather not be making. Broaching separate apartments might push him over the edge. I bit the inside of my check until I tasted blood. *You can do this, Hope. Be Brave.*

"So, are you okay with everything? Can I let Boots know we're good to go and ready to sign a contract?"

"Are you sure you don't want to wait until this summer?"

"Boots says—"

"I'm not asking you what Boots says. I am asking you what you think is best for our family." He folded his arms across his chest and turned his chair to face me.

"Kevin," I said, tears welling in my eyes, "you told me we could move home right away. This is the best time to sell."

He pursed his lips together in thought, his jaw pulsing. "Fine. I thought it would be easier for Michael and Zach if we didn't rip them out of the school year. But, whatever you want. You're in charge."

"Okay." I bit at my lip. I didn't feel right about moving the boys at this time either. It was selfish. They'd already had to switch schools when we moved here. I was a bad mother.

Still, if we didn't move fast, we could lose equity in the house that we might need if we divorced. I also worried I would chicken out completely if I didn't push forward.

"We'll try to time it for moving right after Christmas when the boys are on winter break so they won't be too disrupted. There's a nice apartment complex in San Diego that Michael and Zach and I used to visit friends at all the time. They've got two pools, a big game room, it's like a giant resort hotel that's really kid friendly. Michael and Zach used to ask me all the time if we could sell our house on Kingston Court and move there instead. This was one of their dreams."

The animated men on Kevin's computer screen were running in different directions. The one in silver armor fell over and grabbed his stomach, scarlet blood gushing down his legs.

"We can each get an apartment in the same building."

Kevin's hooded eyes narrowed. "What?"

"That way, the boys can go back and forth easily."

"You never mentioned living in separate apartments. No way, Hope. That's not happening."

Taking a step backward, my mind scrambled for a response. "But, I told you, we—"

"I never agreed to living apart." His voice grew stern. "If that's your plan, we're not selling the house and we're not moving."

The floor fell out from underneath me, dropping me into a free fall. I knew I should have waited until the house sold to tell him my plans. It would have been so much easier. My fingers balled into tight fists, nails digging into the soft flesh of my palms.

If Kevin and I lived in an apartment together in San Diego, nothing would change. He would continue to focus on work and his own interests while I continued to raise our children on my own. Besides that, if I did get there and my friends and my family were no longer enough to fill the emotional void, especially since my Dad was gone, I would have to start all over with the process of separation. It was cleaner to get it done in one shot.

"Why are you pushing for all of this, Hope?" he asked. "Is there another man?"

"What?" I stalled for time, widening my eyes to appear shocked at the question.

My phone chimed in the kitchen. I knew it was Adrian. I'd asked him to give me space. *Fuck him for not listening to me.*

My body went so tense I might shatter. What if Kevin looked at my caller ID? He would see an Oregon area code. I could say it was a telemarketer.

Kevin ignored my phone. "What is going on in your head? Why are you doing this to our family?" He rubbed the back of his neck, his jaw set, his eyes seething with fear and confusion. "The second you told me you were unhappy, I did something about it. Something huge. I'm moving us back to San Diego. I'm commuting to another city for work each week. Doesn't that prove how much I care about you?"

"Yes." I stood frozen.

"How are we going to fix anything if we're living apart and I'm in another city most of the week? Does that make any sense to you?"

"I need to see what it's like without you."

"Why?"

"Because, I told you. I don't feel in love with you."

He winced.

"I need to miss you again," I said.

His eyes flared in recognition. "Is there someone else?"

I considered telling him the truth. As far as I knew, we'd always been honest with one another. The word, *yes*, wouldn't come out of my mouth. If I wanted Kevin back, admitting there was another man would ruin everything. He would never love me the same.

"This is what I want, Kevin. Please." Fat tears rolled down my cheeks. I wasn't being brave and making demands, but I also refused to back down.

He glared at me, taking it all in. His hand raised and I instinctively braced myself for impact. "Kevin," I called out.

He closed his hands into a fist and slammed the top of the desk. A pen reverberated and rolled toward the edge, free falling to the weathered hard-wood floor. I stayed still, almost daring my husband to do something more.

Kevin hadn't laid a hand on me in the two years since he dragged me across the living room in front of the boys. Standing there in the heat of the conversation, I wanted him to hurt me, to crush my guilt, to make my affair all his fault.

His lips curled in despair. "I can't stand the pain on your face right now. I'll do whatever you want."

Shame hit me hard. This was Kevin's sweet side. This was the man who cared for and nurtured me since I was eighteen years old.

"Thank you," I whispered.

"Happy?" he asked.

"Yes."

His expression softened. "Now, can you please tell me what's going on in your head?"

I averted my eyes to the ground. "No," I said, shaking my head and creeping away toward the refuge of our bedroom. I was a coward; a cheating, lying, whore of a coward.

CHAPTER 24

...

WEDNESDAY, OCTOBER 26, 2016
Evening

AS I STOOD in my kitchen, assessing the chaos of moving boxes and piles of chipped or mismatched dishes I planned to donate to charity, my determination deteriorated. Kevin and I hadn't told the boys about our separation yet. What if my children hated me when they found out? What if we arrived in San Diego and Adrian told me he planned to stay in Oregon with his family? What if I missed Kevin so much I couldn't stand it, but he had already moved on emotionally and decided he didn't want me back?

For the first time since I married, I found myself purposely heading toward an uncharted path. Kevin was my safety and security. He loved me and I'd loved him. Perhaps living fearlessly was nothing more than a great slogan, and the reality of following your gut was a big steaming pile of rotten bullshit.

As if he could sense my anxiety, my phone chimed.

Adrian: *I need to talk to you. I found a way for us to be close. Can we please talk?*

It was approaching dinner time. Kevin was at work, and Michael and Zach were playing in their rooms. Eager for an excuse to hear his voice, I set down my packing tape and dashed into the master bedroom, locking the door for privacy.

"Hey, what's up?" I asked, trying not to imagine the feel of his strong arms wrapped around me or the taste of his lips pressed against mine.

"I found a way to get work in San Diego and be close to you."

"Really? What kind of job is it?" I took a deep breath. Nothing he could say would sway me. I would keep my word and give myself a chance to love my husband again.

I peeked out the window to our backyard. Blue-black water lay motionless across our dark pebble-bottomed swimming pool. It was a standard somber autumn evening in Northern California. Our unwavering oak tree stood bare, promising new leaves and dappled shade in the summers to come.

Adrian cleared his throat. "A friend of mine, who's a big shot in San Diego, offered me a deal."

"Doing what?" I closed the curtains and sat down on the bed.

"He's got a big chunk of land and he wants me to build mansions on it, for a gated community." I heard the excitement creeping through his measured tone. He clearly thought he was sealing the deal. If he figured out a way to keep us in San Diego, he had me.

I was skeptical. "Why not someone with more experience?"

"Because I've done things like this before, and I know what the hell I'm doing. He trusts me."

"That's great, Babe."

"Yeah, it is. It's a ton of dough. I can take care of you."

"Enough to move to San Diego permanently with your kids and live with me?" I asked.

"Enough to support you and our kids the way you are accustomed to."

"Seriously?" I had to admit, if this opportunity was legit, it made my choice easier. There would be so much less to sacrifice.

"This is the real deal," he said.

I heard a knock at the door and my heart hammered in alarm. What if Kevin overheard me? He could cancel the whole move.

"Who's there?" I asked.

"Michael. What are you doing, Mama?"

"Getting changed into something warmer. I'll be out in a second." I stood and walked toward the door in relief. "Give me five minutes and I'll take you and your brother out to dinner before I start packing again."

"Where?"

"Tipsy Tomatoes. Your favorite. Five minutes of quiet to get ready, and I'll take you."

"But—"

"Michael, one more word and we're not going."

"Fine," he huffed. I could hear him shuffling away, yelling out to his brother to get ready to go out.

Sitting back down on the bed, my mind began to picture a new scene; me shopping for a beautiful new home, Adrian and all our children living under one roof. A daughter. A big backyard, family nearby, childhood friends, and a man who loved spending time with me. "Do you really think Lisa would let you take the kids?" I asked, searching for holes in his promises.

"She's not going to have a choice. And she's going to follow me, anyway. There's nothing tying her here to Oregon except for me. Her mom's in San Diego, and she can't handle those kids on her own."

"What about her job, Adrian? Are you sure?"

"She can't even handle taking Rose to the dentist and staying there until she has her teeth pulled."

"What do you mean?"

"Lisa took Rose to the dentist the other day without telling me. Rose needed to get two teeth removed. Lisa left her there to go run errands."

"Was Rose upset?"

"Of course she was. She was scared and called me from the dental office. Rose is a tough kid, but she's nine years old and didn't want to be alone. I'm the nurturer. Her mom's not equipped to handle that kind of stuff."

Adrian was having to do all the major lifting himself, just like me. His kids deserved a real mom, the same way my boys deserved a dad who wanted to participate in their lives.

I flopped onto my back. "So why have three?" I resented Lisa's treatment of these children I hadn't met. They were beginning to feel like mine and my instinct was to protect them. "Seems kind of excessive for someone who doesn't want to care for kids, especially if she isn't happy in her marriage."

"She was supposed to be on birth control when she got pregnant last time. We were getting ready to separate and then one night the two of us drank too much and decided to give it a final try. We had sex like it was the Olympics, you know every four years, what was the chance of her getting pregnant?"

"Do you think she did it on purpose?"

"That's beside the point. I love that kid. He's kept me young and he got me back into shape again. Now will you stop changing the subject? The only reason I would be taking this opportunity is to be with you. Do you want me or not?"

"I told you I haven't made up my mind yet. This job doesn't fix everything, Adrian. I still don't want to hurt Kevin or make my boys grow up in a broken home."

"Try a better, happier home," he retorted with confidence.

"How soon would you move?" I asked.

"These kind of projects usually have about a year's lead time. Plans need to be drawn up, permits pulled. He needs me to commit now. I would move out in about six months or so."

"So, say yes, and then go from there."

Before he could respond, I heard another knock on my bedroom door. "Mama?"

"Yes, Michael?"

"Mama, it's been more than ten minutes now."

"Perfect," I said to him. "Adrian, I've gotta go. Talk to you later."

I ended the call and tied my shoe laces. Adrian's words gave me the final punch of courage to move forward. If my marriage failed, I had a solid back-up plan with a man I adored. No matter what happened, my boys and I would stay in San Diego where we belonged.

CHAPTER 25

...

TUESDAY, JANUARY 3, 2017
Evening

KEVIN AMBLED TO where the boys and I stood, huddled below a grand chandelier in the lobby of San Diego's Ocean Villas apartment complex. A gas-powered fireplace blazed behind us, situated between stacked mahogany bookshelves two stories high.

"Hey," he greeted us.

"Hey." I studied the oriental carpet beneath my feet.

Zach ran to hug his daddy while Michael sauntered over to the grand piano to give it a bang.

Ocean Villas was a well-known landing spot for newly single moms and dads. They came here to keep their children in a top school district after divorce ripped their families in half.

"How was the drive?" he asked.

"Good." I nodded to my husband, keeping my distance.

Dressed in a faded baseball cap and an old pair of blue jeans, Kevin's tired eyes and pained expression nearly broke me. I was hurting him. He didn't want this. Neither did my boys. I ached to make them smile, to cave and change my mind to please them.

"Did you check in?" he asked me.

"Waiting for the keys. You'll need to sign paperwork separately for yours." I picked at a piece of lint on my purple yoga pants, and another piece, and then I gave up because I kept finding more.

Thanks to a thriving Silicon Valley economy and our tough realtor, we'd sold our Northern California dream home in less than three weeks, pulling in $200,000 more than we paid for it. Half of that, plus the existing equity, was legally mine should I need it.

Kevin kissed Zach on the top of his curly blond head. "The movers will be here in about thirty minutes," he told me. "They'll unload your things first, and I'll help set up the beds for you and the boys. There won't be enough time to set up both apartments. I'm going to have to spend the night at your place. I can sleep on the couch if you want."

I kicked at the carpet. Letting Kevin sleep over on the first night would set a precedent. I needed to hold strong. "You can have them put the couch in your apartment."

Kevin's jaw tightened. "Sure thing. I'll go take care of paperwork."

"I'll wait here," I said, rubbing my hands together in anxiety.

The sun dropped into the horizon, leaving a cold chill in the air as a woman I recognized from our old neighborhood pushed open the entry doors with her twin three-year-olds in tow. She breezed past us in the direction of the clubhouse.

A beautiful blonde in her mid-forties, I could see from the corner of my eye she had packed on a good fifteen pounds since I last saw her. Her usually perfect hair was hidden under a baseball hat, and her normally immaculate children were dressed in worn pajamas and scuffed tennis shoes.

She reminded me of another mother of three I knew from Kingston Court near our old home here in San Diego. Samantha Chase. She had moved into this apartment complex after learning her husband's secret. She used the experience to turn her whole life around for the better. Samantha wrote a book called, *Becoming*, that turned into a huge bestseller. Maybe I could do the same.

I had watched my former neighbor appear on some big-time talk shows, and read a couple of her interviews in Cosmo and O Magazine. She claimed she discovered she could have easily predicted the outcome of each one of her long-term relationships with men by how they made love to her.

If her theory held true, Adrian was the one for me. Of course, I'd also heard you should never choose a man based on the bedroom. Either way, Samantha had taken a leap of faith, stepped into the dark, and made it through. More than anything, I wanted that for my family, too.

I had a plan. I would live here at Ocean Villas with my boys for three months without speaking to Adrian at all. I would talk with Kevin as little as possible. I would go to therapy and experience life without Kevin and determine if I had the self-control to give up Adrian. Then, I would choose one of the men and make the very best of it. No looking back.

CHAPTER 26

...

THURSDAY, JANUARY 19, 2017
Night

A COUPLE WEEKS after we moved into Ocean Villas, the slam of a distant door rocked me awake. My heart thumped in my chest as I tried to gain my bearings. Before I could, the high-pitched sound of a woman yelling floated up through my floorboards from the apartment below us.

"Don't touch me. Don't fuckin' ever touch me again, you sorry son of a bitch," came her muffled tirade.

It went quiet again. I listened carefully for more. Another slam of a door and then a pitched scream. "Help me! Helllllp."

I reached in the darkness for the cell phone I'd positioned beside my bed. I dialed 911. It was 2 a.m.

When the operator answered, I described my emergency and gave her my downstairs neighbor's address. The operator told me the police would be there as soon as possible, although I didn't sense urgency in her voice.

Lying back down, I contemplated doing something more. My natural instinct was to call Kevin and ask him to come over, or at least get his advice. Obviously, I couldn't do that.

I waited, preparing myself for more screaming, and heard nothing. Maybe I overacted. It was also possible I'd overheard something awful, like a murder in progress. As I waited for any new noises, my eyelids grew heavy and my thoughts drifted toward my own problems.

After spending their first weekend at Kevin's apartment, Michael and Zach had come home distraught. Michael burst through the front door around four in the afternoon, his little brother following close behind, and dumped his overnight bag in the entryway. "I hate you, Mommy."

His anger felt like getting sucker-punched by a weightlifter on steroids. I knew the boys resented my choices. They missed living with their dad. Michael longed for his friends in Andalucía, and Zach wished both his parents would tuck him in to bed at night, in the comfort of our beautiful home.

My stomach curled in tight knots. "Why would you say that to me?"

"Because it's true."

"Do you feel that way too, Zach?"

My youngest son buried his red, teary-eyed face against his older brother's back.

"What happened at Daddy's?" I asked Michael.

He ignored me, stomping toward his makeshift bedroom while Zach nearly tumbled over at the sudden loss of his resting post.

The bare walls and empty spaces no longer seemed practical. Everything about moving into our new apartment felt temporary. I hadn't hung photos, only taped up some of the boys' school artwork. I didn't unpack the *tchotchke's*, those little warm fuzzy items that make a place feel like home, and I opted to use plastic bins for our clothes and ditch the bedframes so that we could keep the heavier furniture in storage.

"Michael?" I followed him into his barren bedroom. "Why are you so angry?"

He turned and glared at me, his little lips twisted in despair. "Daddy told me why you left him. He admitted he pushed you. But he said he was sorry and you refuse to forgive him."

My mind swam for a proper response. "Michael, it's never okay to push a woman."

"I know that. That's why Daddy apologized. Why can't you forget about it?"

"That's not fair. I asked for some time apart for more reasons than that. But pushing is a big deal. It's not something you can say you are sorry for and all is forgiven."

"Why not?"

"Because it's bullying. Men are stronger than women. It's not ever okay for a man to use force to frighten a woman. I don't want you to ever think that is acceptable behavior. There are consequences, even if they don't happen right away."

"Well, I understand that and so does Zach. Okay? So can't we go back to normal now? Can't you stop punishing everybody? You took me away from my best friend. Daddy lies in bed all day and cries. He's probably going to kill himself, and it's all your fault. You're ruining all of our lives for no reason."

His sorrow ripped me open, gravel scraping an already raw wound. Kevin was trying to turn our children against me. Even before we sold the Andalucía house, he had begun shouting at me in front of the boys, saying things like I was destroying the family, hurting him, acting selfish.

He was using Michael and Zach, making this so much harder on them, all to guilt me into forgiving him. Why couldn't he accept responsibility and beg for my forgiveness. Why couldn't he promise to spend more time with us? Would that be so terrible?

Yet, I felt like I deserved the attack, that our separation was my fault. I cheated, broke my vows. What Kevin and I had before Adrian came along was more than good enough. If I hadn't been so eager for something better, we would have all been happier.

Another door slammed downstairs, pulling me out of my thoughts and back to my dark, empty bedroom. Something smashed against a wall. The woman shrieked again, "Bastard. Get your hands off me and get the fuck out of here. This is my house. You don't live here."

The police were taking too long. I rolled out of bed, determined to help her. When Kevin and I were in our twenties and living in Los Angeles, he had heard a woman screaming in the middle of the night from the apartment building across from ours. He was concerned, but decided not to get involved.

The next day I heard from a neighbor that a woman in that apartment complex had been murdered. Her drug dealer boyfriend had tossed her over her balcony to her death. Kevin had felt guilty about it ever since.

What if the man downstairs killed the screaming woman before the cops arrived? Even worse, what if he shot off a gun and it struck one of my sleeping children? Determined to handle this on my own, I threw on some sweat pants and an old t-shirt, and I flew down the cement stairs to confront them.

When I knocked on the door, everything went silent. I rang the bell. Shivering while I waited for something to happen, I watched my breath form small clouds of vapor each time I exhaled into the cold winter air. The door opened and a tall, thin, naked man looked out at me.

I stood my ground. "What is going on in there? What are you doing to that woman?" The authority in my voice surprised me.

The woman appeared behind him, her voluminous breasts billowing inside her tiny negligee. A stunning pin-up version of Jackie O, with jet black hair and porcelain skin, she looked slightly older than the man, probably in her mid-fifties.

"He's beating me. He gave me a black eye." Jackie O pointed to her flawless face, not a mark on her. "He pushed me against the wall and punched me."

I took a step back. Maybe they were playing some weird sex game. I regretted intervening, yet there was no looking back. I was there to protect her and my sleeping children upstairs. "I called the police." I pointed at the man. "You need to leave."

"I'm naked," he said, shimming the bottom half of his body behind the door.

"I can see that. Go get dressed."

He started to close the door. I put my hand out to stop him, thinking of stray bullets and murdered women. "I'll wait here until you go. Leave the door open so I can make sure she's safe."

"Thank you." Jackie O smiled at me as if she'd been invited to the society ball by the most eligible bachelor. "Would you like to come in?"

I shook my head no. She was batshit crazy if she thought I was walking inside her love-torture nest. I may have been a bit reckless, but I wasn't completely stupid.

The naked man crept toward the bedroom and emerged five minutes later clothed, carrying a basketful of laundry, and accompanied by a small curvy blonde following behind him. My mouth fell open as the two of them scooted by me and fled into the night.

Fortunately, the police came around the corner and approached us. "Ma'am, are you the one that called for help?" the tired man in uniform asked me.

"Yes," I wrapped my arms around my chest. "The guy just left. I'm going back upstairs. She can tell you what happened."

I said goodbye and ascended the stairwell, tackling two steps at a time. The adrenaline in my body seeped away and my body shivered from shock at what I'd done. Yet pride stirred in my chest. My children were safe. Jackie O was safe. No boyfriend or husband necessary. I was a total Bad-Ass.

CHAPTER 27

...

FRIDAY, FEBRUARY 17, 2017
Morning

"SOMEONE WE KNOW saw Kevin making out with a younger woman at *Towne*." My former neighbor and close friend, Isabel, was calling to spill the gossip. We'd been in San Diego all of six weeks when her pretty voice trembled through my phone in a horrified tone. "Can you believe it?"

I was out on a hike through the canyons, sucking in the cold morning air, as I tried to examine how this made me feel. "Are you sure it was him?"

Kevin was still traveling up North for work and flying into San Diego on the weekends to spend time with the boys.

"Positive," Isabel said.

I pictured my husband groping a hot young thing at Andalucía's most popular upscale bar and restaurant. He had to know our friends would see him, and that someone would tell me. Still, the scene didn't conjure any surges of jealousy, not an ounce of rage.

Instead, I inhaled sage-scented air, admiring the cloudless blue sky and looping trails hedged in a carpet of velvet green chaparral. I was home. That past month and a half were the hardest of my life as far as guilt and remorse were concerned. Yet, even in my darkest nights and most difficult days, I'd felt grateful to be back. I hadn't missed Kevin.

I still loved him, it wasn't that. But, I'd felt alone in our marriage for so long, his prolonged absence seemed normal and, in many ways, liberating.

Without him around at all, I could play music whenever I wanted and invite friends over without worrying about upsetting him. The boys were free to eat breakfast on the couch. When Kevin took Michael and Zach on the weekends, I could leave the apartment for an hour all on my own without negotiating permission from anyone.

My breath floated away from me in a fine mist as Isabel spoke. "They were all over each other, Hope. It was gross. This friend of ours who saw him was so upset. Who does that? One week after you move, and he's making out with some loser bimbo."

"One week?" I asked in surprise.

"Yeah, this happened right after your move. I thought about keeping quiet. Ed told me not to say anything. But you're my friend and I love you." I heard the turmoil in her voice. "I would want to know."

"You did the right thing." I sped up my pace, breathing harder.

"You have to promise you won't say anything to Kevin. This is between you and me."

"Of course. Was she really that young, Isabel?"

"Early twenties at best. Blonde hair. He took her out in public in front of everyone. Can you believe it?"

I'd had an affair. I was in love with another man. There was no room for me to judge. "I'm relieved he isn't as lonely and miserable as he's been leading me to believe."

"You're not upset?"

I could imagine Isabel's big blue eyes growing wider, her full lips dropping open in surprise. She must suspect the truth, that this was all my fault.

"He's been telling me that I'm destroying his life, that I'm a terrible mother for breaking up the family. The last time I went to his apartment to get the boys, he threatened to kill himself if I didn't get back together with him."

"Oh my God. That's not fair."

"I know, and when I called his therapist and told her he was suicidal, Kevin was furious with me. But what was I supposed to do?"

"You had to call someone."

"Exactly." I made a mental note to check Kevin's expenses. Kevin was sharing an apartment in Northern California with one of his co-workers, if he'd paid for a hotel room that night on a credit card, the charges would show up on the bill. I could confront Kevin without betraying Isabel. "He can't keep treating me like garbage if he's been hooking up with someone since a week after we split."

"I'm glad you're taking this so well." She sounded genuine, but there was hesitation in her voice, a different kind of sadness.

The rising sun glared in my face. I looked at the ground to avoid its scorn. "Is there something else?" I asked.

"No, why would you say that?"

"Because I'm right," I said.

"It's nothing my friend. Don't worry about it."

"Please tell me."

"I've gotta run. I'm on a mission to get—."

"Isabel."

"What?"

"What else do you know?" A man ran past me on the left, scaring the bejesus out of me. Next time I would bring the Taser Mom had given me for Hanukah.

"There's some things you're better off not knowing. It's bad for your health," Isabel said.

"Such as?"

"Fine. But I'm only telling you because you forced me."

I kicked at the dirt and ran my teeth over the seam of my bottom lip, waiting out the uncomfortable silence, refusing to fill the gap.

"He's come over to the neighborhood twice already. Kevin goes to Doug and Karen's house, and then he comes outside and thrashes you. He told Cameron we wouldn't even recognize you, that you've turned into this horrible person. He goes on and on. No one really gives a rat's ass what he has to say, well, except for maybe Cameron, but who cares what Cameron thinks. His wife is about to leave him, too. He just doesn't know it yet."

I didn't want to hear anymore. If she told me Kevin said I'd cheated, I would have to respond. I didn't want to lie to my friend, but I wasn't ready to explain myself either. "I figured he might visit Doug."

"Yeah, what's his deal, anyway? Why are they so buddy-buddy? Doug doesn't seem like Kevin's type."

Doug was Kevin's pot dealer. Kevin probably wasn't comfortable going to one of the local dispensaries. "They weren't that close, but Doug is still a connection to Kevin's old life." Feeling protective, I lied. "I'm sure Kevin wanted an excuse to visit and vent."

"Whatever, dude. Get a life."

"Yeah." I swallowed down the metallic taste in my mouth. "All right, friend. I'm getting another call," I fibbed again to end the conversation. "Talk to you soon."

Despite my growing self-confidence, the shame of keeping so many secrets and the guilt of my betrayal churned acid in my throat. I'd lost more weight off my already petite frame in the past six weeks. Stepping on a scale to check the exact number frightened me. My face looked sunken, my hair was thinning out even more.

Each day the stones of guilt stacked higher on my conscience. I prayed Kevin had found someone new, and I could stop trying to make myself miss him. I yearned for him to set me free.

My ringing cell interrupted my thoughts. When I answered, it was more bad news.

CHAPTER 28

...

FRIDAY, FEBRUARY 17, 2017
Morning

MY RIGHT EYELID twitched in stress. The school nurse told me Zach had another tummy ache and had been crying in class. I agreed to pick him up. As I climbed into the car to retrieve him, my phone rang again.

"Hey." It was Adrian. He sounded nervous.

"What's going on?" I clicked off the car alarm and closed the driver's side door.

"What are you doing?"

"Going to pick up Zach from school. What's wrong?"

"I know we're not supposed to be talking, but I have to tell you what happened. And if you can, I need you to come get me."

"Where are you?" I asked, checking the rear-view mirror and turning the key in the ignition.

"In a parking lot, down the street from Lisa's mom's house."

"In San Diego?"

"She was going down with the kids early over President's Day weekend for an extended vacation, and she asked me as a favor to drive. I didn't think you'd mind."

"Of course not, that's fine." I backed out of my garage and headed for Zach's school. "So what's going on?"

"We got in a fight. She threw me out of her mom's house."

"Okay."

"I was taking a nap. She crawled into bed and tried to come on to me. She was naked."

"What?" I felt like a hungry dog getting her food bowl snatched away mid-bite. It was the first time I'd felt threatened by this woman. "What did you do?"

"I woke right up and told her to stop. She asked me why, and I told her it was over. She asked me if we could try again, and I had to tell her the truth. I told her I was in love with another woman."

I felt ill. I'd begged Adrian not to tell anyone about us. I told him it was because I didn't want Lisa to make any waves in my life. The truth was, I also didn't want Adrian to cut the final string on his failed marriage in case I decided to stay with Kevin. I wanted him to have the option to go back to Lisa if he got lonely.

"What did she say?" I flipped down the sun-visor as I drove out of the apartment complex. The school was only two minutes away. I needed to find out more before we hung up.

"At first, she was mad. She said I should have stopped her before she humiliated herself. Then, she cried."

"You said she never shows emotion."

"She doesn't. I was shocked."

"Did you feel bad for her?"

"No, it made me angry. All these years, she made me feel like there was something wrong with me, that I was unlovable. I thought no one would ever want me. Now I know she was the one with a problem. I was a good husband."

"You said she was crying. Was she crying or was she pleading for you to stay?"

"She said she knew she told me we could see other people, but she didn't really mean it. She didn't think I would actually do it. She said she would do anything if I would take her back."

"Like what? Molest you in bed?" That poor woman just found out the man she wanted most was in love with another woman, and I was the one who felt threatened. Love wasn't reasonable. It was a messy emotion.

"She promised to do more with the kids, treat me better, help out around the house, have sex with me more than once a year."

"Were you tempted?"

"Hell, no. That ship has sailed."

"Are you sure?" I pulled into the school parking lot and searched for a spot to park.

"Babe, I'd rather fuck a dude."

That made me feel better. "Did she ask who I was?"

"Yes."

"Did you tell her?" Heat radiated throughout my body. I already knew the answer.

"She kept asking me if it was someone she knew, and I finally broke down. I'm so sorry. I've wanted to tell her the truth for such a long time. I couldn't stop myself."

I inhaled deeply, trying to control my rising anxiety.

"Please don't be mad I told her."

"I just worry she'll call Kevin and tell him about us. My boys would never forgive me, especially Michael, he holds on to every little thing. This would be catastrophic."

"She won't do that."

"I got a text." I pulled into an empty spot and clicked off my seat belt.

"There's no way she would call Kevin. She's not smart enough to figure that out."

"All she'd have to do is Google me. So many of the articles I've written are posted online and my bio mentions Kevin. If she found his name, it would take her two seconds to find his email address."

"She's not like that. She's not a stalker like you."

"All women are stalkers. Some just don't admit it." I played with the keys in my hand. "I want to check my text messages. Can you hold on?"

"In a minute. I need you to come pick me up. She threw me out. All I have is my wallet and my phone. Do you mind? I know we're supposed to be taking a break."

"Let me get Zach and get him settled at home, then I'll come get you. See if you can book a flight back home. The boys don't know about you yet. This isn't the best way to introduce them."

"Okay."

"Don't sound disappointed, Babe," I said, stepping out of the car. "You know I would spend time with you if I could. This is a complicated situation right now." I took another deep breath. "Hold on, I got another two texts."

Lisa: *If you want him, come and get him. He's all YOURS.*

Lisa: *Hope you enjoy my sloppy seconds!!!*

Lisa: *Homewrecking whore. You two deserve each other!*

"They're from her. How did she get my phone number?" I asked, desperate to contain my frustration before walking in to pick up my troubled son.

"Shit. She must have gone through my cell phone after I told her about you. What do they say?"

I read him the messages. "She's quite articulate," I said, oozing sarcasm. "Oops, here comes another one."

"Don't read it."

"Why?"

"Because it'll make things worse."

I read it anyway.

"She texted me the address to come get you. I'll see you as soon as I can." I shut off the phone and jammed it into my back pocket.

When Lisa went through his cell to find my phone number, she probably read through our old texts and Facebook chats. I would never forgive her or Adrian if she contacted Kevin.

CHAPTER 29

...

FRIDAY, FEBRUARY 17, 2017
Early Afternoon

I PARKED AT the sloped curb in front of a youth center on a quiet residential street, the place she texted me to get him. Looking around, the grass lawn appeared empty.

Skye had offered to watch Zach while I dealt with Adrian. I was in a rush to get back to my anxious son. Leaving him with my sister while I rescued my lover felt all sorts of wrong. I pulled out my phone to double check the address.

"You!" I looked up to find a seething woman with wild dirty-blonde hair exploding toward my car. Adrian chased close behind her.

She ripped open the driver's side door and lunged at me before I could react.

"What's happening?" Instinct took over. I scooched sideways out of my driver's seat and onto the passenger side, away from the psychotic woman.

"Lisa, stop!" Adrian grabbed her wrist and yanked her away from the car. Lisa turned toward him and punched him with violent force in the side of his head.

My heart raced. Rage coursed through my veins with such indignity, I started to shake. Before Adrian could recover, she looked directly at me. "You need to know," she huffed, her face flushed a brilliant red. "You need to know what an asshole he is."

I opened my mouth to speak, to defend him. Adrian was as sweet and sappy as a character in a romance movie. If she couldn't find the good in him, she was doomed to misery.

Before I could form words, Lisa wrenched her wrist free from Adrian's grasp and sank her teeth into the soft flesh of his inner arm.

"Fucking stop." He yelled for her to unclamp her rabid teeth. She jerked her head away, and his skin tore open, gaping and bloody.

I leaned across toward the open door, refusing to allow myself to have a panic attack. "What is wrong with you?" I asked Lisa.

She charged at me again. This time Adrian stepped in between Lisa and the car. He shoved her. She stumbled backward and fell hard on her ample ass.

"You hurt me!" she screamed, an ear-piercing wail. "You attacked me. You son of a—"

I slid sideways, back into the passenger side. Adrian jumped into the car and slammed the door, forcing the seat back for leg room.

Lisa's face appeared in the window like a scene out of a horror movie. Snarling, spittle flew from her mouth. With fierce blows, she pounded the side of her fist against the driver's window.

"She's going to break it," I yelled at Adrian. "That nutcase is going to shatter my window."

He turned the keys in the ignition and stomped on the accelerator, speeding away as she backed up to avoid getting crushed. I could see her in the rearview mirror, standing on the black asphalt, shooting us the bird with both her middle fingers.

"Where are you driving?" I asked.

"To the airport. I booked a flight."

"Pull over. Please pull over." I dropped my head between my knees. The tips of my fingers were turning numb, and my head felt detached. "Oh my God." The heat of my anxiety felt unbearable.

Adrian complied. The car slowed to a stop along the curb opposite a wide-open soccer field. He rubbed my lower back. "Are you okay?"

"Is she gone?"

"Yeah. She's several streets back."

"What happened?"

"She found out you were out here and came out to attack you so, I came to your defense."

"Why?" I raised my head to look at him. "Why did she do that?"

"Because she's angry you came."

"But she told me to pick you up."

"I believe that was more of a dare than her really wanting you to do it." He smirked.

I stared at him in disbelief. "You think this is funny? You're estranged wife punched you in the head and bit a chunk of skin off your arm. There's blood running all the way down to your fingers. Adrian, listen to me," I looked at him dead on. "We need to call the police."

"You do what you need to do but the situation is handled. I will always keep you safe."

"That's not the point. She's crazy." I threw my hands out in exasperation. "What about your kids? Was she drunk?" Adrian had mentioned Lisa had a drinking problem. "What if she drives home to Oregon with them like that? Aren't you worried?"

"She's not drunk. She's just very angry. She's scorned. You took something from her. At least, she feels that way."

Anger ripped through my heart. "I didn't take shit from that woman. She tossed you to the curb. Literally."

Adrian had told me he knew he'd made a gigantic mistake with Lisa only a year into his marriage. They were still living in San Diego at the time, and he was rear-ended on the I-15 North.

He'd encountered a rush hour traffic jam and come to a complete stop. The car behind Adrian was going a good sixty miles an hour when it slammed into the back of his Ford Explorer. The whole back end of his SUV was smashed and totaled. His gas tank landed underneath the car in front of him. According to witnesses, Adrian was knocked unconscious for several minutes.

The next morning, Adrian woke up and could barely stand. His equilibrium was off and the vision in his right eye was dark and blurred. He drove himself to the ER.

A cat-scan revealed there was a buildup of blood inside his skull putting pressure on his optic nerve. Doctors planned to drill into his skull to relieve the pressure.

He called Lisa, who was busy loading up her car for a girl's-only road trip. She was annoyed. Accused him of exaggerating. Refused to cancel her plans.

Lisa never even went to visit him at the ER. Instead she drove off with her girlfriends for a weekend of drinking and dancing. Adrian's swelling went down. The surgery was canceled. His relationship with Lisa was left damaged and broken.

"She was the one who didn't want you anymore. How can she attack you like that and come after me? What is wrong with her?"

"Apparently what she says and how she feels are two completely different things."

"We need to call the police."

"I will never let her hurt you. I will never let anyone ever hurt you."

"But she hurt *you*!"

"I'm a big boy. I can handle myself. All that matters to me is that you're okay."

My emotions were so intense, it hurt to breathe. "That was like something out of a Jerry Springer episode. She makes my brother Pete look normal. Seriously, Adrian, how could you marry a woman like that?"

"She wasn't always this way. Something changed her."

"Like what?

"I'm not sure. All I know is I can't live in the same house with her anymore."

A car crept by. I jerked my head to make sure it wasn't Lisa tracking us down. "Has she ever assaulted you before?"

"Has she ever put her hands on me? Sure."

"What changed her? What made her like that?"

"There were a number of things. After we broke up in high school, she fell in with a bad crowd. She was taken advantage of by someone while she was drugged. God..." He ran his hands through his hair and stared down at the steering wheel. "If I told you what happened to her, it would turn your stomach."

I cracked open my window for fresh air. "Tell me. I want to understand."

"He drugged and raped her inside her own vehicle. He flung his semen all over her and all over the inside of the car and left her there to clean it up."

I fiddled with the silver bracelet on my wrist, wondering what it would have done to me to survive a sexual assault. How would I be different? "When did this happen?"

"When she was much younger, late teens, maybe early twenty's. She never looked at men the same after that. They were either using her or she was using them."

"If you knew this, why did you marry her?"

"I loved her. She was the only other woman besides you who I truly loved. I wanted to show her what it was like to be in a healthy relationship, for someone to selflessly care for her and not want anything from her. I thought I could show her it was okay to be who she was again. It was safe to let her guard down and be vulnerable. I wanted her to know she could be loved, just for the sake of being loved, and not having anything expected in return."

I rested my hand on his thigh. He'd tried to help a woman he loved, even when she hurt him. His desire to nurture and care for her made me love him more.

I also thought it might be time for me to walk away. As much as I loved Adrian and wanted to comfort him, my priority was to protect my children.

I'd watched enough Dateline episodes to know that women like Lisa could snap. If she took me out, everyone would think I had it coming for stealing her man. "She's still your wife, Adrian, and she seems to really want you back now. Maybe you should give it another try."

"No." He shook his head, turning the key in the ignition.

I re-buckled my seat belt. "Why not?"

"It takes a lot for me to love. It takes a lot for me to care for people. In a lifetime of thirty-nine years, I've only truly loved two women. It's hard to move on. But I can't take her back." He pulled out and drove toward the main street.

"Are you sure?" I fished around the passenger side for my missing sunglasses and found them on the floor by my feet. "Maybe we need to take some time apart for you to think about it?"

The light ahead turned green. He accelerated. "She only wants me now because she no longer has me. It's not about love. It's that someone else took her property."

He glanced at me before facing the road again. "Please don't leave me because of this, Hope. I know you. I know you're scared right now, and you're thinking about walking away." He put his hand on top of mine. "I need you."

He deserved so much better. I wanted to be the one to save him.

CHAPTER 30

...

FRIDAY, FEBRUARY 17, 2017
Night

I WAS SITTING on the floor folding laundry when I heard footsteps on the outside stairwell. It was late. I'd taken Adrian straight to the airport that afternoon for his last-minute flight back to Oregon without making any promises about our future.

After spending the rest of the day holding myself together while helping Michael and Zach with their homework and making them an early dinner, I'd dropped them off at their dad's apartment around 5:30.

A key slid into metal. The bolt twisted. My front door swooshed open and whacked the wall.

My body stiffened in fear. What if it was Adrian's psycho soon-to-be ex-wife? He'd told her he was moving out immediately and she'd texted me another three times, reiterating her stance that I was a home-wrecking whore. I knew it wasn't logical she would have a key, but my mind couldn't escape the memories of her biting and punching Adrian.

Two footsteps thudded across the laminate wood entryway. My apartment door slammed shut. I was sitting Indian-style on the floor to the right of the entryway, confined in a narrow hallway. Vulnerable.

Kevin, his eyes heavy-lidded and his body reeking of alcohol, rounded the corner and looked down on me with a sneer. "How quickly you move on."

He scowled at my oversized Chargers football sweatshirt with Adrian's name and favorite team number emblazoned on the back. He'd given it to me before he left. "I wasn't expecting company," I said, trying not to show signs of the panic attack washing over me.

"It makes me sick to think of some other man tasting you with your legs spread open wide."

Shocked, I stared at him. His crude comment set off alarm bells. Kevin didn't speak like that. Yet his words sounded familiar.

"I got a phone call today," he said, brushing his hand over the stubble on his jaw. Dressed in a low cut tank top and designer sweatpants, Kevin had started working out and putting on muscle since our separation. He looked dangerous.

"Did you hear what I said?" he asked me.

"Yeah, you got a phone call." I was determined to stay nonchalant.

"Adrian Sicario's wife." He tilted his head to the side with a smirk.

"Okay."

"She said her phone records between the two of you talking go back at least six months."

"You knew that. We've been friends for years."

"She also emailed me conversations between you and Adrian on Facebook."

My stomach dropped as I fought the urge to vomit. What had Kevin read? My mind raced to past Facebook chats. I'd told Adrian to delete them. He'd promised me he would.

Men were fools. I was positive Lisa went into Adrian's phone. That's why Kevin had made that vulgar comment about imagining another man between my legs. He'd read those intimate conversations. The shame made me dizzy.

I promised myself revenge on Lisa for hurting my husband. I would get her back. She would pay for this.

Kevin cocked his head. "He's still married, you know."

"No, he's not."

His face turned hopeful. Perhaps he thought I would leave Adrian once the truth was revealed. It pained me to hurt him further. "He's moving out next week. They've been separated for years and were living in separate bedrooms to save on expenses."

"That's not true. They're still together. You didn't only ruin our marriage. You ruined two marriages, two families."

"No." My outrage at his false accusation fueled my courage to fight back. "I talked to Lisa about an hour ago. She admitted everything. Adrian sleeps downstairs in his son's bedroom. She told him they should see other people."

"He's completely broke, you know. And he does steroids. She said if I told you she called me, he'd beat her."

"She's a liar, Kevin. If you believed her, you wouldn't have told me."

"So this was an emotional affair?" he asked.

I needed to change the subject. "What are you doing here? Did you leave the boys alone?"

"Zach forgot his special blanket."

"You smell like alcohol," I said, steering him away from my own flaws.

"I knew you were going to say something." His jaw line tensed. "Some guy at the pool spilled his drink on me."

Had he always been such a bad liar? I folded a pair of socks and tossed them in the pile. "Some of my friends saw you at *Towne* making out with a young blonde. The Amex bill showed you spent over a hundred dollars on food and drinks and then another three hundred on a hotel room for the night. That was one week after you moved out."

"God. You're so naïve." His lip curled in a sign of disgust. "I lost the key to my rental place, that's why I got a hotel room that night."

"Right next to the bar on the same night you're making out with some girl? I don't believe you."

"You leave me for a married man, destroy two families, and then you judge me? That girl was throwing herself at me. I needed to know if I was still attractive after you threw me away."

"You finally got what you wanted, a young blonde babe."

"Turns out, it's not that great."

"You didn't have to do it in public. Everybody knows. You made us both look like fools."

"That's what you care about? What your friends think? Not that I was with someone else?"

"What you do is your business. I just wish you'd keep it private. And then you come home from that and tell me how lonely you are, how all you want is for me to wake you up from your nightmare?" I tossed another pair of folded socks in their pile. "How sad could you have been? And why didn't you pay cash at the hotel? I would've never known. Did you want me to see the bill?"

"Speaking of cash." He cleared his throat. "You better get a job."

"I have a job. I've been taking on extra freelance writing work."

"I mean a real job. You want to be independent, time to support yourself."

After twenty years of studying one another, we were master swordsmen in our war of words, each of us stabbing at the most tender spots. I'd already prepared for his move. I transferred half of our savings from the sale of the house into my private account. He couldn't cut me off that easy. "Michael's therapist said it would be detrimental for me to take a job outside the home for at least the next year. Michael needs time to acclimate to this big life transition."

"You know what Michael's therapist told *me*?"

That twitch in my eye started again. For the first time since Michael had begun therapy so many years ago, Kevin had taken our son to a session alone. What if Michael had told the therapist he hated me?

"Dr. Zuluaga said she's worried about you. She doesn't think you're stable. You're not being a good mother. Maybe Zach and Michael should be with me full-time."

Terror took hold. If there was any chance he was right, I'd take sleeping pills and end it all. I couldn't lose my children. "Dr. Zuluaga didn't say that. Two weeks ago you told me our therapist said I was crazy. I called her, she denied it. Dr. Zuluaga would tell me if she was concerned about my parenting. I'm calling her in the morning."

"Don't bother."

"Why not? If it's true, I should know, shouldn't I?"

"How do you even live with yourself?" he asked, changing the subject. "How do you justify your deviant behavior? Don't you care about your children?"

He was the one who had gotten drunk and left them alone at ten at night. I stood up from my spot on the floor and faced him on an equal level.

"Get out." I pointed at the front door. "Get out of my apartment and don't ever come in here again without my permission. You can't take the boys away from me. I'm the one who has raised them, took Michael to therapy, volunteered at their schools."

"Because I was busy supporting us."

"Go home." I clenched my fists in defiance.

"I don't have a home." His shoulders collapsed as he turned to leave.

My power over him took me by surprise. What if I had stood up to Kevin all along? Maybe he wasn't as strong and scary as I imagined. Maybe he'd just been spouting off all along and it was my fault for taking him seriously. "Get out," I shrieked louder, the guilt making my heart race.

CHAPTER 31

...

MONDAY, FEBRUARY 20, 2017
Late Morning

"HOPE." HIS DEEP gravelly voice reached through my phone, sounding steeped in despair. "I have some bad news."

A shaft of sunlight sliced through the window and onto a patch of carpet. Michael and Zach were at school. I was splayed out on our suede couch, trying to wrap up a series of articles I was writing for a fitness magazine.

"I can't take any more, Adrian. Please, don't tell me. My hair is falling out. My boys hate me." It'd been three days since my confrontation with his wife and then my husband. I was ready to dig a large hole and crawl inside. "Kevin looks at me like I'm Hester Prynne. I should have never broken society's number one rule, thou shall not cheat."

"Why do you care what he thinks?"

"Because I've spent my life caring about his opinion. It's a habit I'm trying to break."

"It means you still love him."

"I do love him. I keep telling you, I'm always going to love him, even when I can't stand him. We grew up together. He's the father of my children. But, I'm *in* love with you."

"Maybe you won't be after I tell you this."

I tossed my computer to the side. "Okay, Adrain. Hit me when I'm down. Why not?"

"I'm not getting that job in San Diego."

"No." My whole body went numb. What if he didn't move here? The longer I went without seeing him, the more I missed him. And since Kevin had found out about the affair, our marriage was as good as over. He would never forgive me.

"Yes."

"That's not funny, Adrian."

"My buddy sold the land. Some guy offered him a stupid amount of money, and he took it."

"So you're not moving out here?"

"I don't see how it's possible."

I stood up and began to pace. "Why? You promised. You can't do this."

"I can't afford to live there. Lisa's not going to let me take the kids."

"You said it didn't matter what she said. You said she couldn't take care of them on her own and, even if she said no, she'd end up letting them move anyway."

"How can we afford to live there? If you come here—"

"You promised me if I left Kevin you would move here. You said if I did that, you would handle everything else."

"I was telling you the truth. How could I know this would happen?"

"Fix it," I demanded.

"I can't. You have no idea what I've been through these past couple of weeks."

"You've known about this for two whole weeks?" My pulse quickened. This conversation was taking at least a month off my life expectancy.

"I've been calling everyone I know, trying to make something happen. I didn't want to tell you until I'd exhausted every avenue."

"This isn't going to work," I said, determined to force his hand and convince him to move here with or without a job. I would get extra work if I had to, while he looked after the boys. If he loved me as much as I loved him, if he needed me as much as he claimed to need me, he'd change his mind and come here.

"So you're ending things with me?" he asked.

I flopped back down on my sofa. Splitting up hadn't been my intention, but because he threw it out there, I felt obliged to hold my ground. He needed to believe I was serious about him coming to San Diego. "Yes. You lied to me. I trusted you when I shouldn't have. My mom warned me something like this would happen. She told me I should never leave one man for another, and I was better off being on my own if I divorced Kevin. You made a fool out of me. Your stupid wife keeps pestering me. I've never been more miserable in my entire life."

"So you wish you'd never left him?"

"It'd be better than this."

"Great. I can't give you the money he makes, so you'd rather be with him."

"Don't twist this around." I stood back up and resumed pacing. "You promised me you would move here. Now you want me to pick up my children and go to Oregon?

Your wife outed me. My husband hates me. Soon my children will find out and despise me too. This is a disaster." I inhaled and continued before he could speak. "I'm not moving my boys. They deserve better than that."

"But my kids don't?"

"It's bad enough I left their father and brought them here to San Diego. They've already had to move twice in the past two years. Not to mention, we're all still grieving the loss of my dad." No matter how badly I craved a full life with Adrian, I couldn't displace my boys any more than I already had. I was their mother; they came first.

In a moment of blind fear, I hated Adrian for putting us all in this position. "Don't make this about the money Adrian or your children's hardships. You don't get to do that. Your family was already destroyed when I met you. This is about you lying. You tricked me into giving up a decent life so you could try and drag me to Oregon to live with your kids. I can't believe this is happening."

"I never intentionally deceived you. The circumstances changed. You think I didn't try to fix this? Besides, what's so bad about Oregon? You don't think I could make you happy here?"

"No, I don't."

"Then you don't really love me."

"I guess you're right," I said, fighting back my desire to give him anything he wanted.

"I should have known when you slept with Kevin for the last time you didn't give a shit about me. Was that even the last time?"

I wrapped my hair in a tight bun, ready for battle. "You're trying to change the subject. The last time I had sex with my husband has nothing to do with this. And yes, that was the last time. Don't try to make me the liar."

"How do I know you're telling the truth?"

"I don't care if you believe me or not." I was done with his side-stepping the issue. He must have thought I was a moron not to see what he was doing.

"You already knew you cared about me. How can you have been intimate with me then move on to him?"

I stood still, letting his words sink in. Adrian had told me on several occasions he could never sleep with more than one woman at a time. Adrian believed making love to a woman was the most intimate physical act you could share with another person, and he needed an emotional connection. His old fashioned values weakened my resolve. His romantic beliefs were one of the things I loved most about him.

"He was my husband, Adrian." I punched my thigh in agitation. "If you had such a problem with me sleeping with someone else, maybe you shouldn't have gone after a married woman."

"Are you still breaking up with me?" he asked.

"I have to go."

"Wait."

"What?" I asked.

"If you're going to break up with me, can I see you one last time?"

"No."

"Please, you owe me that. One last time, and I promise I will leave you alone."

"I don't owe you anything. Goodbye." I tapped the end button and collapsed onto the couch in tears.

CHAPTER 32

...

TUESDAY, MARCH 7, 2017
Late Morning

I WISHED I was somebody else. Someone better, someone more well-adjusted. A woman who could make important life decisions all on her own.

While I knew I was in love with Adrian and if I didn't take the leap of faith to be with him, I would spend the rest of my life questioning. I couldn't shake the voices of self-doubt out of my head. What if I was making the wrong decision? What if I was supposed to get over this hump with Kevin and build our marriage stronger? What if Mom was right? What if I was supposed to spend an extended period of time on my own to get to know myself before I made any decisive commitment to either man?

Dr. Thomas, an impeccable redhead in her early sixties, led me into a small office and asked me to take a seat. "Oh,

Hope," she said in her familiar British accent. "It's so good to see you. What's it been, five years?"

I nodded and leaned in for a hug, ready for Dr. Thomas to bathe me in her sage wisdom, to tell me what to do. She would decide my fate.

"Go ahead." She motioned toward the familiar cushy two-seater couch as she settled into her office chair at her tiny black desk. Turning to me with motherly concern, she said, "Hope, dear, tell me what's going on."

I filled her in on the basics, I still loved Kevin, cared about him deeply, but didn't feel in love anymore. "I take my full share of the blame."

"How so?" she asked, her brow furrowing.

"When I gave up my career to look after the boys full-time, I felt like less of a person. I took on all the household duties, paying the bills, doing the grocery shopping, clothes shopping, managing everybody's appointments. I made the decisions for their education."

She nodded her head in understanding, as if to say, standard stay-at-home-mom stuff.

"But even though I was doing my part, Kevin and I both behaved as if his work was more important than what I was contributing. The attitude was, the least I could do was handle all the trivial things since he was the breadwinner."

The air conditioning rattled on, creating a frigid breeze in the warm room. I hugged my thin jacket closer to my body, warding off the chill in my bones.

"After I gave up my career to look after the boys, it was like Kevin threw his hands up. Everything was on me. He'd come home from work, claiming to need a break or alone time, and lock himself in his office to smoke weed and play video games. Even on weekends he'd hole up and get irritated when I asked him to take part in any family outings. I felt like the boys and I were an inconvenience to him, a burden. Over time I started noticing how much other husbands enjoyed their families and liked being with them."

She nodded again with sympathy.

"I can see I was wrong to let him off the hook so easily for checking out. He probably thought it was no big deal. But on the rare occasions I brought it up, he blamed the problems on me, so it became easier to shove away my loneliness and act as if everything was great. Then I snapped. All those years of stored up resentment exploded."

"I'm sure he still loves you. These are normal issues we can work on together in therapy if you like."

"I don't want to. When I think about the two of us, I feel dead inside. Does that make me a bad person?"

"No."

I raked my hands through my hair, swallowing the sour taste in my mouth. "I've asked him for decades, even before we married, to quit smoking and drinking so much. He said he couldn't because I was a nag. Now he says he's stopping. He's seeing other women, and he works out and takes care of himself. It's like I wasn't worth the effort."

She shook her head. "That's natural behavior for anyone going through a traumatic loss. He's doing what he needs to do to feel desirable."

"Well, I don't have the desire to put in the work it would take to make our relationship better. I've bonded so strongly to someone else, my heart isn't in it. Also, Kevin and I met when I was eighteen and he was twenty-three. He was the adult. I stayed the child. How can I make him see me as equal?"

"These things take time when both the husband and wife are committed. You know I've been seeing him this past month. He told me he would forgive you for the affair."

Her comment irritated me. I didn't want his forgiveness. I wanted his understanding. I wanted him to acknowledge that he had done wrong, too. "What do you think I should do?" I waited for her permission to leave Kevin.

"Let me tell you a story about one of my previous clients. She was a woman who lived in La Jolla in a big ten thousand square foot beach front home she had built from scratch. Her husband is Middle Eastern, she's a white blonde woman. Different cultures. He was a bit controlling and he was gone a lot working. She fell in love with one of her construction workers. They had a mad passionate affair."

I nodded. I could see that Dr. Thomas intended to use this woman as an example.

"She came to me because she was positive she wanted to leave her husband. In her case, she would have received half of their fortune and still have plenty of resources to buy a nice home and live comfortably with this new man she met."

I played with the diamond on my necklace. "Sounds nice."

"Well, ultimately she didn't think so. She didn't want to give up her dream home and her easy lifestyle. She realized she wanted to put more into marriage rather than start all over with a more average life."

The story made me feel ill. "I didn't marry Kevin for his money."

"Of course, you didn't."

Why was she telling me this awful story? Did she really think so little of me? "That woman probably didn't truly love her construction worker, and she must have feared he felt the same. If she did love him, she was a coward."

"You have, however, become accustomed to an uncomplicated lifestyle. You have the means to stay home and raise your children. You don't have ex-spouses, stepchildren, the strains of living within a strict budget. Realistically, starting over with a more complicated man would not be good for your anxiety disorder."

"That scares me." I stared out the window, wondering if I was as weak as Dr. Thomas thought.

"It's a serious consideration."

What had Kevin told her and why was she seeing both of us? Wasn't that a breach of ethics? "Okay." I nodded again.

"You don't want to make any rash decisions."

Before responding I cleared my throat in thought. "I don't want to be that person who chooses safety over true love. I've lived in neighborhoods full of those women. Yes, they get to travel, and eat out, and live in beautiful homes. There are so many positives, but honestly, they are sell-outs. Doesn't some big part of them have regrets? Are they really so happy when they go to bed at night?"

I was tiptoeing toward the edge of forty, I wanted a companion, someone who enjoyed my company and conversation. Someone I could spend time with when the kids moved out and left us alone. Once I fell out of love, going back to Kevin in order to maintain a lifestyle felt wrong.

"Listen," Dr. Thomas continued. "You're in love right now and it gives a future with this new boy a hazy glow. Every woman has her regrets. It doesn't mean she would do things differently. The truth is, you don't realize how much easier life is when you don't have to struggle. Stay with Kevin and work on the relationship, and you could have something better than it was before. You also get to stay in the city you love, live close to your family and friends in a lovely home with your own children seven days a week."

I rubbed at my nose, something in the air conditioning was making me itch.

"This new guy with his three children and his ex-wife," she said. "It's going to be a very stressful environment for you. His children may not get along with you or your children. However it works out with him, I promise you it will come with its challenges."

I pressed my hands into my thighs. "If I were watching a movie based on my life, I wouldn't want my character to stay. Her kids already went through a separation. If she went back to her husband and it didn't work out, it would be an even greater disappointment for her children."

Before I married, my motto had been, *do what you fear*. Even before I was formally diagnosed with an anxiety disorder, I instinctively knew that if I gave in to my worries, I would miss out on the best parts of living. I wanted to be that person again.

I rubbed my itchy nose and kept talking, finally feeling confidence in my choice. "I want to be the woman who believes in herself, who chooses love over safety and works hard to make her new life on her terms."

My heroes were all strong women. When Mom left Dad because the relationship wasn't working, she pushed herself to the breaking point, until she made a life she owned.

"I can't un-see what I finally allowed myself to see, and I can't tuck the ugly parts away again." I shifted in my seat, sitting taller. "How many people have the immeasurable good fortune to find someone at this stage in their life; someone they love with a passion and who loves them back even more fiercely? Adrian cares about my children and my extended family. He knows my past and likes me the way I am."

I vowed to call Adrian the moment I left Dr. Thomas's office. It was time to see him again, to commit myself fully to our relationship. Do what you fear. Love wins.

CHAPTER 33

...

SATURDAY, April 1, 2017
Late Morning

AS SOON AS I made the call to Adrian, things happened fast. There was no going back.

Adrian moved out of his family home and filed legal paperwork for a divorce. Kevin found a mediator to oversee our separation. Adrian and I had spent the last two agonizing months trying to be responsible, giving ourselves and our families time to adjust. But two months was long enough, and Adrian was flying in for our first full weekend together--alone.

By the time I reached the airport, my hands were shaking.

I sat a little higher in my seat, heart beating fast as I looked for him amidst the collected travelers. The San Diego airport was an international hub, but he stood out like a bright light in the crowd. I spotted him standing curbside under a radiant sun.

Cars crept by slowly. I waited for an opening so I could pull in and park, watching him search for me.

All the months of what-ifs and maybe-I-shouldn't built to this breaking point, this moment of surrender. He was finally going to be mine. It would only be the two of us. No more guilt, apprehension, or shame. He stood still, his hand across his forehead, shielding his eyes from the sun.

Adrian's grey Diesel jeans fit him just right, a black t-shirt stretched taut across his muscles, and a pair of Beats headphones wrapped around his neck as if they were part of his outfit. God he was gorgeous. He found me and with a confident swagger, he stepped toward my approaching car.

I parked in between two SUV's and nearly tore out of the driver's seat to wrap him in a hug. His lips found me first, in a quick desperate breath before I could get my arms around him. The sound of honking horns and the smell of gasoline dissolved into the background as I let myself soften into his kiss.

Up until this point, a relationship with my childhood sweetheart felt more like a coveted dream than a possible reality. Being with him in that moment, out in public without fear, felt like the ultimate freedom. I loved the taste of his mouth, the fresh soapy scent of his skin.

"Hey, beautiful," he said, pulling back and taking in my face.

I bit my lower lip with nervous excitement. "You drive. I'm too excited to concentrate."

"Let's do it." He nodded, holding the passenger's side open for me. I waited as he threw his bag in the back and strapped on his seatbelt.

"Are you ready for this?" His right hand strayed from the steering wheel and rested on my bare thigh. "God, your skin feels incredible. I can't believe I finally have you."

I brushed my left hand over the top of his, lacing our fingers together. "Me, too."

"Where are we going?" He laughed. "I can't even concentrate."

"Take the 5 North. I'll tell you where to get off." I grinned at him. We were heading straight to my apartment. No distractions.

"Come here," he said, giving my thigh a gentle tug. "Get closer. I can't stand it."

I leaned over the center console to kiss him as he drove. Being forced to wait through the drive taunted the sexual tension already building in me. I moved my lips to his neck, his heavy breath and the low rolling hum of his voice intensifying my need for him.

Without asking, his hand slid further up my thigh, until it was hidden beneath the white eyelet lace of my dress. I didn't stop him. For once, I didn't have to.

My lips froze against his neck as he pulled my satin panties to the side. Allowing myself to feel the pleasure of it, I spread my legs apart.

With a shudder, I leaned back into my seat and gripped the headrest with my hands as he touched me. "Oh my God, Adrian."

A sudden jolt shook me as he slammed on the breaks. Adrian must have lost concentration. The driver behind us flipped us off as we nearly rammed into the car in front of us.

"We should stop," I breathed.

He kept his eyes focused on the road. "If we don't, I won't be able to wait until we get to your apartment."

After a torturous drive, Adrian pulled into my attached garage and opened the passenger door to let me out. He pressed me against the car, reaching his warm hands up my thighs and leaning his weight into me.

I kissed him hard, trailing my hands over the firm contours of his back, and then gently pushed him away. "I want our first time to be in bed together." I'd thirsted for this moment with him since our first reunion. So far, being near him was everything I'd wished for.

"I think I can wait for that."

We'd already discussed protection. Both of us were safe. We wanted to feel each other completely, skin on skin. I grasped his hand, led him up the dark stair well, and into my bedroom.

"Can I freshen up first?" I asked, wanting to be perfect for him.

"No. I like you exactly the way you are. I want to taste you while you're wet." He kissed me, lifting me up and wrapping my legs around him while I grasped his shoulders.

"I've been dying to kiss you again," he whispered into my mouth.

He held onto my back as the two of us sank into the bed, the pressure of his body strong and heavy on top of me. We fell into a space where nothing mattered but us.

"I love you, Hope." He slid off the bed with his knees on the floor.

I shivered as his fingers swept beneath my dress, grazing the bare skin of my hips, and dragged my panties along the tops of my thighs.

I drew in a long breath as he buried his face between my legs. "How do you do that?" I asked.

My body warmed at the touch of him gripping my legs. "Baby," he spoke. "Baby."

"Huh?" I was lost in him.

"Relax." He gently pried my legs loose from his head. I had him in a vice grip. He grinned before putting his mouth back on me.

I tried to let him continue, but being so close to the edge was agony. "Please, Adrian," I begged. My hips wouldn't stay still. "It's too much of a tease. I can't take it." I wiggled my way out from under him and began to lift my dress up over my head. As I did, his hands moved up the sides of my waist, reached around and unclasped my bra in a single stroke. He traced his hands along my breasts and the backs of my arms.

Kissing him on the lips, I tugged his shirt up, the heat of our skin together warming us both.

He told me he loved me, needed me, just being near me was enough to make him happy. Kissing me deeper, he poured these emotions into his lovemaking; his words, his touch, his scent, the ultimate aphrodisiac. I tugged his shirt off completely and reached my hands up his torso, grasping his chest.

Adrian pulled away from me and removed his pants and then his underwear. He was beautiful. Almond shaped amber-green eyes, light brown skin, thick hair that fell into his face.

"How are you this hot? You look like one of those male models from a sexy man-calendar."

"You banned me from fighting. I've been hitting the gym. It's my only outlet."

"Lucky me." I reached out to touch him again, pulling him closer.

He looked into my eyes.

My mouth opened, my lips heavy. He lay back down on top of me. I let my hands grasp his hips, nudging him closer, needing him to continue.

"You have no idea how many times I've fantasized about doing this with you, Hope, how many different scenarios have run through my mind."

"Show me," I whispered.

He ran his hands through my hair. "I'm about to have everything I've ever wanted."

I felt the same. I wanted to give him all of me.

As he slid inside I wrapped my legs around his body, gasping at the feel of him. He was harder than I expected. A breathy moan escaped me.

I couldn't speak. He moved slowly, in and out, and just when I expected him to lay all his weight on me, he'd pull out and go down on me again.

When he came up for air, he kissed my belly and worked his way up to my breasts, licking my nipples.

This was the kind of lovemaking I'd read about, but never expected to find. My body was his. He owned me. I would give him anything.

"Stop teasing," I begged.

He eased himself in again, warm, silken and full, and moved faster. I rolled him over and crawled on top. I was in charge, I was going to come.

"I'm all yours," he said.

He was urgent and tender, and we had a level of intimacy I'd never allowed with another man. I moved faster, building my own rhythm. Leaning down, I laid my right breast into his mouth and he flicked my nipple with his tongue while I let out a moan of pleasure.

My orgasm was happening fast, I could feel the release taking over. I didn't want the experience to end. "We have all night," I spoke out loud to myself. "We can do this again."

He gripped my hips and moved me. I was going to have a big one, on our very first time. That never happened.

"Fuck, you feel good." His hands clutched me firmer, increasing my speed. "I want to watch it happen. I want to see your face when you come."

Inhaling hard, shockwaves tore through me. I heard my own screams and he pressed his mouth to mine, muffling my moans. As my body collapsed on top of him, spent and sweaty, he rolled me over onto my back for his turn.

I lay catching my breath as he moved, every deep thrust sending a rush through my body.

"I'm so in love with you, Hope." He breathed harder.

I smiled up at him, watching his face tense with pleasure.

He moved on top of me, steady, and then fast, quick bursts. Tiny beads of salted sweat ran down his chest. I reached up and took his handsome face in my hands, making him look at me. I loved his noises, his looks of pleasure. He finished and lay sprawled atop me, hot and satisfied. We belonged to one another.

Honest. Sincere. Tender. My Adrian, my perfect.

CHAPTER 34

...

SUNDAY, APRIL 2, 2017
Morning

I WOKE EARLY to the scent of eggs, buttered toast, and turkey bacon. Adrian stood over me with a handsome grin, my breakfast plate in his hands.

"Is that for me?" I asked.

"What do you think, babe?" he asked, dressed in nothing but his blue jeans. His body looked so perfectly tight and toned, his light caramel skin, better than candy.

"Thanks." I smiled, reaching out for the plate. "Where's yours?"

"In the kitchen, I'll grab it in a minute."

"Set it on my bedside table. I want to wait for you."

He fidgeted with the fork as he set down my food. Adrian looked nervous. "First, I have to ask you something."

"Okay." I watched him settle down onto one bent knee.

"Adrian, you're not—"

"Shhh," he said gently. "Let me—"

"But it's too soon."

"Hope, I have wanted to do this since I was fifteen. Please?" His green eyes melted my protest.

"Okay," I said, knowing what was coming. I wanted it as much as he did, but we had adult responsibilities, other people besides ourselves to consider.

"Hope Rains Sullivan?"

"Yes?"

He remained firmly planted on one knee, looking up at me from my perch on the bed where I sat with crossed legs.

"I always felt parts of me were broken or missing. When I'm with you I feel whole, like such a stronger man. There is no other woman who compares to you or has come anywhere close to making me feel the way you make me feel."

His words made me want to drag him back up into my arms. How did I get so lucky? What I had done right to deserve him?

"I promise you," he continued, "from the bottom of my soul, my love for you will never diminish, never waiver. It will only grow stronger. I will love you till the day I die."

I reached out to touch his face. "I love you, too."

He shook himself free of me. "I don't just love you, I want to hold you every night, kiss you every morning. I want those photos on the wall to be our family pictures. I want to be the one you spend your life with."

He pulled out a small silver ring from his back pocket, sparkling chips of diamonds inlayed throughout.

"It's pretty."

"It's a token for now, a promise ring until I can afford something better."

I reached out for it. "No, it's perfect."

He held on tight. "I still have to ask you."

I smiled, the sun peeking through the blinds. "Yes, dear. You were saying?"

"Stop. I'm being serious." His sensitive eyes crinkled in hurt.

"I'm sorry. Go ahead."

He cleared his throat and looked directly into my eyes. "Yes, I do want you now. Yes, I will work like a goddamn slave to support all of us. I would do anything to be with you, push myself to my limits. But I will wait for you if I have to. Hope Rains Sullivan?"

I nodded.

"When you are ready, will you marry me?"

"Yes," I said, feeling my heart pound faster. This man was going to be my husband. I felt like I had won the greatest prize.

He slipped the ring on my finger. I twisted my hand to catch the sparkles.

"When?" he asked.

"So persistent." I kissed his cheek. "After our children meet and some time has passed. When we're both legally available. An engagement isn't appropriate right now. But when the time is right, I would love to be your wife."

"Hope Sicario," he said.

I played the sound of his last name in my head. "I like it."

"Will you change your name?"

"For sure." I nodded. "Is Lisa going to change her last name? I don't want to have the same last name as her."

"Babe, she'll probably want to keep it, to have the same name as her children."

"Maybe I should do the same thing for my kids," I teased.

"You're such a pain in the ass." He stood and leaned over me, putting his hands on my shoulders. "I want you to have my name."

"Fine. I'll think about it. In the meantime," I reached out and set his promise ring on the end-table next to my breakfast. "I'll keep this tucked away somewhere special. My boys need to meet you and your children before anything else." I wrapped my arms around his neck. "Time for me to ask you a serious question."

His eyes grew wider. "What?"

"When are we going to eat? I'm starving."

He leaned in and nuzzled my ear. "Later."

CHAPTER 35

...

SATURDAY, MAY 14, 2017
Late Afternoon

IT WAS A pretty ride through Oregon's rolling greenery. Adrian and I drove along the Rogue River highway, heading south toward East Park Street. He wanted to show me the first house he'd ever worked on with his uncle. It was one of the few positive family memories from his childhood.

We sped past tall pine trees, magnificent white oaks, and sprawling big-leaf maples. A flock of birds sailed in formation across the robin's egg blue sky, puffy clouds lingering in their wake. "It's gorgeous, Adrian." I rested my head on his shoulder as he drove.

The boys and I had flown into the Rogue Valley the previous night and Adrian met us at the baggage claim with all three of his children. Adrian and I had visited one another each weekend for the past month and a half so I could get to know his kids and he could spend one-on-one time with mine. This was their first time meeting each other.

Michael and Zach hit it off with Adrian's well-behaved children right away. They talked Pokémon, Xbox, and YouTubers React videos on the drive from the airport to his apartment complex. Michael and Adrian's daughter, Rose, stayed awake throughout the night, playing on their iPads and sharing whispered secrets. Zach had gotten along well with Adrian's younger two.

Having left our kids with his mom, the two of us turned left on East Park Lane, a quiet rural road. A handful of the homes lining the street were large and modern. Most, however, were smaller, well cared for, single story homes skirted by tidy picket fences, featuring proud American flags waving in a gentle breeze. Corvettes parked beside RV's and pickup trucks. Everything about this place epitomized sophisticated country charm.

"So tell me more about this house," I said.

"When I was fifteen, John, my mom's younger brother, got a contract to build an addition to this place. He took me with him, and the plans expanded into other projects inside the home. John and I spent most of the summer here, him teaching me all the basics of home renovation. It was one of the best times of my life, besides when I was with you."

"I'm excited to see it." I clasped my hands together in anticipation.

"You're going to love it. Original hardwood floors from the 1920's, big bedrooms, a giant kitchen. The whole place overlooks the Rogue River. I haven't been back since that summer. When I saw it was up for sale, I had to show you."

With our windows rolled down, I inhaled the scent of fresh pine. "It really is gorgeous around here." I looked down at my cell. "You think the kids are okay? Maybe I should text Michael and check-in."

He kissed the top of my hand. "The kids are getting along famously, they're fine."

"Yeah, I guess they would call if they needed me."

"Those boys are attached to your hip. Let them hang out. It's good for them to have some independence."

I pursed my lips in thought. His children were so subdued and well-mannered. I joked after I met them that he and his ex must drug them up on Valium.

My children were maniacs in comparison, jumping off the couch, talking five decibels higher than necessary. Zach's nickname at swim class was The Screamin' Demon. I'd worried they would overwhelm Adrian, but the first time he met Michael and Zach, he got right down on the floor of my apartment and taught them mixed martial arts moves. They thought he was a blast.

Adrian's Dodge Ram pickup slowed. "It's right up here." He pointed to the left. I saw a large home, the green paint peeling off the sides with a white picket fence and a for sale sign on the yellowing lawn.

Adrian parked in the gravel off the driveway. "The realtor said there's a spare key in a rock near the front door."

"They don't do lock boxes out here?" I asked.

"Yes, Princess. This isn't the boondocks. She put it out there for special guests like us. The agent is a friend of a friend, and she knows I'm a good guy." He unbuckled his seatbelt and opened his door, walking around the car to open mine.

"Thanks," I said, taking his hand as I stepped out into the sunshine.

"What do you think?"

I took in the view. "It's nice. I love the big Japanese maple tree and all the rose bushes. It looks a little overgrown and neglected, but nothing a loving owner couldn't fix." I tilted my head, listening. I could hear the river flowing behind the house.

Adrian searched for the key while I took a for-sale flyer.

"There's some great fishing down there. The back has stairs leading straight to the water." He held up the key. "Come on. Let's go inside, and I'll show you around. I'm curious to see what's changed over the years."

We walked up the cedar steps to the small porch, admiring the stained-glass window in the center of the front door. "I installed that myself." He puffed with pride. "It still looks great after all these years."

"It does." I held my breath as he pushed open the door. This place was important to him. I wanted to love it.

A grand living room stood before us, light spilling inside from hazy floor-to-ceiling windows. The back of the home faced the Rouge River, thrashing wild and free as we stood in admiration. "It's gorgeous," I said, and I meant it.

He squeezed my hand as I looked around the interior. Stained beige carpeting covered the floor, a peek of the kitchen to the left called my attention. I stepped forward, wanting to see more.

"They covered the floors." He kicked his toe at the dirty carpeting, clearly disappointed.

"Babe, it's been over twenty years. Things are going to have changed."

"Yeah," he sighed. "The owners didn't even live here full time. It was their vacation home."

I gazed out again through the glass windows, appreciating the lush greenery that edged the rolling river. "It'd be a great home to write in and raise children. Maybe get a dog?"

"Don't get excited. I'm just sharing my past with you. This is way out of my price range."

I walked into the expansive kitchen and ran my fingers over dusty green porcelain countertops. The home was still fully furnished with mismatched floral patterned sofas and funky artwork, including Van Gogh's sunflower painting nailed nearby, and an overhead lighted ceiling fan that featured purple glass blown flowers encasing the light bulbs. It looked like a troupe of blind bohemian grandmas had decorated the place. "I read the flyer while you were digging out the key. It's not out of *my* price range."

"I thought you weren't ever going to move here. Besides, you can't buy us a house. That's my job."

"It's not the 1950's, Grandpa Adrian. I have my own money, and if you were willing to put in the man hours for renovation, this property would be an incredible investment."

He grinned. "I could totally fix up this place."

"Four thousand square feet." I slid my index finger along the counter. "Whitewater views. What kid wouldn't want to grow up here? They could run down the stairs in the backyard to the river and spend their days off the iPads, exploring, like the way we grew up... way back in the eighteen-hundreds." I rolled my eyes at him. I liked the idea of buying our first home for the two of us.

He waved his hand at me with a grin. "Stop."

"Even if the boys and I never moved in full time, you could pay the mortgage and handle all the maintenance. We could spend our summers here together. Whenever Kevin has the boys for spring break or winter holidays, I'd come visit. You'd make this house so beautiful, Adrian."

"The first thing I'd do is rip out this carpet and restore the floors." He began looking around the room, no doubt considering future projects.

"Our house would be our refuge," I said, building in excitement. "The boys could collect tadpoles and frogs and learn to fish, experience country life. We could get a dog."

"Next thing I'd do is strip down that hideous floral wallpaper in the bathroom. This place fits right in with some long-gone century."

"Not by the time you were done with it." I pictured him with his shirt off, his muscles flexing, hammering nails, pulling wood beams, doing manly things.

"I'm getting turned on thinking about it."

"Are you serious about this?"

"Dead serious." I laced my fingers into his. "Let's go upstairs. I want to see the rest of the place."

He led me up the generous formal stairway, covered in the same dirty beige carpet. "Where to?" he asked when we hit the landing.

"There." I pointed to a cluttered pale yellow room with landscape art covering the walls. A stack of blank canvases leaned against a heavy wooden easel. Various shapes and sizes of paint brushes filled glass cups on a small particleboard countertop.

We walked inside. To our left, a small window provided a flood of natural light and graced us with views of the river.

A full-service kitchenette ensured whoever stayed in this room could cook their own meals. In the center of the large space, rested a twin-sized bed. "This is an artist's studio." I squeezed his hand, bouncing at my knees. "I love it. This must have been the previous owner's special retreat." I imagined myself writing award-winning articles here, maybe even a novel.

"Adrian." I looked at him, feeling inspired by the beauty and possibilities surrounding us, positive this was where we were meant to be. All the fighting, pain, and struggle had led us to this space. "This is it. This is our home. Let's buy it."

CHAPTER 36

...

FRIDAY, JUNE 23, 2017
Late Afternoon

AFTER CHANGING OUTFITS several times that evening, I'd settled on a red top and green slacks decorated with sewn-on patches of colorful fireflies. I pushed through Mom's heavy front door into her dimly lit, empty living room. Bishop shot through the kitchen's doggie door and galloped across hardwood floors, rubbing against my thigh. My brand new King Charles Spaniel puppy wriggled in my arms and yipped a hello at Bishop.

As soon as I had signed on the line for our dream house in Oregon, I realized I wanted to live there full-time. Right afterward, Adrian surprised me with a family dog to celebrate.

We'd decided to make the move over the summer. It gave Adrian some time to work on home renovations, for my boys to finish their school year, and for me to stick around and help my sister plan Dad's long awaited Celebration of Life.

Standing in Mom's living room, the rich scent of marijuana drifted down from her deck. I stuffed my phone into my back pocket and dropped my purse on the bookshelf beside the door. Peals of laughter carried through the open windows.

Only a week away from my big move to Oregon, I was meeting up with my family for a special reunion. It had been eight months since Dad died. My throat constricted as a wave of grief unexpectedly washed over me. Dad would never get to meet the final missing piece of our family puzzle.

"Hey," I said, ascending the roof deck stairs. The sweet lingering scent of weed grew stronger. Flames flickered in lanterns set around the patio table.

Under a quarter-moon, Mom, my brother Pete, Skye and my newfound brother, Robert, gathered around the white patio table passing a fat joint. It didn't feel real. We were meeting Dad's son and he wasn't here to experience it.

"Hi," I said to my brother, feeling shy.

Robert looked the same as he did in the pictures. At nearly fifty years old, he boasted a full head of thick brown hair and big bushy eyebrows, exactly like Dad's.

"Hey, Hope," Robert said, standing for a hug. "Who's this?" He scratched Maui's neck.

The sound of his voice made my hands shake. Robert had grown up in Chicago, my parent's hometown. With his nasally Great Lakes accent, he sounded so much like Dad's brother Sean, I had to search Robert's face again to confirm he wasn't my dead uncle reincarnated.

"Oh my gosh," I said in surprise.

"What, I sound like Sean?" He chuckled.

My mouth fell open. "Yes."

He laughed, "heh, heh, heh," just like Dad. "The others mentioned that."

"And you look so much like Dad, only taller." *And with a Jewish nose*, I thought. Dad had been around five foot eight. Robert stood closer to six feet.

I reached out to give him a big hug while Maui squiggled in my arms, trying her best to break free. "This is Maui, by the way."

"She's adorable. Cool name."

"Thanks." I smiled. "My best friend moved to Maui a while back because that's her paradise. I thought since my boyfriend got Maui as a gift for me to start our new life together, she represented my paradise."

Mom stuck her index finger in her mouth as if to gag herself. "That's nauseating."

Robert ignored Mom. "Very cool." He gave Maui another scratch on the head before I set her down.

"It's so nice to finally meet you in person," I said, feeling even shyer without a warm puppy cradled in my arms.

"Yeah." Robert rubbed out a flake of ash that had settled on the table. "I had no idea Sharon had been looking for me all this time. This is so surreal."

"No kidding." I tucked a strand of hair behind my ear. "How are you feeling now that you've met us all?"

"Surprisingly comfortable," he said, sitting back down.

"See." Mom looked at him, her glassy eyes sparkling with joy. "I told you."

"Mom's always right." I grinned at her, settling into the empty chair beside Robert.

Mom nodded. "Robert said he's felt different and weird most of his life. He was worried we wouldn't like him. I told him when he met us, he'd realize it's the rest of the world that's crazy. We're the normal ones."

Pete passed me the joint, and I handed it over to Robert.

"You don't smoke?" he asked.

Skye smiled. "Hope's the straight one in the family."

"Whatever." I uncrossed my legs. "What else did they say about me while I was gone?"

"Nothing really." He shrugged. "That you're moving to some small town in Oregon to live with your boyfriend, and that your sons are with their dad in San Francisco for the summer."

"That about sums up my life." I smiled.

"You're lucky your ex let you take them out of state." Robert rolled the joint between his fingers. "I've heard horror stories from friends who wanted to move their kids."

"Kevin was against it at first." I rubbed my hands on my thighs and then leaned over to pick up Maui and place her on my lap. "Lawyers got involved. We went back and forth, but in the end, he agreed to let me move Michael and Zach as long as he got them for the summers." I bit the tip of my tongue. "I miss them already, and it's only been three weeks. They're having fun, though."

"Are you excited about the move?" Skye asked.

"Yeah, really excited." I nodded with enthusiasm. "It's been tough these past couple of months away from Adrian."

I looked at Robert to explain. "He's been so busy working on the house. Adrian hasn't let me visit since I bought the place, because he wants everything to be perfect. It's supposed to be this big surprise."

He nodded. "Sweet."

Mom leaned forward. "I think it's weird. It's your house. You should visit it whenever you want."

"It's romantic," I said, doing my best to defend Adrian. I trusted him to do a great job, and although I wasn't getting to see him as often as I liked, he called several times a day with updates and stories. We'd grown even closer in our time apart.

"I do miss him though, a lot. I would have moved there a little sooner if we weren't planning on Dad's Celebration of Life this weekend."

Robert cleared his throat and looked at the ground. "Thanks for waiting for me."

"Of course," Skye said, a large wave crashing in the ocean. "Dad would be thrilled to know you are going to his memorial."

"Yeah." Pete took a deep hit, then blew the smoke out in perfect rings. "We planned a Hawaiian luau with food from the Jewish deli he ate at all the time, and everyone is going to wear T-shirts representing his favorite bands."

Skye and I glanced at one another knowingly. Pete was taking credit, yet he hadn't helped with a single thing.

Mom drummed her fingers on the table. "Both of you girls did a great job planning the party. You did your dad proud."

"Thanks, Mama." I reached out and squeezed her hand. "I'm so glad Kevin is flying down with the boys so all three of them can be here." The thought of them missing the memorial made my tummy ache.

Pete took another long drag before passing the joint back to me. "I'm shocked the jack-ass is making an effort. Is Mr. Antisocial actually going to show up?"

"Don't be a jerk," I said.

"What?" He threw up his hands in mock surrender. "I'm only stating the truth. He's a total douchebag."

"Kevin's a good guy, and he's really stepped it up since our divorce. He flies out here almost every single weekend, and he's been much more involved in the boys' lives. He just needed a wake-up call. And you're not one to talk, Peter the Great. How's your love life? What happened to that baby mama of yours? The one who's supposedly pregnant again?"

"I plead the fifth." Pete held up his hands in surrender.

"Do you ever miss him?" Skye asked me.

"Kevin?"

"Yeah."

I couldn't help wonder why she was asking. Was she losing interest in her own husband?

"Honestly?" I placed the joint between my lips, finally giving into the peer pressure, and took a puff, holding it for a beat before slowly blowing out the smoke, and relishing the satisfying burn in my throat. "I miss the stability and his cooking. Kevin's a great cook."

My fingers tingled and my head began to feel weightless. I was an inexperienced lightweight when it came to smoking out and the weed took immediate effect. "Now that Kevin's checked back into his own life again - started lifting weights, spending time with the kids, going on dates and traveling with his girlfriend - it does make me wish he would have made those changes for me. We could have been happy together."

"He'd probably still take you back." Skye leaned her head back to take in the stars.

"I don't know about that." I held onto the joint, considering taking a second hit. "Kevin moved in with his girlfriend two months after our separation. She's older and more educated than me. She also makes a boatload of money. Kevin gets to live in a gigantic house, they eat at the best restaurants, and donate money to charity." I decided to go for it and take another tug. Inhaling deeply, I held the smoke in my lungs until I choked.

Tapping my palm against my chest, I passed the joint to Skye and continued. "I put Kevin on a strict budget when we were married, and I was never interested in his hobbies with his robots and remote-control helicopters. Maybe we're just too different. Maybe his girlfriend is in to that kind of stuff." I took a deep breath and exhaled, releasing my sadness.

"Anyway, our marriage is over. I'm in love with Adrian, and I like the woman I've become since my divorce. I'm stronger now. I have so much more self-confidence."

"That's good," Skye said, her eyes shutting for a moment.

The furrow in Mom's brow deepened. "Well, I think moving to Oregon is a big mistake."

"I know that, Mom. You wanted me to be alone and miserable so I could find myself. But, guess what? Adrian makes me happy, and I like being happy. Michael and Zach love him. Our kids get along. We're going to have a beautiful home on the river."

Her eyes squinted in agitation. "You know Robert is thinking about moving out here with his daughter after she graduates high school? Your whole family is in San Diego."

I felt bad for Mom. My move was hard for her, but I also wanted her to drop it. I was thirty-nine years old, and this wasn't her choice to make. It was mine. "I'm sure this isn't what Robert wants to be discussing the first night he meets us. Can't we focus on him?"

I turned to my newfound brother. "Is there anything special you want to do while you're out here?"

Robert mumbled something about the San Diego Zoo and Mexican food while my mind drifted toward memories of Dad and my move to Oregon. Not only would Dad never meet his second son, he would also never meet the man I'd fallen in love with. Dad wouldn't ever visit my new home.

CHAPTER 37

···

THURSDAY, JULY 6, 2017
Early Morning

IT WAS 2 am. I'd just driven up to Oregon with Maui and a car full of my belongings. Knocking on our front door, my fingers shook in the cold predawn air.

This was it, I was finally here. Adrian and I would start our lives together. We were going to be a real family. Joy pulsed throughout my entire body.

A light switched on inside, and the lock twisted. I realized I didn't even have a key yet to my own house.

"Hey." Adrian stood in the entryway, fully dressed in street clothes and looking wide awake. Maui lunged out of my arms and straight for him. Falling to the floor, she planted her furry front paws on his legs, eager for a pet on the head.

His appearance surprised me. "I didn't call you for the past few hours, because I was sure you were sleeping."

"Nah." Ignoring Maui, he stepped aside from the stained-glass door to allow me inside. "I was trying to get some stuff done. Couldn't sleep."

I scanned the entryway. Maui gave up on Adrian and ran past us both, disappearing into the shrouded darkness of our quiet home. The rough wood floors beneath my feet remained unfinished, the scrapes on the white walls, unpainted. "I hope the rest of the place doesn't look like this," I joked. "Why aren't you hugging me hello? You don't seem very excited to see me."

He wrapped his arms around me and then leaned in for a kiss. I nudged him away. The stiffness in his posture, the way he was fully dressed and full of energy in the middle of the night, something was wrong.

"No." I broke free from his grasp and flicked on the nearest light switch. A layer of dirt covered the porcelain kitchen countertops, the ones he said he had replaced with the gleaming granite I'd paid for. The flooring lay warped, the sliders to the backyard looked nothing like the French doors he said he had installed.

Fear gripped me hard. These past two months, Adrian had insisted I stay away so he could surprise me with renovations. Anxiety flushed my body in a hot layer of sweat. He'd lied. "What's going on?"

His eyes hardened, as if he'd anticipated my reaction. Adrian raked his hand through his hair. "I told you it wasn't ready yet. I asked you to give me a few more weeks."

"A few more weeks? How about a few more centuries? Minus the dirty carpeting, everything looks the same as when I bought it. Have you been working on the upstairs? Is this a prank?"

"I've been busy with other projects, Hope." He scowled at me. "You expect so much of me. The pressure is too much."

"But you told me you were working on the house. You sent me pictures of the new granite slab for the kitchen and the French doors to the backyard." I had stumbled into an alternate reality. "Where is it? Where's the granite? Where are the doors? Babe, what have you been doing all this time?"

"They're in the garage. I've been busy with work and the kids. Not everyone can live a life of leisure." He began to pace as he talked. Maui showed back up and trailed behind him, still eager for attention.

"Aren't you going to pet her? Don't you even care?" Tears stung my eyes. My mind raced as I tried to make sense of his sudden hostility.

"You've been so hard on me from the beginning. You want me, you *don't* want me. One day you say you're going to grow old with me, the next you never want to see me again. I couldn't take it. I cracked."

I reached out to touch him. Maybe he was scared. He was finally getting the life he dreamed of, and he'd panicked. We could fix this. "Why didn't you tell me you were feeling this way? I'm so sorry, Adrian."

I felt the familiar pangs of guilt for hurting someone I loved. Then I looked around the unfinished house again. "Where have you been staying this whole time? Does the upstairs look like this, too? You said you made our bedroom perfect. You said you couldn't wait to stop sleeping alone." I turned to rush up the stairs and he grabbed my arm to stop me.

My fear intensified. The upstairs was just as unfinished, I felt sure of it. There was no perfect bedroom, he hadn't kept me away to surprise me.

"This was everything we've been working toward," I whispered in hurt, struggling to wrench my arm free. "...a home together, our children together, us together – no more lonely nights longing for our other half. Why aren't you happy to see me? What is going on?"

My stomach dropped. "Have you been staying at Lisa's?"

"No." He released his grip on my arm. "I've been here. Sleeping on the couch." He pointed to an old sofa with a blanket strewn across it, pushed up against the living room wall. A large, brand new TV hung on the opposite wall.

Maybe he was telling the truth.

"Listen, Hope, I don't know if I can do this."

"Do what?" I asked.

"Stay here with you."

My body froze in horror. The pain of his words was so intense, it felt like being buried. "I moved my entire life to be with you. I sacrificed my marriage, my hometown, my savings to buy this house so we could fix it up. We planned to get married and have a life together."

My lips trembled as I struggled to finish my response. "Why would you wait until I got here to tell me you didn't want me? My boys are coming home early from Kevin's in three days." I gave up on investigating the upstairs and stumbled toward the back door.

"I only needed a little time to get my head together," he pleaded, sounding repentant. "You're like a serpent when you're angry."

I stared outside into the inky darkness, the unseen river roaring below. "I don't understand."

"You really messed me up, Hope. I wanted to please you so badly, but I couldn't live up to your grand expectations. You broke me."

"I bet you didn't even put up the fence in the backyard for the puppy," I murmured. "You didn't do anything, did you?" My head swirled in a deafening panic. "Everything you told me was a lie."

"I need to go," he said, his footsteps falling away from me, as he headed to the front door.

I turned to face him in disbelief. "Go where?"

He looked back at me. "To my buddy Joe's, one of the guys I spar with at the gym."

Tears ran down my cheeks. "The movers arrive in the morning with all my stuff. What am I supposed to tell them?"

"Have them put everything in the garage. I'll handle it."

"Like you've handled everything else? You said I was all you ever wanted. You said just being near me was enough to make you happy. I was your dream come true. What is going on?"

"You hurt me more than anyone else ever could. Lisa had rage issues, but I never let her get to me. I was vulnerable with you, because I loved you so deeply. You messed with my heart, Hope."

"How?" I sucked in my lower lip and fought back the torrent of tears. "No matter how unsure I was in the beginning of our relationship, I'm here now. I gave up my life for you. What you're saying doesn't make any sense."

The two of us stood in silence.

"You said 'loved' in the past tense?" I wrapped my arms across my chest. "You don't love me anymore?"

"I still love you," he came over to give me a hug and I remained frozen, unsure how to react. "I just don't know. I need time."

"You had to know what you were getting into when you pursued a married woman. It's not fair to punish me for my indecisiveness." I shook my head back and forth.

I wasn't going to let him do this to us without a fight. "You either stay in our house with me and work this out," I stared at him, "or I'm telling the movers to turn around and take my stuff back to San Diego. I need to know where to register my kids for school. I can't play around with their lives."

"So you're going to leave?" His eyes looked flat and uncaring. He wasn't my Adrian anymore. He was someone else.

"No. I want you to stay here and forgive me. You are my Prince Charming. This is supposed to be the beginning of our happily-ever-after. We've worked so hard to get to this point. Don't ruin it."

"I can't right now. My head's not good. Can't you give me a few days, Hope? Is that so much to ask?"

"Not when I just moved here and my boys are going to arrive in a couple of days. You either deal with me now or say goodbye forever. I'm not waiting for you."

I shook my head again, feeling stronger. Adrian would snap out of this if he knew I meant business. "I can't confuse Michael and Zach. I can't sit around with them in this empty house and tell them you're not sure about us anymore. That's ridiculous, Adrian. This isn't how grown-ups behave. You don't do that to children. They need stability. All of our children need some damn consistency."

"Fine. Have it your way." He left me standing frozen, walked over to the flat screen TV and lifted it from its base in one swift move. Adrian's arms stretched wide with his heavy load as he pushed past me toward the opened front door. Maui trailed after him.

I rushed to grab her before she disappeared into the night.

"This isn't what I want. Please stay," I sobbed, pressing Maui's warm, panting body into my chest. "Where are you going?"

"I already told you, my buddy Joe's. He said I could crash there for a couple of nights."

I stood in the doorway and watched in astonishment as he lumbered toward the back of his red truck and shoved the gigantic television into his flatbed. His rejection was a vicious slap across my face.

"If you take off Adrian, don't come back." I stood rigid and tense, pleading with him in my mind to return to me. "I'm not bluffing. I'll sell this house and drive back home to San Diego. You'll never see me or the boys again."

The dead look in his eyes as he glanced at me told me what I didn't want to know. He wasn't going to fight for me. He didn't care.

Adrian closed the tail gate and held his hand up as if to bat away an irritating swarm of gnats. His farewell salute. With the flick of a hand, the girl he professed he would do anything to have, meant nothing to him.

CHAPTER 38

...

THURSDAY, JULY 6, 2017
Pre-dawn

DENIAL. THIS WASN'T happening. This wasn't real. How could he have kept his true feelings bottled up this whole time and lied to me about working on the house? How could I have not noticed? What kind of human being did this to another person, especially to the woman he claimed to love more than any man had loved any woman?

Shutting the front door, I pulled my phone from my purse with trembling fingers and searched for his ex-wife's cell number. I didn't believe he was going to a friend's house.

Gulping for air, I called. No answer. It was the middle of the night, I guessed she was probably sleeping. Frantic heartbeats thundered in my chest as my fingertips tapped out a text.

Me: *Is Adrian staying with you?*

Moments later, the text message dinged. She was awake.

Lisa*: Yes*

Bile rose in my throat. I imagined the man I loved sleeping with another woman all this time. This wasn't real.

There must be another explanation. Maybe he was only sleeping on her couch. Adrian was a big baby at heart. He needed to be close to his kids and in his comfort zone when times got tough. He hated being alone.

He must have panicked as my move here pressed in closer. Knowing the house was in shambles, he probably feared I would leave him.

Me*: How long has he been staying with you?*

If Lisa said more than three days, I would never let Adrian forget it. I didn't care how lonely he was, or afraid, when he came pleading for forgiveness, he would owe me big time for doing something so cowardly.

Her text came through. Heart thumping, I checked Lisa's response.

Lisa: *2 months*

My vision blurred. Heat rippled across my chest. He wasn't sleeping on her couch.

I rushed to the guest bathroom and placed my hands on the cool porcelain sink to steady myself. Standing very still and breathing in through my nose and out thorough my mouth, I told myself, *I'm okay. I will be okay.*

David Foster Wallace once said, the truth will set you free, but not until it is finished with you. I was terrified to learn more, to dive into the pain the truth would unleash.

Sitting down on the toilet top, I texted Lisa again.

Me: *How long have you been together?*

Lisa: *In the beginning, when he first left me for you, so much I'm embarrassed to say. Then I took him back again four months ago. Huge mistake. Why did you call me? What happened?*

I leaned toward the sink, vomiting as heat stung my nerve endings. My organs felt like they were shutting down. Adrian told me he could never be with another woman. He said he'd rather fuck a dude than get back with Lisa.

Previous inconsistencies flooded my mind, all those little details, in retrospect, made sense. He said he'd saved that card he'd written me when we were teens, the one where he wrote he was still in love with me and asked if we could try again. Yet, whenever I asked about it, he told me he was still looking for it.

My account on his family Netflix disappeared two months ago. Adrian told me his son had accidentally deleted it, and he would take care of it. He never did.

Then there was the time Adrian cancelled his visit to see me last minute. He'd said Lisa asked him to stop by her house and then she snuck off and left him alone with kids. I texted Lisa, and she said she had no idea what I was talking about. I assumed she was lying.

Another recent incident surfaced. Adrian disappeared for twenty-four hours, didn't return any of my texts, his contractors claimed to have no idea where he was. I called Adrian's brother-in-law. He seemed hesitant, almost confused by my questions and concerns, as if he couldn't figure out why I cared.

The cold realization sliced me open. I was going to be alone. No one would love me the way Adrian pretended to.

I lay down on my side on the dusty bathroom floor and curled up in the fetal position, begging the universe to suck me under. I wasn't strong enough to withstand another blow.

She texted again. I ran my index finger along the grain of the old heart pine floors, scratched and neglected. At least Adrian had torn out the shag carpet and linoleum. He had done something. I peeked at my phone as Maui licked my face.

Lisa: *What happened tonight that you felt the need to contact me?*

I texted her back from my spot on the floor, still wanting to retreat into denial. There had to be an explanation, something that would fix this and make it all make sense.

Me: *We were supposed to start our new life together, but when I got here tonight to officially move into our home, he said he was hurt that I was so mean to him in the past. He said he was going to stay with one of his fighter friends that he works out with while he got his head straight.*

I hit send and waited for her response.

Lisa: *Where did you think he was living this whole time?*

Me: *Here. He said he was living here while he did all the renovations. He told me he wanted everything to be perfect and it was going to be a big surprise. That's why I haven't visited in so long.*

Her text shot back fast.

Lisa: *Adrian was never working on the house. He stayed there sometimes after we fought. Also, he isn't a fighter. He used to tell me that shit too, and he has no friends. Have you ever met one of them? I haven't!!! He is a pathological liar and probably a narcissist. You are lucky you don't have kids with him, no ties. You can leave.*

Me: *Lucky me.*

Tears slipped down my cheeks and onto the sleeve of my ragged sweatshirt. I wanted so desperately to believe in him again, for him to staunch my misery. I couldn't bear the pain. Lisa had to be lying. Adrian went to his friend's house. She was using his momentary weakness to drive a wedge between us.

Me: *You are making this up, Lisa. I saw what you did to Adrian that day you attacked him, bit him and ripped off his shirt. Why would you say such terrible things? Who are you?*

She texted back immediately.

Lisa: *You know who I am. I was you once. Believed the stories of love and romance. I divorced him, because he was an asshole. Probably still is. I hoped he would find happiness with you, so I could move on.*

Her words stung. Deep in my bones, her response rang true. This nightmare was real.

Me: *Why did you take him back when you knew he was with me?*

Lisa: *Because I'm an idiot. I finally started getting over him, and he couldn't stand it. I was seeing other men, and he hated it. He begged me to take him back. He called all day long. He would break into my house and show up in my bedroom in the middle of the night. He told me he had been going to therapy, and he realized he was still in love with me.*

You sent me an email saying he left you. Why did you send me that email???

My body shivered.

Me: *I never sent you an email.*

She forwarded me a copy of it. He had clearly hacked into my emails. It was some bullshit he'd typed to Lisa. He pretended to be me. The email said, *Adrian doesn't want me anymore, you can have him.*

Me: *I never sent that. But afterwards, you must have figured out we were still together. Why did you keep him?*

I was searching for sanity.

Lisa: *He tells me he loves me every day. I don't respond because I know he's lying. I've heard him on the phone with you. I've read his text messages. When I tell him to leave, he threatens to destroy me. He knows what to say to scare me. I'm getting better at not caring, but it is scary not knowing what he will do. I have to suck up my fucking pride and listen to his lies so he doesn't hurt me.*

I had sacrificed my marriage and my savings. I'd packed up my children and yanked them out of their school with the grand promise of a bigger house and a permanent family. They were going to hate me.

The weight of the loss was excruciating. Adrian's betrayal was another death. First my dad and then my future.

Lisa: *You don't need to put up with it. You can leave. I'm living in hell. Please don't say anything to him about this. He is going crazy that you are going to find out about me, and he takes it out on me and the kids. He's in a constant state of anger.*

The truth kept getting sicker. I needed to end our conversation. I couldn't take much more.

Me: *He's on his way back there now. We should probably stop texting.*

Lisa: *Okay*

I crawled out of the bathroom and looked around our looming empty house, the one we were going to grow old in. A large trash can overflowed with fast-food wrappers and oily paper napkins. Adrian told me he was a neat freak. He said he did all the cleaning in his marriage with Lisa.

How could I have not seen the signs? I'd known him since we were teenagers. How could he have fooled me for so long? Another terrible thought ran through my head. I wanted to ask Lisa one last question, something I needed to know for my children's safety.

Me: *How does he threaten to hurt you?*

I stared at the wall until I thought I saw it move, and then in a daze, picked at the chipped pink paint on my shaking finger nail. Time expanded and contracted, going nowhere, moving in a numb, endless elastic loop.

Finally, my phone chimed.

Lisa: *I went into debt after the divorce. He's giving me money. He helps with the kids. It's temporary until I get back on my feet. But he threatens to cut me off completely. He is taking advantage of me, and it's so sad this is his example to his kids. Are you going to stay here?*

I bit off the tip of my pinky nail and spit it out on the floor.

Me: *No.*

Lisa: *I hate having to live with him. He isn't a good person! Never met anyone like him. Never noticed he was so psychotic. You should see what he sent me Saturday. He was so awful!!!! Please do not let him know I'm talking with you. He will lose his shit.*

Me: *What did he send you on Saturday?*

She sent me a screen shot of dated text messages between her and Adrian. They looked legit, and I couldn't imagine how she could possibly have faked it, let alone anticipated I was going to call her and announce he'd left me.

His text message to her was chilling:

Adrian: *If you speak with Hope and tell her the truth about us, and I get wind of it, I will push this as far as I possibly can. You could have been nice to me, and I would have helped you but you can't control yourself.*

My fingers shook as I typed her back.

Me: *You need to get help, Lisa. He sounds dangerous, like a certified sociopath.*

She didn't disagree.

Lisa: *Last night I got woken up to him calling me a cunt because I won't please him sexually. I hate having sex with him.*

Me: *So then DON'T. Why would you when he treats you like that?*

Lisa: *I know it sounds absurd but if I don't have sex with him he starts such big fights and threatens to financially destroy me. Drag me back to court so he doesn't have to pay child support. Take away my car. I get so tired of fighting.*

He says, 'I'm helping you, so I deserve something in return.' I hate myself for it. But I hate him more for taking advantage of me. How can he say he's a good man and do this to us both?? How is that a good man???

He'd played make-believe about his steadfast monogamy, his desire to only love me. He'd faked being a family man. He'd even exaggerated his experience as a mixed martial arts fighter, made up a social life, and claimed friends who didn't exist.

The enormity of Adrian's lies was obscene. He had created a whole new identity. My mind struggled to make sense of it all. Did he lie to woo me, to play out a fantasy, or to punish me for not loving him the way he wanted when we were kids? Maybe the answer was D – all of the above.

Looping my arms around my knees, I rocked back and forth. I ached for a man who'd never existed, for a life that would never be.

CHAPTER 39

...

THURSDAY, JULY 6, 2017
Morning

THE FIRST SHARDS of daylight flooded through bare windows, searing my face as I remained tethered to my spot on the floor. I'd been mostly awake for twenty-four hours, only occasionally drifting into the respite of sleep before waking, the memories of what happened bombarding me all over again.

It was 7 a.m. I thought about the full bottle of Xanax in my overnight bag. I imagined the master bathtub upstairs the size of a kiddie pool; how easy it would be to fall asleep. Then I pictured my two boys. Staying alive was an obligation.

I called my mom. When I heard her reassuring voice on the other end of the line, my lips quivered and a fresh torrent of tears rolled from my eyes. "Mama, I need you."

"What's wrong?" She sounded frantic.

"Adrian's a very bad man. He's been living with his ex-wife. He took the TV and left me. I need you to come here."

"When?"

"Now." I choked down the vomit rising again in my throat. "Please."

"Okay." She spoke in a controlled voice, trying to sound tough. "I'll book a flight. If there's anything available, I'll fly out this afternoon. Should I rent a car, or will you pick me up at the airport?"

"I'll get you. The boys fly in tomorrow." My voice scratched in my throat. "I can't do this."

"Yes, you can."

CHAPTER 40

...

THURSDAY, JULY 6, 2017
Evening

MOM MANAGED TO book a flight, landing in the early evening. A dimming sky flaunted streaks of deep oranges across wispy white clouds as she pulled my car into the driveway. Dusk was falling. Before she was able to put the car in park, we spotted a red pick-up truck taking up space in the carport.

"It's his," I told her, my heart thrashing inside my ribcage. Maui, sensing my anxiety, uncurled her body from my lap and placed her front paws on the window. Her tail pointed straight in high alert.

"You stay here," Mom instructed. I'd already filled her in on my text conversation with Adrian's ex-wife. Neither one of us expected him to let me go easily.

I nodded my head, relieved Mom was taking charge. The heat and humidity, even this late in the day, made it hard to breathe. Besides that, I hadn't eaten a thing all day, and I'd barely slept. My body was ready to collapse. Adrian would have the advantage over me in any sort of confrontation.

Mom rang the doorbell and peeked inside through the stained-glass window. She was getting ready to push the bell again when he appeared in the entryway, dressed in last night's blue jeans and a clean gray t-shirt. The slogan *No Excuses* blazed across his chest. My skin prickled with heat at the sight of him, longing mixed with a deep sense of betrayal.

I sucked in a ragged breath. Shattered pieces of me ached to reach out to him, beg for him to wrap his arms around my waist, rest his chin on the top of my head, and hold me until my heart rate slowed to a steady, comfortable rhythm. I remembered the way his warm hand would brush across my cheek and tuck a loose strand of hair behind my ear when I was upset. His gentle ways of showing me love. I hated that I still wanted him. Emotions hadn't kept time with reason.

After a few minutes of what looked like a heated debate, Mom stepped aside and allowed Adrian to rush toward the passenger-side window where I sat trembling. He jammed his hands into his front pockets. "Hope, I need to talk to you," he begged, his amber-green eyes imploring me to listen. "It's not what it looks like. You need to let me explain."

I wanted to believe in him. What if Lisa lied to me? What if Adrian could explain everything and fix us?

"What are you doing here?" I asked.

"Picking up some of my things. Are you going to get out of the car?"

I shook my head no, reminding myself of the dead look in his eyes when he'd left the previous night. I needed to be strong.

"Please." Tears welled in his eyes. "I love you, Hope. Hear me out."

Wiping the sweat from my brow, I cracked the window down several more inches and looked toward Mom for direction. "See what he has to say." She waved her hand for me to exit the car. "I'm going to unload my things before we figure out the game plan."

With her approval, I clicked on Maui's leash and opened the door. Adrian offered his hand to help me out. I shooed him away.

"Let's go for a walk." I refused to make eye contact, taking off along the narrow gravel path that separated cheerful front yards on our right, from the lonely two-lane country road to our left.

"Don't you want to cut down to the river?" he asked.

"No. This isn't some romantic stroll along the water."

I gathered up my courage. Lisa may have over-dramatized her twisted relationship with Adrian, but there were a few things I couldn't deny. I knew for certain he had lied to me about working on the house. Even worse, it was obvious he'd hacked into my email account and sent at least one fake message on my behalf. Also, while I waited for Mom's flight, I'd messaged some of his old friends via Facebook and verified he had a history of inventing his own reality. Nausea rolled in my stomach at the thought of their validation.

"Say what you need to say, Adrian." I squeezed Maui's purple roped leash in my fist.

"If you'd let me explain."

"I *am* letting you explain," I snapped, maneuvering around a set of trash cans someone had left curbside well after pickup. "Go! What's your excuse?"

His hand brushed against mine as I momentarily lost my footing. Denial lingered, craving his touch.

"I didn't do this for the reasons you believe."

"Do what exactly?" I couldn't cave, couldn't give into my desire to forgive him and make-believe we had a chance. "Can you explain why you fucked your ex-wife nearly the entire time we were together? Made up lies about your whole existence? Or maybe you want to enlighten me as to why you dragged your children back and forth between two women?"

I felt an overwhelming need to scream. "What kind of father does that to his kids?"

"I wasn't with her that much. Lisa was exaggerating." Adrian stepped on a fallen magnolia flower, crushing its sweet perfumed petals into the coarse gravel.

"How do you know I talked to her?" I asked, suddenly worried about Lisa's safety. I'd promised her I wouldn't tell Adrian about our conversation.

"She told me."

"Oh." I felt betrayed by her too. I hated them both. "How long were you having sex with her?"

"Three months. That's all."

"That's all," I scoffed. One time would have been heartbreaking. Three months crushed me. "And you were with her when we first agreed to be together?"

"A few times in the beginning. It was so easy for you to be away from me, you could be so cold. Lisa accepted me whenever I wanted her."

A hauling truck lumbered down the road, belching fumes of exhaust. No wonder Lisa attacked him that day I picked him up from her mother's home. He was capable of driving any woman to violence.

"I made a mistake," he admitted.

"Yeah, you did. You told me you could never be with someone you didn't love. You said that just being near me was enough to make you happy. Yet I gave up my whole life to be with you, and the moment I get here you grab the television off the wall and abandon me."

"I wasn't in my right mind. I was so worried about losing you, I sabotaged my own damn self. Give me a chance to fix this. I'll do anything." He reached for my hand.

I hesitated. My heart was still weak. I could do it. Forgive him...

"I'm calling a realtor," I said, listening to my gut and pulling free of him. "I'm putting the house up for sale tomorrow. Kevin is keeping the boys an extra week so I can get back to San Diego."

"He was supposed to have them the whole summer. Now he's doing you a favor by keeping them an extra day?"

I held up a hand to tell him to stop. "I said one *week,* not one day. Quit pointing out other people's supposed inadequacies and look at yourself."

"You don't understand."

"Then tell me. Why did you do it?"

"You won't listen to me."

I stopped dead in my tracks, ready to punch him in the side of the head and bite his arm the way Lisa had. "I *am* listening. You have my full attention." Maui tugged at her leash to keep moving, and I leaned over to scoop her up.

"You're so angry," he pouted.

"Talk! Give me your story."

"Okay." He ran his fingers through his hair. "Lisa started drinking again, getting so wasted she was passing out on the couch in front of the kids. Twice she got pulled over for drunk driving. Then she began dragging guys home who only wanted to get in her pants. I was worried about my kids. What if one of those sick fucks she was bringing around tried to molest Rose while Lisa was passed out cold? If I stepped in, I knew she'd stop the nonsense. I thought it was my job to save her."

His explanation pulled at my conscience. "What about your responsibility to me?"

"I was wrong. That's why I asked you for a couple of days to straighten things out. If you would have just given me—"

"What? A few days would erase all the lies, the sex, the pretend life you made up?"

"No, but—"

"You blamed your problems on me." Maui squirmed in my arms. "You said you were going to live with a friend to get your head on straight, because I'd been mean to you. Not once did you mention anything about the ex-wife you were fucking."

"I was afraid if you knew the truth, you'd disappear. I messed up. I fell so far short of who I truly am." He put his hand on my arm, but I shrugged away from his touch.

"I've talked to a therapist," he continued. "I'm better now. I know my priorities. Hope, I promise it will never happen again. I will spend the rest of my life and beyond making up for all my wrongs. I will worship the ground you walk on."

My throat rose up inside me, tears threatened to spill down my cheeks. "I want to believe you. You have no idea how badly I want to trust you again, but I can't."

"You can. I will prove it to you every single day. It will be even better than it was before because now I have no doubts. I have no lingering responsibility to any woman besides you."

"Adrian, I talked to some of the girls you dated before you married Lisa." I swiped away an escaped tear. "They all told me they'd caught you in lies. You exaggerated about your work, too. You don't even fully renovate homes, you only specialize in drywall and painting."

"That's not true." He shook his head.

"The point is, I could probably forgive you for cheating. But I can't get over all your lies. How can I have a relationship with someone who makes up his friends, his sport, his work? It's too much. I would spend the rest of my life questioning every single thing you told me."

"Those people are trying to hurt me. Give me a chance to prove it to you. Give the man you said you loved the benefit of the doubt."

I stood in silence for a painful moment. Birds didn't chirp. Trees did not sway. The whole world went quiet.

This was it, let him back in or cut the cord.

Too much of what Lisa had said rang true. I could see it, imagine how he must have gone back and forth between us. Me on the weekends and holidays, her on his regular schedule. All those times he claimed to be working late, or hanging out with friends, he was giving his affection to another woman. None of it could be undone.

"No." I forced myself to choke out the word, then turned back to the house before he could convince me to stay.

My boys would start school soon. I needed to get us resettled before I messed up their lives even more than I already had. "Go back to Lisa and pray she allows you to stick around," I spoke with as much resolve as I could muster.

"Stop," he said in a low commanding voice that gave me the chills. "Don't do this. You will never find anyone who loves you as much as I do."

I squeezed Maui closer to my chest, refusing to show weakness. "I'd rather be alone than spend my life with a con artist."

He walked behind me, keeping up with my pace. "You're angry and blowing things out of proportion. You're going to regret this, Hope."

"I'm not her." I stomped my foot in the dirt. "You can't frighten me into taking you back. I don't need your financial assistance. And thank God we didn't have children together. Go home to your family."

"I don't want her, Hope. I want you. I made a mistake, and I will spend the rest of my life— "

"You said that already." Adrian's behavior was pathological.

He quickened his pace and caught up with me, reaching out to pet Maui. "Are you leaving her with me?"

"Why would I give you my dog? You bought her for me as a gift."

"I bought her for us. She's mine, too."

"Are you joking? You're actually asking me to give up my dog now? Haven't you taken enough?"

"If you go back to San Diego, how are you going to keep her? Lock her up in a tiny apartment?"

"She's not that big. I'll figure something out."

"This isn't fair to me, Hope. You're taking away my heart."

His inability to think of anyone other than himself blew my mind. How could he beg for my forgiveness and then act like I was taking something from *him*? He'd done this. Not me. Where was the man who could read my mind and put me before anyone?

"At least let me take her on a walk and say goodbye. I love her, too."

"You don't love anyone Adrian." I could feel my nose turning red as my eyes filled with tears. "You're broken inside. Something is deeply wrong with you."

"I'll let you go without a fight. Please, Hope, let me take her on one last walk." He reached out again to lift Maui from my arms. I held her closer.

"Fine." I was tired of arguing. "I'll give her to you for one walk. Then you go. Give my mom and me space to take care of things before we drive back to San Diego. Be enough of a man to let me go in peace." Another truck rattled past us, kicking up lose dirt in the road and making me cough.

"You're the one who fucked up," I reminded him. "You are the one who walked out and ruined us. Allow me to leave on my terms. Have the decency to do that."

Setting Maui on the ground near a dense row of tall Cypress trees hedging a stately home from the road, I handed Adrian the leash.

"Can I give you one last hug?" he asked.

I narrowed my eyes at him, willing my sorrow to fade. "No. Goodbye, Adrian."

CHAPTER 41

...

THURSDAY, JULY 6, 2017
Evening

I WALKED INTO the house and collapsed on the lumpy sofa, tears streaming down my face.

Mom looked up from her notepad. She stood at the kitchen counter, making a to-do list. "Where's the dog?" she asked.

"Adrian wanted to take her on a walk by the river. He claims he's sad we're leaving."

"You sure that's a good idea?"

"Yeah, she needs to use the bathroom so she doesn't go in the house again. Hopefully, he won't bring her back all dirty."

"She already pooped in the house, and she peed in two different places. I cleaned it up with old napkins I found in the garbage can."

The sharp scent of piss and shit hit me. I looked at the overflowing trash, knowing the filth Adrian had left behind bothered Mom almost as much as it upset me.

"What did he say?" she asked.

"Some crap about how he was trying to rescue his ex and protect his children. He tried to make himself the hero."

"I'm glad you're not buying it." She shook her head. "That man has a screw loose."

I pulled my knees to my chest, memories pelting me like stones. His stories played through my mind.

I had flowers for you. He'd messaged to me that night I spoke with him on Facebook in my Andalucía kitchen. *I spent my last fifteen dollars buying you a dozen roses. It wasn't even enough, but the lady felt sorry for me and sold them to me at a discount.*

My car was out of gas. I used my last dollar to buy you those flowers.

I peeked up at Mom, my body prickling with reality. He'd made me feel like the center of his existence.

I completely straightened out my life to make myself worthy for you. I dropped my old friends, found a real job, enrolled in college. I eventually got my education because of you. When I called you that day, it was because I was ready for you. Ready to be the man you deserved.

At every opportunity, Adrian fed me beautiful lies, telling me what I wanted to hear. I ate his words like a starving woman.

Mom swiped her hand across the green tiled countertop. Particles of dust floated in the air, trapped in a dying beam of sunlight. "So what do you want to do?" she asked.

"Nap." I rested my forehead on my boney knees, a thin pair of colorful yoga pants doing little to soften the edges.

"I'm being serious."

"So am I. I'm exhausted, my whole body hurts."

"Do you still want to come back to San Diego?" The floor creaked as she shifted her weight. Her face dripped perspiration.

"Yes."

"Are you sure? It's a nice house." Mom wrinkled her nose, betraying her true feelings. I knew she didn't really like it here. "The boys were looking forward to having their own bedrooms and having some land to roam."

Adrian had told me he wanted the pictures on the walls to be pictures of our family. The children were going to all play together by the river, Maui was going to trail along. He told me I'd always been his perfect. The girl he would do anything to be with.

"No, Mama. I can't stay here. The house still needs a ton of renovations, and it will do nothing but remind me of what was supposed to have been. Besides," I added, knowing Mom wouldn't be as swayed by my sappy emotions. "Adrian will never leave me alone if I'm close by."

"It's going to be hard to sell in this condition. Most people don't want a fixer-upper. It's too much of a hassle."

"I know I'm going to lose a ton of money. It doesn't matter. I can't survive here. I have to go home." My eyes drifted toward my bare finger on my left hand, the one I wished was wearing his engagement ring. "I told the movers not to unpack my things. They shoved everything in the garage, because they said they had another delivery to make after mine and they couldn't haul everything back to San Diego."

"Then get off the couch and let's get started. I've made a list." She waved her notepad in the air. "We need to get the locks changed, call a realtor, clean this place up. You have to figure out where you want to live when we get back to San Diego, and then we should call the moving company and make arrangements for them to bring your things there."

"I can't right now. Please, can we do this in the morning?"

"Why did you call me out here? To do it all for you?"

"I don't know." My empty stomach rumbled in pain and my eyes felt gritty from all the dust. "I'm tired. I can barely keep my eyes open."

"Then sleep for one hour while I find a store and get some cleaning supplies and food for us to eat for the next few days." She opened the bare pantry and looked inside with irritation. "There's nothing in this house."

My body felt like it weighed five hundred pounds. "I can't do this."

"What do you mean?"

"I mean, I don't know how I can do all this. It's too overwhelming." All my courage and resolve were spent. I gathered myself back into a sitting position as tears fell in streaks down my face and onto my hands.

The crease in between Mom's brow furrowed. Her lips formed into a sharp line. "Look at me," she said.

"I am."

"You have two choices." She put her left hand on her hip and walked around the kitchen counter, her right index finger pointing at me. "You can curl back up into a ball and give up. I'll put you in the hospital while I handle everything with the house."

"Okay," I nodded. Her idea didn't sound half bad.

"I'm not finished. You go give up in the hospital and I call Kevin and tell him to keep custody of your boys. Your life could be only downhill from here."

She took a seat next to me and rested her hand on my shoulder. "Or," she said, her voice softening. "You take a quick nap while I run to the store, and then you pull yourself together. You do what needs to be done. You put your boys first, and you take care of your life."

CHAPTER 42

...

THURSDAY, JULY 6, 2017
Late Evening

MOM'S THREAT TO call Kevin and give away my boys
scared me more than a life without Adrian. I had asked her
to wake me as soon as she returned from the store.

"Where's Maui?" she asked as she removed food from
brown paper bags and placed her purchases on the kitchen
counter.

I rubbed at the sleep in my eyes and shivered. It was
dark. The house had cooled in her absence. "She's not
back?"

"She didn't come running when I opened the door. I
thought she might be curled under the blanket with you."

I flopped the blanket on the floor and looked at my
empty lap in a daze. "You sure she's not here?"

"Adrian's truck is gone," Mom said, no longer unloading
the groceries.

I reached out for my cell phone, a small wave of panic pulling me further awake. Maui was a snuggler, never far from my lap.

"There's a bunch of text messages," I told her, my fingers scrambling to open them.

"Adrian?" Mom asked.

"He lost Maui." I sat straight up, my body going rigid.

"No." Her lips narrowed into a frown.

"He's coming back to the house now so we can help him look for her." I took a deep breath. "He said as soon as they got down to the river, she took off. He's been searching for her this whole time."

"He took her leash off?"

"He shouldn't have. I've told him a dozen times never to take her off the leash."

"Is it normal for her to run away?"

"Oh, my God. Why are you asking me so many questions when I just woke up?" I leaned over to shove my feet into my sneakers. Panic squeezed my heart until it hurt to breathe. "The boys call her our joy bomb. We need her." I ran nervous fingers through my hair. "He's such a piece of shit. I wouldn't be surprised if he did this on purpose."

"He's trying to get your attention."

"Well, he better not have actually lost her. He better be fucking joking."

The doorbell rang. Before Mom or I could answer, Adrian let himself inside with his key.

"Where were you?" I asked, standing up from the couch.

Mom put out her hand, palm up. "This isn't your home. Give me the key."

Adrian smirked at her, shoving his keyring into his back pocket. "I was looking for the dog." He patted his back pocket as if to ensure the house key was safe from Mom's grasp. "I haven't taken all my stuff yet. You can't evict me without warning."

"Evict you?" Mom asked.

"I've been living here since April. According to Oregon law, that makes me a tenant." Adrian spoke in near monotone. He was untouchable.

"Hand me the key." Mom thrust her palm out further as she approached him.

Adrian took a step back, staring her down with that hideous dead look in his eyes, not saying a word. I sucked in too much air and began to choke. He turned his attention to me. "Are you going to help me look for the dog or what?"

The late evening sun had already surrendered to the darkness. She might not make it through the night.

"Get out of here," Mom said to Adrian. "Leave."

"Is that what you want, Hope? Maui listens to me better than you. She responds to a man's voice."

"Like she listened while you were out calling for her?" Mom asked. "You've been gone for more than an hour. Where did you drive to if you were down by the water searching for her?"

Another memory sucker-punched my heart. It was right before I'd kissed Adrian on the bench at Sunset Cliffs. He told me he'd spent the past twenty plus years thinking of what he could have done differently to be with me. What he could have tweaked. What he should have said. If he'd had a little more fight in him back then. He said he would have done anything for a second chance to be with me.

Nothing he said was real. Every piece of our relationship was founded on a lie.

"Go home, Adrian," I told him. My panic over Maui started to simmer into something stronger. "Get whatever it is you came here for and leave."

"I'll be back tomorrow. Rose will come with me to help me carry things."

"You barely have anything here." I walked closer to him, raising the tone of my voice. "You don't need to come back with Rose. Take your shit now, and get out."

"I have a right to be here, Hope."

"Then come back with the police," Mom said. "We don't want to be alone with you anymore. You're making us uncomfortable."

"What about the puppy?" He cocked his head at me with defiance.

"Leave!" I shouted. My fury was sky-rocketing.

"Watch what you ask for, Hope. That dog shot off like a bullet when I removed her leash. You're not going to find her without help."

I was a wild animal cornered. I charged at Adrian and punched him with my left fist and then my right. Over and over. I pounded against his rock-hard chest. "Get out of my house. I hate you, Adrian. I hate you more than I've ever hated anyone in my entire life."

I swiped at the spit on the side of my lip. "What did you do to my dog? Where is she, you sick son of a bitch?"

I dropped to my knees sobbing, snot pouring from my nose. "I wish you would light yourself on fire and burn to death."

Adrian turned to my mom without emotion. "You see what she did to me? You're my witness."

Mom picked up her cell phone. "Walk out the door right now or I'm calling 911."

I let out a violent wail. All that built-up rage tore free from my chest. How could I have fallen in love with such a monster? Where was Adrian's heart? "You made up that job you supposedly had in San Diego, didn't you? You never planned on moving there to be with me. It was all bullshit. I was your fantasy world. You don't care who you hurt. Was it fun, Adrian? Was it an entertaining game?"

He inched backward. "You don't know what you're talking about."

"I need to go look for Maui," I sputtered, shaking too hard to speak clearly.

"Stay where you are," Mom instructed me. "You're not going out in the dark alone." She sneered at Adrian. Her fingers dialed quickly. "Hello? Yes, this is Sharon Edwards, my daughter's name is Hope Sullivan. I'm at Hope's house right now on East Park Street and her ex-boyfriend won't leave." She cupped her hand over the phone. "What's your exact address?"

I gave it to her as Adrian stood clenching his fists.

After filling the operator in on our situation, Mom told her she didn't want to hold the line any longer. When she hung up the phone, she scowled at Adrian. "They're on their way over."

"Good," he said, glancing down at me as I sobbed. He had to realize this wouldn't look good to the police.

"You want to give me the key?" Mom asked him.

"No." He cleared his throat, gripping the hemline of his jacket and tugging it downward to smooth it out. "You ladies can look for the dog yourselves. Good luck with that." He turned to leave. "I'll be back tomorrow with Rose to get the rest of my stuff," Adrian called over his shoulder. "If you damage anything, you'll be liable."

CHAPTER 43

...

THURSDAY, JULY 6, 2017
Night

THE TWO POLICE officers who eventually showed up on my doorstep offered to skip their dinner breaks and help Mom and me search for Maui. They carried large heavy flashlights next to the guns holstered on their thick black belts. The men said they were familiar with the terrain.

We walked down the wood steps that lead to the Rogue River. It was possible Adrian was lying about the location. For all I knew, he'd locked Maui in his car and taken her with him.

Officer Mike, a big man, at least six feet with a wide upper body, wore delicate wire glasses. He pushed them up his nose as we trekked to the west. Mom headed east with Officer Dawson. A tall squeaky-clean blond no older than twenty, he was young enough to be my son.

I couldn't bear the thought of explaining to the boys that Adrian had lost our beloved dog. Telling them we were moving back home would be terrible enough.

I called for Maui as Officer Mike's flashlight swept through the darkness. The air had cooled, leaving my skin clammy and uncomfortable. I wished I'd brought my sweater. "Maui," I cooed. "Here girl, here sweet puppy."

I tried not to imagine her getting scooped away by an owl or devoured by a large animal. It was impossible not to worry that she might have drowned in the Rogue's racing waters. I peered into the river and shivered at the thought of Adrian throwing her in. She'd never make it out. She wasn't strong enough to fight its current.

Never seeing my sweet puppy's face or stroking her silky brown ears made my heart hurt.

We had to find her.

"Maui," I heard my mom holler in the distance. "Here, puppy, puppy, puppy. Mau-iiiii."

Mom shouted my name. Officer Mike and I turned around, tramping over rocks and debris, rushing in her direction.

We found Mom standing with Officer Dawson beside the river's edge. "Did you find her?" I searched Mom's empty arms.

"Look," she held up Maui's purple dog collar instead, its fake diamond-studded tag flashing in Officer Dawson's beam of light. "I found it in the mud next to the water," Mom said.

My hand shot to my mouth in fear. "She's been wearing that since I got her. It's never fallen off."

"Then he must have taken it off her." Mom concluded. "I think he threw her in the river."

I hated to acknowledge the possibility Adrian could to be that cruel. "She's only five months old."

"Why else would her collar be here?"

"Maybe he took it off and set her loose. We still need to look for her." Fresh tears welled in my eyes. "Why would he do this?"

"Why would he do any of the other things he's done, hon? He's a troubled individual," Mom said, walking over to rub my back.

Officer Dawson's nostrils flared with indignation. "Going after the family dog is cold-blooded."

Tears trailed down my cheeks. "We have to keep looking. If she's out here, she's scared and she needs us."

"Ma'am," Officer Mike said. "We can help you search a little longer. But after that, we need to get back to work and you ought to go inside and call for a locksmith."

"Do you think we're in danger?" I asked.

Officer Mike rubbed his thumb across his chin. "It's hard to say. You're better off taking precautions."

"What if he comes back?"

"We call 911," Mom answered for him.

I looked at the other officer. "My mom is recovering from a stroke. Stress isn't good for her."

Officer Mike tapped his finger on his flashlight. "Your mom said you're planning on putting the house up for sale. I think that's your best bet. Get out of the state and put some distance between you and that guy. Let your mom have some peace of mind. If you don't need to be here, why invite trouble?"

"This is a nightmare," I sobbed.

Mom wrung her hands. "This is life, Hope."

CHAPTER 44

...

MONDAY, JULY 10, 2017
Afternoon

WE NEVER DID find our sweet puppy. Four days later, when the house was packed up and I'd moved past crying to more of a catatonic zombie state, we had to leave without her.

Mom drove my car, and I wondered, as I watched my happy ending grow smaller in the side mirror, if Maui would live. I hoped she would and tried to imagine a family taking her in, how excited a little boy would be to find her running behind his bike.

That make-believe story was a distraction from the reason my dog was missing, the betrayal her loss represented. I could hardly face my true heartbreak, the one that numbed me, threatening to crush my spirit and pull me under completely.

Once in San Diego, Mom helped unload the car-full of boxes. We carried the remnants of my life up the stairs to a one bedroom apartment she'd arranged last-minute.

"Well, it's not the most beautiful place, but it'll do," Mom said, setting a box on the counter.

"It smells like old milk," I mumbled, finding it hard to be anything but angry and negative.

"So open up some windows and air it out. It'll feel more like home when the rest of your things arrive in a few days."

I shrugged.

"Are you going to be okay here?"

"I guess."

"I'll go blow up the air mattress and put it in the bedroom. You can sleep in there tonight." She dragged the box into what would be the boys' shared room and began unloading. I heard the whir of the air pump as she filled the plastic bed.

I had that one day in San Diego to get my apartment set up before the boys came home. *Home*...the word no longer held meaning for me.

Weak, and stinking from days without showering, all I wanted to do was sleep. It was my new drug of choice, my escape. When I closed my eyes, I imagined Adrian's lips pressed to mine. I could taste him and smell his familiar citrus scent. The sound of his voice rumbled through my dreams, telling me he loved me and we would grow old together.

My fantasies were so much better than my reality.

"All righty, the bed is good to go." Mom walked back into the living room and clapped her hands together. "I put clean sheets on and there's some pillows for you to share with the boys until you get yours. You've got some food and bathroom toiletries in the boxes in the kitchen."

"Thank you, Mama. I couldn't have done it without you."

"Well, I'm not going to be around forever to keep bailing you out. You need to start depending on yourself, Hope, not some stupid man to complete you. Just because someone's got a penis, doesn't make him better than you."

My body tensed, another headache brewing behind my eyes.

"Put one foot in front of the other," she continued, "and do what you gotta do. It's like AA. One minute at a time. Then, one day, you'll wake up and be amazed at all you've accomplished."

"Okay." I looked around the cramped apartment, wishing she would leave.

"Don't allow yourself to wallow in self-pity. Your boys need you. And if that scumbag calls, you tell him to fuck off. Better yet, ignore him. He blew it, Hope. There's no going back."

"I know, Mama."

"Do you?"

CHAPTER 45

...

TUESDAY, JULY 11, 2017
Morning

THE ALARM ON my cell phone woke me the next morning. Harsh sunlight burned my swollen, itchy eyes. I threw up, told myself repeatedly I was okay, and brushed my teeth. My phone chimed, flashing Mom's number on my caller ID.

"Hello?" I said.

"I wanted to make sure you were up. Do you want me to go to the airport with you to pick up the boys?"

"Ummm." I looked around the room, trying to unscramble my brain.

"Are you dressed?" she asked.

"Yeah." The sweatpants and old t-shirt I wore to sleep last night would work for my daytime ensemble as well.

"Why don't you come over to my place? We can grab some breakfast on the way to the airport."

"Nah." I could feel the acid churning and rising in my gut. Everything tasted metallic or stale. "I'm not hungry."

"Well, you better eat anyway. You need to keep your strength up."

How many times did I have to beg her to eat after her stroke?

"Hope? Did you hear what I said?"

I thought I better say something before she went on another roll. "I'll get the boys on my own. They're going to want to come straight home and see the new apartment. Michael already told me he's furious he doesn't get to have his own room. They both said Adrian ruined their lives."

"Well, show them you can have an even better life."

"Yes, Mama. I'll talk to you soon."

* * *

I found a space in short-term parking and slogged across the deserted pedestrian tunnel toward the bank of check-in agents. Sound, touch, taste, light. They all felt like an attack on my overloaded senses.

Someone issued me a pass to get the pat down with airport security and wait for Michael and Zack at their gate. I barely remembered to make eye contact.

Their plane was delayed and then delayed again. Fog in San Francisco, even in the summer, affected takeoff.

I thought about my favorite aunt, the one who shot herself after she found out her husband had been cheating on her. She'd left behind three of my young cousins. I remembered how her suicide divided the family. One faction blamed her husband for cheating. Another alliance thought my aunt had been selfish to not suck it up and do what was best for her children.

I secretly understood. As devastated as I was by the loss of Aunt Sher, it wasn't hard to imagine myself inside her head. She was on her second marriage, with the love of her life, and he was preparing to leave her. She was going to have to start all over again. Depression can blind you from seeing an expiration date on your misery. She probably told herself she was so useless, her children would be better off without her.

Who was to say that wasn't true for my own children? Kevin could give them a big home with a stable partner. Michael and Zach would attend elite private schools and never need to shuttle back and forth between parents. Also, wasn't it true that, as they grew older, boys needed their dads more?

I saw the plane touch down and then a light went on announcing they would be deplaning. As a crowd of travelers began to exit through the passageway, Zach popped his little head off the runway first, a bright eager smile pasted across his freckled face. "Mommy," he said, flinging his arms open and racing toward me. The weight of his hug nearly knocked me backward. I picked him up and squeezed him tight. Tears of joy and pride slipped down my cheeks. I had made this boy, and he loved me as much as I loved him.

Michael gave me a shy smile. Transitioning from one parent to the other still made him nervous. He sidled up beside me as I set Zach down on his feet. "Hey, Mom," he said. "It's really good to see you." He put his arm around my waist as I pulled him tighter. "I missed you."

"Yeah," Zach piped up. "We really missed you. I made you a wood-working project. Do you want to see it?" He slid the little backpack off his right shoulder and twisted it forward so he could open it. "Here." He pulled out a sanded piece of wood about the length of half my arm and handed it to me. Engraved on it were the words, *I love Mommy*.

"Oh Zach, it's beautiful."

"I know. Daddy taught me how to use a drill bit, and this is what I wanted to make with it."

Michael cleared his throat and dropped his duffle bag to the ground. "I got you something, too."

"No way."

"Yeah," he said, digging into his bag. He pulled out a giant handmade card and straightened up. He looked away from me as he waved the blue construction paper for me to grab.

"What is it?"

"Read it."

The card inside said:

Mom,

If it were not for you, I would not be happy. I would not have such a good life. Thank you for taking me to therapy when I did not want to go. Thank you for teaching me things I needed to learn even when I said I hated you. You are my hero. I love you very much.

It was hard to stand in front of my boys and feel anything but love. In their presence, I realized my truth. Their love was worth more than any emotion I'd ever receive from a man. It was deep and fulfilling. It gave me purpose.

Nothing was a mistake. Every difficult day with Kevin had been worth it, because our relationship gave me my children. And even in the darkest depths of my heartbreak, they'd be there, with me, loving me.

Standing in that quiet corridor of the San Diego airport, I felt the first rush of freedom. My life was mine. I could be whoever I wanted to be. This was a fresh start.

I could build my own consulting business to match writers with contract work. I could follow my dream of writing a novel. We could adopt a puppy, whichever one my boys and I liked best.

They were what mattered. We had each other, and though the fresh cut of my broken heart remained, I willed my sudden surge of hope to staunch the ache.

We would be okay.

EPILOGUE

I CALL IT my year of goodbyes. I lost a lot, but I found myself. Sometimes the simplest joys come from having nothing. Losing so much forced me to appreciate life's little gifts, like the hot sun on my shoulders or the light sprays from the Pacific that beat against the cliffs and kiss my cheeks.

As I traverse the sharp lava rocks of La Perouse Bay, a stunning location just south of Wailea, on the Hawaiian island of Maui, I remind myself that all that sorrow served a purpose.

I am here today on my own to release my half of Dad's ashes and to give thanks to the universe for its many blessings.

It's been a year since I moved back to San Diego, a time of recovery and growth. I thought I'd found a man who would save me, help me skip over any painful life lessons and dive straight into love.

The universe had other plans.

Those first few weeks on my own were the most difficult. I spent my waking hours arranging our new apartment, making the boys basic meals, and registering and preparing them for school.

Michael and Zach watched as I struggled to eat, to take them outdoors for fresh air, and to simply stay awake. We were in survival mode, and I did the bare minimum to muddle through each painful hour.

Adrian texted me and called my friends and family, pleading with them to help convince me to take him back. As soon as he knew the boys were in school, he flew in unannounced from Grant's Pass and showed up at my apartment, crying and begging for forgiveness. I chose not to open the door, imagining how my boys would feel if I caved. I wanted to let him in, so badly it made me ache. One final kiss, I reasoned, and I would have closure. Instead, I called the police and waited for him to leave.

Other days he would send messages threatening to ruin my life, or say things like it was my fault the two of us were miserable, because I couldn't find it anywhere in my cold heart to forgive him.

The therapist I saw in emergency sessions twice a week told me that the attachment hormone, oxytocin, stays in our blood stream for about three months. If I avoided all physical contact with Adrian during that time period, the longing would dissipate.

I clung to that biological fact, and after three long months, I did miss him less. Even better, sometime around the five month mark, the thought of Adrian actually repulsed me. Progress.

There was still work to be done.

I realized I'd been longing for a man to come along and magically make me happy since I was a teenager. The moment I first saw Luke smoking a cigarette on his balcony, that boyfriend of mine who slept with my stepsister, I was certain he was the one.

I remembered how I pictured myself looping his name on my notebooks in red sparkle nail polish. I was positive, ten years down the road he would marry me and we'd live happily ever after.

Luke became the first leading man in my own make-believe romantic comedy. I was positive, if I could have him, my life would be perfect.

And then I thought it would be Kevin, and then Adrian.

I was the girl, waiting for the boy, to make her feel special.

These days I'm following Mom's advice to remain single for the time being as I grow myself. I get down on my knees throughout each day, and I pray for strength and guidance. I practice yoga, spending most of the class lying face up, with my left hand on my chest and my right hand on my belly, quietly telling myself, *I love you.* At night before bed, I write one thing I am grateful for on a post-it note and stick it to my bathroom mirror.

Perhaps most powerful of all, I have mentally revisited each defining step in my childhood, teens, twenties and thirties. I have observed each of my former selves, the good and the bad, and found the intrinsic value in her at every stage. The younger versions of me made mistakes and learned. She did her best. I love and accept her.

As I tighten my back-pack, which carries my dad's remains, I step closer to the rocky crevice of cliff I've been searching for. Sydney has brought me here many times before. We would come to throw rocks into the ocean and make wishes to the universe.

Pulling off my backpack, I feel the wind sweep across the back of my dampened t-shirt. I take out the Mason jar I've been storing Dad's ashes in and unscrew the metal lid. Peeling off the top, I wait for the wind to calm.

The ocean thrashes down below. I am finally ready to let go, to set him free to the waters where he asked me to release him. "Thank you for being my father," I whisper as I hold out the jar and let his ashes scatter in the wind. "I'm keeping my promise to you, and doing my very best to live fearlessly and with intention. I love you, Dad."

He drifts and swirls and lifts in the warm air. The sun shines high on the horizon, its light glimmering along the sea of blue. Waves collapse, then explode against the cliffs.

My throat stings as I try to hold back tears, until I realize it's okay to cry. Dad would love it here. He'd say it was the perfect day and the ideal place, to take a solo dip in the Maui ocean.

A breeze cools my wet cheeks, and I wipe them clean with the hem of my t-shirt, smiling to myself as I do. *This* will be my year of letting go.

Mine is not a story of miraculous epiphany. I haven't healed overnight. There are days I take leaps forward and on others, come crashing two steps back.

Nevertheless, I'm glad it happened. Adrian was the only reason I was brave enough to leave my marriage. The difficult path that brought me back to myself.

I have learned that love is not allowing someone to make your world smaller. Love is not found when we lead with fear. True, healthy love, is self-care, and is at its very best when it builds you up and makes you stronger.

Each morning I make a choice. I choose to love myself. I choose to act as if I am the woman I want to be, and moment by moment, decision by careful decision, I am becoming the kind of woman I admire most, one of the battle-strong who has overcome hardships and nourishes her own dreams. A woman who can save herself. I've had the power all along. Now I know it.

I am choosing Hope.

AUTHOR'S NOTE

If you or a loved one has experienced a harmful relationship like the one described between Hope and Adrian, I strongly encourage you learn more about narcissists, sociopaths, and psychopaths. All three of these personality disorders exhibit similar traits and make having a healthy relationship an impossibility.

Men and women with one of these personality disorders do not think, or eventually behave, like the average person. Though it seems impossible to believe, they have no conscience nor are they capable of feeling empathy. After they charm you, they will do harm, and sociopathy is far more common than we realize.

Studies show anywhere from 1 in 100 people to as many as 1 in 25 people are sociopaths. The best way to protect yourself is to recognize and understand their tell-tale signs and patterns. Knowledge is power. You are not alone.

Some books I recommend reading are:

Women Who Love Psychopaths: Inside the Relationships of Inevitable Harm With Psychopaths, Sociopaths & Narcissists, by Sandra L. Brown

The Sociopath Next Door, by Martha Stout, Ph.D

Husband, Liar, Sociopath: How He Lied, Why I Fell For It & The Painful Lessons Learned, by O.N. Ward

ACKNOWLEDGEMENTS

My kind-hearted, smart, resilient boys, Joshua and Alexander, you are my sunshine. Jennifer Pudlow, a world-class therapist, you planted the seeds for hopes of a brighter tomorrow. Jessica Therrien, my writing bestie, biz partner, and irreplaceable friend; your edits and encouragement make me strive for my very best. Shelly Stinchcomb and Laura Taylor, my talented editors, you pushed me to take my writing to the next level. And thank you to all my wonderful beta readers, Leslie Acabela, Danielle Foerster, Janet Jackson, Steve Kenney, Michelle Myers, Olga Rosenmayer, Mary Jane Therrien, Caitlyn Toropova, Mandy Urena, and Christa Yelich-Koth.

ABOUT THE AUTHOR

HOLLY KAMMIER is a former journalist who has worked everywhere from CNN in Washington, D.C. and KCOP-TV in Los Angeles, to the NBC affiliate in small-town Medford, Oregon. A UCLA honors graduate, she is the author of *Kingston Court*, her debut novel. *Choosing Hope,* her second published novel, is a spin-off from best-seller, *Kingston Court,* with overlapping characters and locations. The California native and mother of two, lives in San Diego, California close to her family and friends. Co-Founder of Acorn Publishing, Holly is available for speaking engagements and content editing.

WWW.HKAMMIER.COM
WWW.ACORNPUBLISHINGLLC.COM

If you liked this book, please leave a review on Amazon,
Goodreads, etc. and tell your friends.
Word of mouth is an author's lifeblood.
Thank you so much for reading!